Elijah

The Unseen Hand

Elijah Kellogg

The Unseen Hand

1st Edition | ISBN: 978-3-75235-048-7

Place of Publication: Frankfurt am Main, Germany

Year of Publication: 2020

Outlook Verlag GmbH, Germany.

THE UNSEEN HAND

BY

ELIJAH KELLOGG

PREFACE.

A vast majority of the noblest intellects of the race have ever held to the idea that,—

> "There's a divinity that shapes our ends,
>
> Rough hew them how we will."

By its influence they have been both consoled and strengthened under the pressures and in the exigencies of life. This principle, to a singular degree, assumes both form and development in the story of James Renfew, the Redemptioner.

He comes to us as an orphan and the inmate of a workhouse, flung upon the world, like a dry leaf on the crest of a breaker; his mind a blank devoid of knowledge, save the idea of the Almighty and the commands of the Decalogue, whose force, in virtue of prior possession, held the ground and kept at bay the evil influences by which he was surrounded. And in consequence of thus holding aloof from all partnership in vice, he was brow-beaten, trampled upon, and made a butt of by his companions in misfortune.

His only inheritance was the kiss of a dying mother, the dim recollection of her death, and a Bible which he could not read,—her sole bequest.

The buoyancy, the frolic of the blood, the premonition of growing power, which render childhood and youth so pregnant of happiness, and so pleasant in the retrospect, were to him unrevealed. At nineteen the life seemed crushed out of him by the pressure, or, rather puncture, of a miserable present and a hopeless future. In the judgment of the most charitable, he was but one remove from fatuity.

From such material to develop the varied qualities of a pioneer, a man of firm purpose, quick resolve, and resolute to meet exigencies, might well seem to require supernatural power; and yet, by no other alchemy than sympathy, encouragement wisely timed, and knowledge seasonably imparted, was this seeming miracle accomplished.

The pity of Alice Whitman, the broad benevolence of her husband, the warm sympathy of Bertie and his young associates, the ripe counsels of the glorious old grandfather,—sage Christian hero,—and the efforts of Mr. Holmes, who honored his calling, while sowing good seed in the virgin soil of a young heart, were but visible instruments in the grasp of the Hand Unseen.

CHAPTER I.
"THE MOTHER'S BREATH IS WARM."

It was the autumn of 1792. The beams of the declining sun were resting peacefully upon the time-worn walls of a log house of large dimensions, evidently built to serve the purposes both of a dwelling and a fortress, and situated upon the banks of the Swatara Creek, in the State of Pennsylvania.

A magnificent chestnut-tree, whose trunk and lower branches were all aglow with the long level rays of the retiring light, shadowed a large portion of the spacious door-yard.

This was the homestead of Bradford Whitman, a well-to-do farmer, and whose family consisted of himself and wife, his aged father, and three children, Peter, Albert and Maria, aged respectively sixteen, fourteen and eleven.

Upon one of the highest branches of this great tree was seated Bertie Whitman. The eyes of the lad were eagerly fastened upon the road that, skirting the rising ground upon which the dwelling stood, led to a distant village.

At once his features lighted up with a jubilant expression; he rapidly descended from his perch, and ran to the door of the house, shouting, "Mother! Maria! Grandfather! They've got him; they are coming down Liscomb's hill this minute, and there's three in the wagon. Oh!"

He would have run to meet the approaching team, and had taken a few steps when he was met by his elder brother.

"Bertie, we've got the *redemptioner*, and I jumped out of the wagon while the horses were walking up our hill to tell you and Maria not to laugh if you can help it, 'cause it would make him feel bad; but you can't think how funny he does look; he's lame besides, and his name's James Renfew."

This conversation was interrupted by the rumbling of wheels as their father drove up, where his whole family were grouped around the door. Mrs. Whitman stood on the door-stone, the old grandfather beside her, leaning on his staff, the children in front, while Fowler, the house-dog, with his fore-legs

4

on the shoulders of old Frank, the near horse, his particular friend, was trying to lick his nose and Frank was arching his neck to accommodate him.

Mr. Whitman helped James to get down from the wagon. The boy made no return to the salutations of the family save by a stony stare, not even taking the hand extended to him by Mrs. Whitman. He, however, manifested some token of sensibility by offering to help in unharnessing, and would have limped after the horses to the barn, but his master told him to go into the house and keep still till his leg was better; nevertheless there he stood staring after the horses, and evidently would much rather have followed them to the barn.

The dog then came and smelt of him. Mrs. Whitman told Peter to take him by the hand and lead him into the house. She placed an arm-chair for him, and a smaller one to put his lame leg on, and in a few minutes he was fast asleep.

Judging by appearances Bradford Whitman had drawn a blank at this his first venture in the redemptioner lottery. The children got together (with the dog) under the great chestnut-tree to free their minds and compare notes.

"Isn't he queer?" said Bertie.

"Did ever anybody see such funny clothes? I guess they were made for him when he was small and so he's grown out of them, but he'd be real handsome if he had good clothes and his hair combed, and didn't have such a pitiful look out of his eyes," said Maria.

"I tell you what he puts me in mind of," said Bertie, "Mr. William Anderson's oxen that are so poor, their necks so long and thin; and they look so discouraged, and as though they wanted to fall down and die."

Peter now related all he had heard Wilson tell their father, and dwelt with great emphasis upon Mr. Wilson's statement that the lad had not a friend in the world and no home.

"He's got one friend," said Bertie, "Fowler likes him, 'cause he smelt of him and wagged his tail; if he hadn't liked him he would have growled. Mother's a friend to him, and father and grandpa and all of us."

"We will be good to him because he never had any chestnut-tree to play under and swing on, nor any garden of his own," said Maria.

"How can we be good to him if he won't say anything, Maria!" said Bertie.

"Can't we be good to the cattle, and I'm sure they don't talk?"

"If they don't they say something; the cat she purrs, the hens prate, Fowler wags his tail and barks and whines; and the horses neigh, and snort, and put down their heads for me to pat them; but how could you be good to a stone?"

5

and he's just like a stone, when mother put out her hand to shake hands he did not take it, nor look pleased nor anything."

"Perhaps 'twas 'cause he was afraid. When we first got our kitten she hid away up garret, and we didn't see her for three days, but she got tame, and so perhaps he will."

They finally made up their minds that James was entitled to all the sympathy and kindness they could manifest towards him, when they were called to supper.

It now became a question between Mr. Whitman and his wife, where to stow James that night.

"Put him in the barn and give him some blankets to-night, and to-morrow we will clean him up."

"I can't bear to put him in the barn, husband, I'll make him a bed of some old 'duds' on the floor in the porch. Send him right off to bed; I'll wash his clothes and dry 'em before morning. I can fix up some old clothes of yours for him to work in, for I don't want any of the neighbors to see him in those he has on."

Mr. Whitman now ushered James to bed, waited till he undressed, and brought in his clothes that were soon in scalding suds. Had Mr. Whitman gone back he would have seen this poor ignorant lad rise from his bed, kneel down and repeat the Lord's prayer, and though repeated with a very feeble sense of its import may we not believe it was accepted by Him who "requireth according to that a man hath and not according to that he hath not," and whose hand that through the ocean storm guides the sea-bird to its nest amid the breakers, has directed this wayfarer to the spot where there are hearts to pity and hands to aid him.

A blazing fire in the great kitchen fireplace so nearly accomplished (by bedtime) the drying of the clothes, that in the morning they were perfectly dry, the hot bricks and mouldering log giving out heat all night long. In the morning Mr. Whitman carried to the porch water in a tub, soap and his clean clothes, and told James to wash himself, put them on and then come out to his breakfast.

When James had eaten his breakfast (Mr. Whitman and Peter having eaten and gone to the field), the good wife cut his hair which was of great length, gave his head a thorough scrubbing with warm soapsuds, and completed the process with a fine-toothed comb. Removing carefully the bandages she next examined his leg.

"It was a deep cut, but it's doing nicely," she said, "there's not a bit of proud flesh in it; you must sit in the house till it heals up." When having bound up the wound she was about to leave him, he murmured,—

"You're good to me."

This was not a very fervent manifestation of gratitude, but it betokened that the spirit within was not wholly petrified; as Alice Whitman looked into that vacant face she perceived by the moisture of the eyes, that there was a lack not so much of feeling as of the power to express it.

"God bless you, I'll act a mother's part towards you; it shall be your own fault if you are not happy now. I know God sent you here, for I cannot believe that anything short of Divine Power would have ever brought my husband to take a redemptioner."

Bertie and Maria, who had been looking on in silence, now ran into the field to tell their father and Peter all their mother had said and done, and that the redemptioner had spoken to her.

"Father," said Maria, "if mother is his mother, will he be our brother?"

"Not exactly; your mother meant that she would treat him just as she does you, and so you must treat him as you do each other, because your mother has said so, and that's sufficient."

"Then we mustn't call him a redemptioner?"

"No; forget all about that and call him James."

"When we have anything good, and when we find a bumblebee's nest, shall we give him part, just like we do each other?"

"Yes."

Mrs. Whitman sent for Sally Wood, one of her neighbor's daughters, to take care of the milk and do the housework; and then set herself to altering over a suit of her husband's clothes to fit James, who, clean from head to foot, sat with his leg in a chair watching Mrs. Whitman at her work, but the greater portion of the time asleep.

"Let him sleep," she said; "'twill do him good to sleep a week; he'll come to his feeling after that and be another boy. It's the full meals and the finding out what disposition is to be made of him, and that he's not to be hurt, makes him sleep. I doubt if he had any too much to eat on the passage over."

By night the good woman, with the aid of Sally (who, besides doing the work, found some time to sew), had prepared a strong, well-fitting suit of working-clothes and a linsey-woolsey shirt, and, after supper, James put them on. He made no remark in relation to his clothes, but Maria reported that she knew he was as pleased as he could be, because she peeped into the door of the bedroom and saw him looking at himself in the glass and counting the buttons on his waistcoat and jacket.

James improved rapidly, and began in a few days to walk around the door-yard and to the barn, and sit by the hour in the sun on the wood-pile (with Fowler at his feet, for the dog had taken a great liking to him), insomuch that Mrs. Whitman asked her husband if it would not make him better contented to have some light work that he could do sitting down.

"Not yet, wife. I want to see if, when he finds us all at work, he won't start of his own accord. He has no more idea of earning anything, or of labor in our sense of that word, than my speckled ox has. When I hold up the end of the yoke and tell old Buck to come under, he comes; and so this boy has been put out to hard masters who stood over and got all out of him they could. He has never had reason to suppose that there are any people in this world that care anything about others, except to get all they can out of them."

"If, as you say, he has always had a task-master, perhaps he thinks because we don't tell him what to do, that we don't want him to do anything."

"We'll let the thing work; I want to see what he'll do of his own accord before I interfere. It is my belief that, benumbed as he now appears, there's enterprise in him, and that the right kind of treatment will bring it out; but I want it to come naturally just as things grow out of the ground. He's had a surfeit of the other kind of treatment."

Affairs went on in this way for a week longer, till the boy's leg had completely healed, during which time it became evident that this apparently unimpressible being was not, after all, insensible to the influence of kindness, for, whenever he perceived that wood or water were wanted, he would anticipate the needs of Mrs. Whitman nor ever permit her to bring either.

Mr. Whitman still manifested no disposition to put the boy to work, and even shelled corn himself, till his wife became somewhat impatient; and though even the grandfather thought the boy might, at least, do that much. Whitman, however, paid no attention to the remonstrances of either, and matters went on as before.

CHAPTER II.
THE REDEMPTIONER.

The reader of the opening chapter will, doubtless, be disposed to inquire, "What is a redemptioner? By what fortunate chance has this singular being been flung into the path, and at once domesticated in the family of Bradford Whitman, and admitted without scruple to the inner sanctuary of a mother's heart."

Not by any chance as we believe, and will, therefore, endeavor to satisfy these demands by introducing to our young readers Mr. Robert Wilson, a *soul-driver*, as the occupation in which he was engaged was then termed (and one of the best of them) and permit him to tell his own story.

The great abundance of food and coarse clothing in America, and the anxiety of the farmers to obtain cheap labor, led to this singular arrangement.

They contracted with the masters of vessels to bring over able-bodied men accustomed to farm-work, the farmers paying their passage, which included the captain's fees, the laborers contracting to serve for a certain term of years to reimburse the farmer for his outlay; the farmers agreeing to furnish the laborers with wholesome and sufficient food and comfortable clothing.

These people were called redemptioners, and the term of service was generally three years, and, in the case of boys, four.

The system, however, which operated very well for a while, had its disadvantages that brought it into disrepute, and resulted in its abolition. The principal of these was its falling into the hands of speculators, who went to the other side and took whomsoever they could pick up, without regard to their honesty, industry, or capacity of labor, some of them parish-poor, not only ignorant of agricultural labor, but even thieves and vagabonds. These persons collected them in gangs of twenty, and even more, and drove them through the country and delivered them to the farmers, ostensibly at the rate of their passage-money and a reasonable compensation for their own trouble and expense in seeking and bringing them over.

Mr. Wilson naturally a man of kindly feelings, that had not been entirely blunted by the business in which for many years he had been engaged, and who—having been well brought up by godly Scotch parents—could by no means wholly ignore the lessons of his youth, was now on board of the "Betsy" brig, in Liverpool, bound for Philadelphia, and had engaged berths for thirteen persons, eleven of whom different farmers in Pennsylvania had agreed to take off his hands. He had paid the passage of the twelfth at his own risk, and wanted, but had not been able to obtain, one more, having been disappointed in a man whom he had engaged on the previous voyage, and, as he would be compelled to pay for the berth, whether occupied or not, he was, of course, anxious to obtain another man. The vessel was not to haul out of the dock under two days, and he resolved to make a final effort to find another man.

Mr. Wilson was well known among the neighboring population, and therefore possessed peculiar facilities. The persons already obtained he had brought from the country, and he doubted not from his extensive acquaintance that he could dispose of almost any man who was sound in limb, accustomed to labor, whether much acquainted with farm-work or not. "If he is only honest," said Wilson to himself, "and young enough, it will do; for what he don't know he can learn, and must work for his employer a longer time, that's all."

In regard to character he was able, in many cases, to obtain references, but a shrewd judge of men, he trusted much to his own judgment, and had seldom cause to repent it, although, as we shall see, he was deceived in the character of one of the men then on shipboard which led to his relinquishing the traffic not many years after.

He set out early in the morning for a village about ten miles from the city, and where he had often found men to his liking, especially on the previous voyage. He found quite a number eager to go, but some were Irish, whom he did not like; some were boys, some old and decrepid, or too much labor-worn.

He was returning from his bootless search in no very satisfactory state of mind, when he stumbled upon a company of young persons, who late as was the hour, had just started out from the shelter of some old crates filled with straw that had been piled against the brick wall of a glass-house, in which were built the chimneys of several ovens, and which had afforded them warmth, for the nights were quite cool.

They were shaking the straw from their garments and evidently preparing to break their fast. One had a fish in his hand, another meat, and another vegetables, but all uncooked.

The group presented such a hardened vagabond appearance, that Wilson who had paused with the intention of speaking, was about to pass on, when upon second thoughts, he said within himself, "They look like thieves, but they are a hard-meated rugged looking set and all young. Perhaps there may be among them one who taken away from the rest, and put under good influences, and among good people, might make something."

Turning towards them, he said,

"Young men, do any of you want to go to America?"

"Go to 'Merica," replied a dark-complexioned fellow of low stature, with a devil-may-care-look, and quite flashily attired, apparently in the cast-off clothes of some gentleman.

"Yes, some people are going over to the States with me as redemptioners, and I want one more to make up my number, it's a first-rate chance for a young man who's smart, willing to work, and wants to make something of himself. There are scores of men there whom I carried, that are now forehanded, have large farms, cattle and money at interest, who when they left here lived on one meal a day and often went without that."

"Don't you know Dick," said a red-headed, saucy, but intelligent-looking chap, with sharply cut features, "that's the genteel name of those poor devils who sell themselves for their passage and this 'ere likes is the boss what takes the head money."

Without noticing the interruption, Wilson continued,—

"Here, for instance, is a young man who can get no work these hard times, which means no clothes, no bread, no place to put his head in. A farmer over there who wants help pays his passage. He works for that farmer till he pays up the passage money; and the farmer takes him into his family, and feeds and clothes him while he is doing it."

"How long will he have to work to pay for his passage?"

"Three or four years; three if he is used to farm work."

"What does he do after that?"

"Then he is his own man and can always have plenty of work at good wages and found, and won't have to lay up alongside of a glass-house chimney to keep from freezing. Land is so cheap that if he is prudent and saves his money, he can in a few years buy a piece of land with wood on it that he can cut down, build him a log house, plant and sow and be comfortable. In some places the government will give him land to settle on if he builds a house and stays five years, or he can pay for it by working on the highways."

"Go, Dick," cried the red-head, "they say it's a glorious country, plenty of work, plenty of bread, and no hanging for stealing, just the place for you my lad."

"You shut up. What is he going to do after he gets the land!"

"Work on it to be sure, make a home of it, have cattle, and sheep, and hogs, and lashings to eat."

"Then all the redemptioners, as you call 'em, go to 'Merica for is to work?"

"To be sure, to get a chance to work and get ahead, and that's what they can't do here."

"Well, grandfather, I won't be a redemptioner, because work and I have fallen out. Ain't it so with you, Tom Hadley?"

This interrogatory was addressed to a tall pale youth, clothed in a suit of rusty black, that might have belonged to a curate, with finger nails half an inch in length, and on his fingers three valuable rings and a broad-brimmed hat on his head.

"Yes, I never fell in with it yet. Don't think I am fool enough to work three years for the sake of getting a chance to work all the rest of my life, a thing I am altogether above and do despise."

"If you won't work how do you expect to live?"

"By stealing," replied the lank boy, displaying his rings.

"By working when we can't do any better, granddaddy, and begging for the rest," said Tom Hadley.

During this conversation this select company had gradually gathered around Wilson, and one of them was in the act of purloining a handkerchief from the latter's pocket, when he received a blow from a stout cudgel in the hand of the Scotchman, that felled him to the ground.

"Why don't you take Foolish Jim?" said the red-headed chap, "he'll work; rather work than not."

"Who's Foolish Jim?"

"There he is," pointing to a boy leaning against the wall of the glass-house, aloof from the rest.

"Why do you call him Foolish Jim?"

"'Cause he's such a fool he won't lie, swear nor steal; but we are dabsters at all three."

"What makes him so much worse dressed than the rest?"

"'Cause he's a fool and won't steal. Now we all get one thing or another, meat, fish, vegetables; and we're going down to the brick yards to have a cook and a real tuck-out, but he's had no breakfast, nor won't get any, till he runs some errand for the glass-house folks, or gets some horse to hold, or some little job of work, just 'cause he won't steal nor beg either. If you'd a dropt that handkerchief on the ground and he'd a picked it up, instead of putting it in his pocket, he'd a run after you crying, 'Mister you've lost your handkerchief.' Now there's no work to be had by those who are fools enough to work, so he's just starving by inches."

"And to help him out of the world you keep him with you to make sport of him."

"That's so, as much as we think will do, but we can't go but about so far, 'cause he's strong as a giant and he's got a temper of his own, though it takes an awful sight to git it up; but when its up you'd better stand clear, he'll take any two of us and knock our heads together. When the glassmen have a heavy crate to lift, they always sing out for Jim."

"Ask him to come here."

"Jim, here's a cove wants yer."

Mr. Wilson scanned with great curiosity the lad whom his companions termed a fool because he would neither lie nor swear, steal nor beg, but was willing to work. He was tall, large-boned, with great muscles that were plainly visible, of regular features, fair complexion and clean, thus forming a strong contrast to his companions, who were dirty in the extreme. He might be called, on the whole, good looking, as far as form and features went, but on the other hand there was an expression of utter hopelessness and apathy in his face that seemed almost to border upon fatuity, and went far to justify the appellation bestowed upon him by his companions.

His movements also were those of an automaton; there was none of the spring, energy or buoyancy of youth about him.

He was barefoot, with a tattered shirt, ragged pants and coat of corduroy, the coat was destitute of buttons and confined to his waist by a ropeyarn. On his head he wore a sailor's fez cap, streaked with tar and that had once been red, but was faded to the color of dried blood.

"What is your name, my lad?"

"Jim."

"Jim what?"

"Jim, that's all."

"How old are you?"

"Don't know."

"Where are your father and mother?"

"Haven't got none?"

"Any brothers or sisters?"

"No."

"Where did you come from? Where do you belong?"

"Work'us."

"Do you want to go to America with me, and get work?"

"I'll go anywhere if I can have enough to eat, clothes to keep me warm, and some warm place to sleep."

"Will you work?"

"Yes; I'll work."

"What kind of work can you do?"

"I can dig dirt, and hoe, and pick oakum, and drive horses, and break stones for the highway, and break flax."

"What other farm-work can you do?"

"I can mow grass, and reap grain, and plash a hedge, and thrash (thresh) grain."

"Where did you learn these things?"

"They used to put me out to farmers once."

"How long was you with the farmers?"

"Don't know."

"Mister," broke in the lank youth, "he don't know anything. Why don't you ask 'em up to the work'us; like's they know who he is, where he came from, and all about him. They feed him, but he's so proud he won't call upon 'em if he can help it, 'cause he thinks it's begging. He might have three good meals there every day if he would, but he's such a simpleton he won't go there till he's starved within an inch of his life."

Upon this hint the Scotchman, whose curiosity was now thoroughly aroused, taking the lad for a guide, started for the workhouse.

CHAPTER III.
JAMES RENFEW.

As they went along, Wilson, feigning fatigue, proposed that they should sit down to rest, but his real motive was that, undisturbed by his companions, he might observe this singular youth more at his leisure and be the better able to form some more definite opinion in his own mind respecting him.

After long contemplating the features and motions of Jim at his leisure, Mr. Wilson came to the conclusion that there was no lack of sense, but that discouragement, low living, absence of all hope for the future, ignorance and being made a butt of, were the potent causes that had reduced the lad to what he was; and that, under the influence of good food and encouragement, he would rally and make an efficient laborer and perhaps something more, and resolved to sift the matter to the bottom.

From the records of the workhouse he ascertained that the boy's name was James Renfew, that he was not born in the institution, but was brought there with his mother, being at that time three years of age. The mother was then in the last stages of disease, and in a few weeks died. He was informed that the boy had been several times put out to different farmers, who, after keeping him till after harvest, brought him back in the fall to escape the cost of his maintenance in the winter.

Wilson mentioned what he had been told in respect to his character, to which the governor replied it was all true, and that he should not be afraid to trust him with untold gold, that he came and went as he pleased; and when starved out, and not till then, he came to them and was housed, fed and made welcome.

"Where did he get ideas in his head so different from those of workhouse children in general?"

"I am sure I don't know except they grew there. You seem to have a great deal of curiosity about the history of Jim, there's an old Scotchwoman here, Grannie Brockton, who took care of his mother while she lived and of the boy after her death; she's a crabbed venomous old creature, deaf as a haddock, but if she happens to be in a good mood and you can make her hear, she can tell you the whole story."

"I'll find a way to make her agreeable."

He found Grannie Brockton, who seeing a stranger approach, drew herself up, put one hand to her ear, and with the other motioned the intruder away.

Wilson, without a word, approached and laid a piece of silver on her knee. This wrought an instantaneous change, turning briskly round she pulled down the flap of her right ear (the best one) and said,—

"What's your will wi' me?"

"I want you to tell me all you know about James Renfew and his parents."

"It's Jeames Renfew ye want to speer about, and it's my ain sel' wha' can tell you about him and his kith, and there's na ither in this place that can."

The interrogator felt that the best method of getting at the matter was to leave the old crone to her own discretion, and without further questioning placed another small piece of silver in her lap.

"What countryman may ye be?"

"A Scotchman."

"I kenned as much by the burr on your tongue; ay then, ye'll mind when the battle o' Bannockburn was."

"The battle of Bannockburn was fought on the twenty-fifth day of June."

"True for ye. It was sixteen years ago Bannockburn day that this boy's mother was brought here sick, and this Jeames wi' her a bairn about three years old. A good woman she was too. I'm not a good woman, naebody ca's me a good woman, I dinna ca' myself a good woman, but for all that I know a good person when I see one.

"She had death in her face when she was brought in, would have been glad to die, but her heart was breaking about the child to be left to the tender mercies o' the work'us.

"When she had been here little better than a week, a minister came to see her; a young, a douce man. Oh, he was a heavenly man! She was so rejoiced to see him, she kissed his hands and bathed them wi' her hot tears. She thanked him, and cried for joy. I could nae keep from greeting my ain sel'."

"Where was he from?"

"He was the curate of the parish where she used to live, was with her husband when he was sick, and read the service at his funeral; and he had christened this child, and aye been a friend to them."

"She told me the parson o' the parish was a feckless do-little, naebody thought he had any grace; this curate did all the work and visited the people, who almost worshipped him."

"Did he come any more?"

"Ay, till she died, and then attended the burial. For four years after her death he came three times a year to see the child, and would take him on his knees and tell him stories out of the Bible and teach him the Lord's prayer. He made the child promise him that he would never lie, nor swear, nor steal, and taught him a' the commandments. He likewise made me promise that I would hear him say the Lord's prayer, when I put him to bed, and that I would be kind to him. I did hear him say the prayer, but I was never kind to him, for 'tis not in my nature to be kind to any body, but I used to beat him when he vexed me."

"Who was this boy's father?"

"He was a hedger and ditcher, and rented a small cottage, and grass for a cow, in the parish where the curate lived. After his death, his widow came to Liverpool, because she had a sister here who had saved money by living at service, and they rented a house, and took boarders, and washed and ironed; but her sister got married and went to Canada, and she was taken sick, and came here to die."

"What became of the curate?"

"He came here till the laddie was seven years auld, and then he came to bid him good-by, because he was going to be chaplain in a man-of-war, and the laddie grat as though his heart wad break.

"The curate gave him his mother's Bible, but little good will it do him, for he canna read a word, nor tell the Lord's prayer when he sees it in print." Finding her visitor was about to leave, she said,—

"Mind, what ye have heard frae me is the truth, sin a' body kens that cross and cankered as auld Janet may be, she's nae given to falsehood."

The relation of auld Janet had stirred the conscience of Robert Wilson, and probed his soul to its very depths.

"I cannot," he said within himself, "leave the boy here. The curse of that dying mother would fall on me if I did. He must come out of this place. Let me see what can I do with him? Could I only hope to prevail upon Bradford Whitman to take him—I know he hates the very sight of me and of a redemptioner, but a friendless boy of this one's character, that I can get a certificate from the governor of the workhouse to establish, might operate to move him, and he's a jewel of a man. I'll try him. If I can do nothing with him, I'll try Nevins or Conly, but Whitman first of all. If none of them'll keep him, you must take him yourself, Robert Wilson; take him from here, at any rate."

Mr. Wilson made his way back to the authorities, and said to them:—

"I'm taking some redemptioners to the States; if you'll pay this boy's passage, I'll take him off your hands, but you must put some decent clothes on him."

To this the chairman of the board replied: "We cannot do that. We will let you have the boy and put some clothes on him, and that's enough. You make a good thing out of these men; you don't have to advance anything, the farmers pay their passage and pay you head-money."

"Thank you for nothing, that's not enough. The rest of my redemptioners are able-bodied men used to farm-work, but this creature is but nineteen, don't know much of anything about farm-work; only fit to pick oakum or break stones on the highway, and there's none of that work to be done in the States. He'll be a hard customer to get rid of, for he don't seem to have hardly the breath of life in him; these Americans are driving characters; they make business ache, and will say right off he's not worth his salt. I shall very likely have him thrown on my hands (if indeed he don't die before he gets there) for I have no order for any boy."

"You are very much mistaken, Mr. Wilson, that boy will lift you and your load, will do more work than most men, is better fitted for a new country than one who has been delicately brought up."

"Mr. Governor, I have made you a fair offer. This boy has got a settlement in this parish, and you cannot throw it off, so you will always have him on your hands more or less. By and by he'll marry some one as poor as himself, and you'll have a whole family on your hands for twenty, perhaps fifty years. You know how that works, these paupers marry and raise families on purpose, because they know they will then be the more entitled to parish help. Give him up to me and pay his passage, you are then rid of him forever and stop the whole thing just where it is. I've told you what I'll do. I won't do anything different."

After consultation the authorities consented to pay his passage and give him second-hand but whole shoes, shirts, and stockings enough for a shift, and a Scotch cap.

Mr. Wilson then took him into a Jew's shop, pulled off his rags, furnished him with breeches and upper garments, and put him on board the brig.

Mr. Wilson was an old practitioner at the business of soul-driving. His custom was to stop a week in Philadelphia in order to let his men recover from the effects of the voyage, which at that day, in an emigrant ship, was a terrible ordeal, for there were no laws to restrain the cupidity of captains and owners. This delay answered a double purpose, as his redemptioners made a better appearance, and were more easily disposed of and at better prices. He also improved the opportunity to send forward notices to his friends, the tavernkeepers, stating the day on which he should be at their houses; and they in turn notified the farmers in their vicinity, some of whom came out to receive the men they had engaged, and others came to look at and trade with Wilson for the men he might have brought on his own account, of whom he sometimes had a number, and not infrequently his whole gang were brought on speculation.

It was about nine o'clock on the morning of the second day after his arrival in Philadelphia, and Mr. Wilson, having partaken of a bountiful meal, was enjoying his brief rest in a most comfortable frame of mind. He had good reason to congratulate himself, having safely passed through the perils of the voyage, and, on the first day of his arrival disposed to great advantage of the man he had brought at his own risk; the other eleven were engaged, and the boy alone remained to be disposed of.

His cheerful reflections were disturbed by a cry of pain from the door-yard, and James was brought in, the blood streaming from a long and deep gash in his right leg.

The tavern-keeper asked him to cut some firewood, and the awkward creature, who had never in his life handled any wood tool but an English billhook, had struck the whole bit of the axe in his leg. The blood was staunched, and a surgeon called to take some stitches, at which the boy neither flinched nor manifested any concern.

The doctor and the crowd of idle onlookers, whom the mishap of James drew together, had departed, the landlord had left the bar to attend to his domestic concerns. Mr. Wilson, his serenity of mind effectually broken, paced the floor with flushed face and rapid step, and talking to himself.

"Had it been his neck, I wad nae hae cared," he muttered (getting to his Scotch as his passion rose) "here's a doctor's bill at the outset; and I maun stay here on expense wi' twelve men, or take him along in a wagon.

"I dinna ken, Rob Wilson, what ailed ye to meddle with the gauk for an auld fool as ye are, but when I heard that cankered dame wi' the tear in her een tell how his mother felt on her deathbed, and a' about the minister taking sic pains wi' him, it gaed me to think o' my ain mither and the pains she took tae sae little purpose wi' me. I thocht it my duty to befriend him and gi' him a chance in some gude family, and aiblins it might be considered above, and make up

19

for some o' thae hard things I am whiles compelled in my business to do. I did wrang altogether; a soul-driver has nae concern wi' feelings, nor conscience either. He canna' afford it, Rob, he suld be made o' whin-stone, or he canna thrive by soul-driving."

Mr. Wilson arrived in Lancaster county, within a few miles of the residence of the Whitmans and their neighbors, the Nevins, Woods, and Conlys, with only three redemptioners, who were already engaged to farmers in the vicinity, and the boy Jim, who was so lame that he had been obliged to take him along in a wagon.

CHAPTER IV.
THE WHITMAN FAMILY.

The starting of a boy in the right direction, and the imparting of that bent he will retain through life, is a work the importance of which cannot be overrated. That our readers may appreciate the force of these influences about to be invoked to shape the future,—to fling a ray of hope upon the briar-planted path of this pauper boy, and quicken to life a spirit in which the germs of hope and the very aroma of youth seem to have withered beneath the benumbing pressure of despair,—we desire to acquaint them with the character of Bradford Whitman, to whose guiding influence so shrewd a judge of character as Robert Wilson wished to surrender his charge (and moreover resolved to leave no method untried to effect it), and in no other way can this object be so effectually accomplished as by our relating to them a conversation held by Whitman and his wife in relation to the building of a new dwelling-house on the homestead.

Several of Whitman's neighbors had pulled down the log-houses their forefathers built and replaced them with stone, brick, or frame buildings, but Bradford Whitman still lived in the log-house in which he was born; it was, however, one of the best of the kind, built of chestnut logs, with the tops and bottoms hewn to match, and the ends squared and locked.

Whitman was abundantly able to build a nice house, and only two days before the event we are about to narrate occurred, mentioned the subject to his wife, saying that several of the neighbors had either built or were about to build new houses, and perhaps she felt as though they ought to build one, but she replied,—

"Bradford, you cannot build a better house than the old one, a warmer or one more convenient for the work, nor could you find a lovelier spot to set it on than this. It is close to the spring from which your father drank when he first came here a strong lusty man, stronger, I have heard you say, than any child he ever had. There's many a bullet in these old logs that were meant for him or some of his household."

"True enough, Alice, for Peter dug a bullet out last fall that came from an

Indian rifle, and made a plummet of it to rule his writing-book; but the same may be said of many other houses in this neighborhood that have been taken away to make room for others, for there are but few on which the savage did not leave his mark."

"But I fear it would give the good old man a heartache to miss the house in which his children were born, his wife died, all his hardships and dangers were met and overcome, and his happiest days were spent.

"A little jar will throw down a dish that is near the edge of the shelf; the least breath will blow out a candle that's just flickering in the socket, and though I know he would not say a word, I am sure it would make his heart bleed, and I fear hurry him out of the world. Besides, husband, while your father lives your brothers and sisters will come home at New Years, and I have not a doubt they would miss the old house and feel that something heartsome and that could never be replaced, had dropped out of their lives. I hardly think you care to do it yourself, only you think that as we are now well to do, I have got ashamed of the log-house, and want a two-story frame, or brick, or stone one, like some of the neighbors."

"It would be very strange if you didn't, wife."

"No, husband; I am not of that way of thinking at all. We have worked too long and too hard for what we have got together to spend it on a fine house. Here are some of our neighbors whom I could name who were living easy, had a few hundred dollars laid by that were very convenient when they had a sudden call for money, or wanted to buy stock, or hold a crop of wheat over for a better market, but their wives put them up to build a fine house. It cost more than they expected, as it always does, and when they got the house, the old furniture that looked well enough in the old house, didn't compare at all with the new one, they had to be at a great expense to go to the old settlements to buy fine things; it took all the money they had saved up, and now those same people, when they want to buy cattle or hire help, have to come to you to borrow the money."

"That is true; for only yesterday a man who lives not three miles from here, and who lives in a fine house, came to me on that same errand."

"No, husband; you and I are far enough along to be thinking less of mere appearances than we might have done once. We have three children to school and start in the world; a new house won't do that, but the money it would cost will."

"May the Lord bless you," cried Bradford Whitman, imprinting a fervent kiss on the lips of his wife, "and make me as thankful as I ought to be for the best wife a man ever had. You have just spoken my own mind right out."

Alice Whitman blushed with pleasure at the commendation of her husband so richly deserved, and said,—

"Husband, that is not all. If we have something laid by we can open our hearts and hands to a neighbor's necessities as we both like to do, and I am sure I had much rather help a poor fatherless child, give food to the hungry, or some comfort to a sick neighbor, than to live in a fine house and have nice things that after all are not so comfortable nor convenient as the old-fashioned ones."

"You are right wife, for when John Gillespie was killed by a falling tree last winter and all the neighbors helped his widow and family, William Vinton said his disposition was to do as much as any one, but he hadn't the means, and the reason was that the cost of his new house had brought him into difficulties. I knew it gave him a heartache to refuse, and I believe he would have much rather have had the old chest of drawers and the log-house and been able to give something to the fatherless, than to have the new house and the nice furniture and not be able to help a neighbor in distress. I hope Alice you won't object to having the old house made a little better and more comfortable, providing it can be done without much expense."

"If you will promise not to make it look *unnatural*, like an old man in a young man's clothes and wig, and if you meddle with the roof (as most like you will) not to disturb the door that bears to-day the gash cut by the Indian's tomahawk who chased your mother into the house, and that took the blow meant for her, nor meddle with the overhang above it, through which your father fired down and shot him."

Bradford Whitman put a new roof on the house and ceiled the wall up inside with panel work, thus hiding the old logs. He also laid board floors instead of the old ones that were laid with puncheons (that is, sticks of timber hewn on three sides) that were irregular, hard to sweep over and to wash. But in his father's bedroom he disturbed nothing, but left both the walls and the floors as they were before. The grandfather, though he made no remark, yet manifested some trepidation in his looks when the roof was taken off, and the floors taken up, and seemed very much relieved when he found that the walls on the outside were not disturbed, that the old door with its wooden latch, hinges and huge oaken bar, the former scarred with bullets and chipped with the tomahawks of the savages, remained as before. And when he found that his son, with a thoughtfulness that was part of his nature, had, after ceiling up the kitchen, replaced in its brackets of deer's horns over the fireplace, the old rifle with which he had fought the savage and obtained food for his family in the bitter days of the first hard struggle for a foothold and a homestead, not only expressed decided gratification with the change but to the great delight of Alice Whitman desired that his bedroom might be panelled and have a board floor like the rest of the house. And the delighted daughter-in-law covered it with rugs, into the working of which were put all the ingenuity of hand and brain she possessed.

This was the family in which Robert Wilson desired to place James Renfew, for notwithstanding in his passion, he had wished that James had stuck the axe into his neck instead of his leg, he was really interested in, and felt for, the lad, and wanted to help him.

He knew Bradford Whitman well, knew that he was as shrewd as kindly-affectioned, and that he was bitterly prejudiced against the business of soul-driving in which he was engaged, as Wilson had for years vainly endeavored to persuade him to take a redemptioner; but he had heard from the miller that Mr. Whitman was coming to the mill in a few days with wheat, and he resolved to make a desperate effort to prevail upon him to take James.

"He's a kindly man," said Wilson to the miller, "perhaps he'll pity the lad when he comes to see him."

"Yes, he is a kindly man but if he could be brought to think that it was his *duty* to take that boy, your work would be already done, and if he *should* take him, the boy is made for life, that is, if there's anything in him to make a man out of."

"Can't you help me old acquaintance?"

"I would gladly, Robert, but I don't feel free to, for this reason. Bradford Whitman is a kindly man as you say, and an upright man, and a man of most excellent judgment, a man who knows how to make money and to keep it and is able to do just as he likes. We have always been great friends, but he is a man quite set in his way, and if I should influence him to take this boy, about whom I know nothing, and he should turn out bad (or what I think is most likely, to be stupid and not worth his salt) he never would forget it."

But notwithstanding the backwardness of the miller to aid his friend, the Being who is wont to shape the affairs of men and bring about events in the most natural manner, and one noticed only by the most thoughtful, was all unbeknown to the soul-driver preparing instrumentalities and setting in operation causes a thousand times more effective than the efforts of the miller (had he done his best), to bring about the purpose Wilson had at heart.

CHAPTER V.
THE UNSEEN HAND.

As the Whitmans were seated at the supper-table of an autumn evening, Peter, the eldest boy, who had just returned from the store, reported that Wilson, the soul-driver, had come to the village and put up at Hanscom's tavern, with some redemptioners, and that Mr. Wood, one of their neighbors, who had engaged one the last spring, was going over to get his man, and they said there was a boy he hadn't engaged, and wanted some one to take him off his hands.

"From my heart I pity these poor forlorn creatures," said the mother; "brought over here to a strange land with nothing but the clothes on their backs, and how they will be treated and whose hands they will fall into, they don't know."

After the meal they all drew together around the fire, that the season of the year made agreeable.

The children, hoping to obtain some old-time story from their grandfather, drew his large chair with its stuffed back and cushion, worked in worsted by the cunning hand of their mother, into his accustomed corner. Bradford Whitman sat in a meditative mood, with hands clasped over his knees, watching the sparks go up the great chimney.

"Bradford," said the old gentleman, "I have sometimes wondered that you don't take one of these redemptioners; you are obliged to hire a good deal, and it is often difficult to get help when it is most needed."

"I know that there are a good many of these people hired by farmers; sometimes it turns out well, but often they are villains. Sometimes have concealed ailments and prove worthless; at other times stay through the winter, and after they have learned the method of work here, run off and hire out for wages in some other part of the country."

"Husband, Mr. Wilson has been many years in this business, and I never knew *him* to bring any people of bad character."

"He is too shrewd a Scotchman to do it knowingly, but he is liable to be deceived. I have thought and said that nothing would ever tempt me to have anything to do with a redemptioner, but when Peter came to tell about that boy it seemed to strike me differently. I said to myself, this is a new thing. Here's a boy flung on the world in a strange land, with nobody to guide him, and about certain to suffer, because there are not many who would want a boy (for it would cost as much for his passage as that of a man), and he will be about sure to fall into bad hands and take to bad ways; whereas he is young, and if there was any one who would take the pains to guide him he might become a useful man."

"That, husband, is just the light in which it appears to me."

"So it seemed to me there was a duty for somebody concerning that boy, that there wouldn't be allowing he was a man. When I cast about me I couldn't honestly feel that there was any person in this neighborhood could do such a thing with less put-out to themselves than myself. Still I can't feel that it's my duty; he might turn out bad and prove a great trial, and I am not inclined to stretch out my arm farther than I can draw it back."

"My father," said the old gentleman, "was a poor boy, born of poor parents on the Isle of Wight. His father got bread for a large family by fishing, and by reaping in harvest; and his mother sold the fish, and gleaned after the reapers in wheat and barley harvest. The children as they grew large enough went out to service."

"What was his name?" said Peter.

"Henry."

"What relation was he to me?" said Bert.

"Your great-grandfather. When he was sixteen years old, with the consent of his parents, he came to Philadelphia in a vessel as passenger, and worked his passage by waiting on the cook and the cabin passengers. The captain spoke so well of him that a baker took him into his shop to carry bread. A farmer who hauled fagots to heat the baker's oven offered to hire him by the year to work on his farm, and he worked with him till he was twenty-one. After that he worked for others, and then took what little money he had, and your grandmother who was as poor as himself, for her parents died when she was young and she was put out to a farmer, and they went into the wilderness. They cleared a farm and paid for it, raised eight children, six boys and two girls. I was the youngest boy; my brothers and sisters all did well, they and their husbands acquired property and owned farms. Your mother and I came on to this land when it was a forest. I with my narrow axe, she with her spinning-wheel; and a noble helpmate she was as ever a man was blessed with."

The old gentleman's voice trembled, he dashed a tear from his eye and went on. "We raised eleven children, they all grew to man's and woman's estate, the girls have married well, the four boys are all well-to-do farmers and prospering. There are nineteen farmers and farmers' wives without counting their children, and not a miserable idle "shack" among them; all of whom sprang by the father's side from that poor boy who was the poorest of the poor, and worked his passage to this country, but found in a strange land friends to guide him. So you see what good may come from a friendless boy, if he is well-minded and helped."

"You know, husband, the children have a long distance to go in the winter to school, and a boy like that would be a great help about the barn and to cut firewood, or go into the woods with you. The clothing of him would not be much, for I could make both the cloth and the clothes, and as for his living, what is one more spoon in the platter? And in regard to the money for his passage you know we haven't built any new house, and so you won't need to borrow the money."

"Wife, if you want to take that boy, I'll start off to-morrow morning and get him."

"I want you to do just as you think best in regard to taking anybody, either boy or man. We are only talking the matter over in all its bearings, and as you brought up the disadvantages and risks, your father and myself were bringing up something to balance them; it is not a very easy matter to decide, at any rate."

"But father," cried Peter, "Bertie and Maria and I want you to take him."

"Why do you want me to take him?"

"'Cause we want him to come here and grow up to be a great, smart, good man, just like our great-grandfather—and as grandfather says he will."

"And we want to help about it and befriend him," put in Bertie.

"And me, too," cried Maria; "I want to befriend him."

"No, Peter, I didn't say he *would* become a good man, because no one knows that but a higher Power. I said that to my certain knowledge one boy did, and that ought to be an encouragement to people to put other boys in the way of making something."

"Well, that's what grandpa means," said Peter, resolved to carry his point.

"Father," said Maria, "I want you to take him, 'cause if Peter or Bertie was carried 'way off where they didn't know anybody, and where their father and mother wasn't, they would want somebody who was good, to ask 'em to come to their house and give them something to eat."

"Wife, where did Peter get all this news that seems to have set him and the rest half crazy?"

"At Hooper's, the shoemaker. He went to get his shoes, and Mr. Hooper told him that his father-in-law, John Wood, was going to-morrow to Hanscom's tavern to get a redemptioner Mr. Wilson had brought over for him, and that neighbor Wood wanted him to get word to you that Wilson had a man and a boy left. Mr. Wood wants you to go over with him to-morrow and take the boy; he says you couldn't do better."

"I am going over there day after to-morrow to haul some wheat that I have promised; if the boy is there I shall most likely see him."

"Oh, father, before that time somebody else may get him."

"Well, Peter, let them have him; if he gets a place, that's all that is needed."

"But perhaps 'twon't be a good man like you who'll get him."

"He may be a great deal better man."

More enthusiastic and persistent than her brothers, and unable to sleep, the little girl lay wakeful in her trundle-bed till her mother and father had retired, and then crawling in between them, put her arms around her father's neck and whispered,—

"Father, you will take the boy, won't you?"

"My dear child, you don't know what you are talking about. I have not set eyes on him yet, and perhaps when I come to see him he will appear to me to be a bad, or stupid, or lazy boy, and then you yourself would not want me to take him."

"No, father; but if you like the looks of him, and Peter likes the looks of him, 'cause if Peter likes him Bertie and I shall, will you take him then?"

"I'll think about it, my little girl, and now get into your bed and cuddle down and go to sleep."

Instead of that, however, she crept to the other side of the bed, hid her face in her mother's bosom and sobbed herself to sleep.

Notwithstanding the entreaties of the children, their father remained firm in his purpose, but, at the time he had set, started, taking Peter with him, as the lad was to have a pair of new shoes. He was also to buy the cloth to make Bertie a go-to-meeting suit, as the cloth for the best clothes was bought, and made up by their mother who wove all the cloth for every-day wear. He was also to buy a new shawl for Maria, and get a bonnet for her that her mother had selected some days before. In the mean time Peter had received the most solemn charges from both Bertie and Maria, "to tease and tease and tease their father to take the boy." Just as they were starting Maria clambered up to the seat of the wagon and whispered in his ear,—

"If father won't take him, you cry; cry like everything."

Peter promised faithfully that he would.

When the sound of wagon wheels had died away in the distance, Bertie and Maria endeavored to extract some consolation by interrogating their mother, and Bertie asked if she expected their father would bring home the boy.

"Your father, children, will do what he thinks to be his duty, and for the best, but there is an unseen hand that guides matters of this kind. I shall not be very much surprised if the boy should come with them."

No sooner was the wheat unloaded than Peter entreated his father to go and see the redemptioner.

"Not yet, my son, I must go and pay a bill at Mr. Harmon's, he is going to Lancaster to-day to buy goods and wants the money. And then I must get your new shoes and the cloth for Bertie's suit, and a bonnet and shawl for Maria, and *then* we will go."

"Couldn't you pay the bill please, and get our things after you see the redemptioner?"

"I don't know, I'll see."

The truth of the fact was, Mr. Whitman was sorry that he had expressed before his family the transient thought that crossed his mind in regard to the boy, because he felt that his wife and father were anxious that he should take him, although they disclaimed any desire to influence his actions; and being an indulgent parent, the clamorous eagerness of the children aided to complicate the matter. He likewise felt that he had so far committed himself, he must at least go and look at this lad, though inclined to do it in that leisurely way in which a man sets about an unpleasant duty. But, to the great delight of Peter, before the horses had finished their provender, Mr. Wilson himself appeared on the ground.

"Good morning, Mr. Whitman. I understand from Mr. Wood, to whom I have brought a man, that you want a boy. I have a boy and a man at the public house and would like to have you step over and look at them."

"I have never said to neighbor Wood nor to any one that I wanted a redemptioner; he must either have got it from Peter here, through some one else, or have imagined it. All I ever had to do in the matter was to say, when we were talking in the family about your having a boy among your men, that I did not know but it might be my duty to take the boy. It was however merely a passing thought. I have about made up my mind that I will have nothing to do with it, and I do not think it is worth while (as I have met you) for me to go and see either of them."

"You had better go look at them, your horses have not yet finished eating."

"I am an outspoken man, Mr. Wilson, and make free to tell you I don't like this buying and selling of flesh and blood. It seems to me too much like slavery, which I never could endure. I think a capable man like you had better take up with some other calling, and I don't care to encourage you in this. If you'll buy oxen or horses or wheat I'll trade with you, but I don't care to trade in human bodies or souls."

"I know, Mr. Whitman, that we are called *soul-drivers*, and a great many hard things are said of us, but just look at the matter for a moment free from prejudice. Here is a young able-bodied man on the other side, willing to work, but there is no work to be had, and he must do one of three things—starve, steal, or beg; there is a farmer in Pennsylvania who wants help but can't get it. I introduce these men to each other and benefit both. The farmer gets help to handle his wheat, the poor starving man bread to eat, he learns the ways of the country, and when his time is out can find work anywhere and become an owner of land. You know yourself, Mr. Whitman, that within ten, twelve, and twenty miles of here, yes, within five, are living to-day persons, owners of good farms and one of them a *selectman*, another of them married to his employer's daughter, who were all brought over by me, and came in rags, and who would not care to have their own children know that they were redemptioners."

"I've no doubt but that like everything else almost in this world, the business has its benefits. And by picking out the best and leaving out the worst parts of it, you may make a plausible showing so far as you are concerned, but you know yourself that it is liable to be abused, and is abused every day, and I don't care to have anything to do with it."

"But father," cried Peter, with the tears in his eyes, "you *promised* me you would go and see him when the horses had done eating."

"I forgot that, then I will go; I never break a promise."

"I will bring the boy here," said Wilson, "it is but a few steps."

"Perhaps that is the best way, as, now I think of it, I want to trade with the miller for some flour."

Wilson soon returned with our old acquaintance Foolish Jim, very little improved in appearance, as his clothes, though whole, did not by any means fit him. His trowsers were too short for his long limbs, and his legs stuck through them a foot, and they were so tight across the hips as to seriously interfere with locomotion. As to the jacket, it was so small over the shoulders and around the waist it could not be buttoned; a large breadth of shirt not over clean was visible between the waistcoat and trowsers, as instead of breeches he wore loose pants or sailor trowsers and no suspenders. The sleeves, too short, exposed several inches of large square-boned black wrists, and on his head was a Highland cap, from under which escaped long tangled locks of very fine hair; and his skin, where not exposed to the weather, was fair. Jim was so lame that he walked with great difficulty by the help of a large fence stake, his right leg being bandaged below the knee, and he was barefoot. He wore the same stolid, hopeless look as of old, and which instantly excited the pity and moved the sympathies of Peter to the utmost.

His father, on the other hand, could not repress a smile as he gazed on the uncouth figure before him.

"Do you call him a boy, Wilson? If he was anything but skin and bones he would be as heavy as I am, near about."

"Yes I call him a boy, because he's only nineteen, though there's considerable of him."

"There's warp enough, as my wife would say, but there's a great lack of filling."

"He's a wonderfully strong creature, see what bones and muscles he's got."

The miller rolled out three barrels of flour for Whitman, and he and Wilson went into the mill leaving James seated on one of the barrels.

"What do you think of him?" said Wilson when they were inside?

"I think I don't want anything to do with him. What do you think I want of a cripple?"

"That's nothing; he cut himself with an axe after we landed, and I had to carry him in a wagon, but it's only a flesh wound. He's got a good pair of shoes, but has been so used to going barefoot that they make his feet swell."

"The boy looks well enough, Mr. Wilson, if he was put into clothes that fitted him; is handsomely built, has good features, good eyes and a noble set of teeth, and that's always a sign of a good constitution. But there don't seem to be anything *young* about him, and if he had the use of both legs seems to have hardly life enough to get about. He is like an old man in a young man's skin. Then he has such a forlorn look out of his eyes, as though he hadn't a friend in the world, and never expected to have."

"Well, he hasn't, except you and I prove his friends. It is the misery, the downright anguish and poverty that has taken the juice of youth out of that boy. He never knew what it was to have a home, and no one ever cared whether he died or lived, but there is youth and strength; and kind treatment and good living, such as I know he would get with you, will bring him up."

"Where did you get him that he should have neither parents, relatives, nor friends?"

"From a parish workhouse."

"I judged as much."

"They gave him up, and he is bound to me."

"It was not much of a gift; I wonder so shrewd a man as I know you to be should have taken him with the expectation that anybody would ever take him off your hands."

"I know, Mr. Whitman, you think we are all a set of brutes, and buy and sell these men just as a drover does cattle, but there's a *little* humanity about some of us, after all."

He then related the circumstances with which our readers are already familiar, saying, as he concluded the narration,—

"When I saw those miserable wretches with whom he was brought up, dressed up in stolen clothes, and he in rags that were dropping off him; heard them call him a fool because he would neither beg, lie, swear nor steal; and when, being determined to know the truth of it, I inquired and heard the story of the old nurse at the workhouse confirmed by the parish authorities,—a change came over me, and I determined to take this boy, but from very different motives from those that influenced me at first."

"How so?"

"You see I had engaged, and had to pay for, berths to accommodate thirteen men, had been disappointed and had but twelve. The vessel was about ready for sea, I had to pick up some one in a hurry and thought I would take this boy. I knew I could get rid of him somehow so as to make myself whole in the matter of trade. But when I heard about the poor dying mother, and the good minister, I determined to take that boy, bring him over here, put him in some good family and give him a chance; and that family was yours, Mr. Whitman, and I have never offered this boy to any one else, never shall. If you do not take him I shall carry him to my house."

"Body of me, why then did you come within two miles of your own house and bring him here? And what reason could you have for thinking that I of all persons in the State would take him?"

"I will tell you. You and I have known each other for more than twenty-five years. I have during that time felt the greatest respect for you, though you perhaps have cherished very little for me. I know how you treat your hired help and children, and believed that there was something in this boy after all, —stupid as misery has made him appear,—and that you could bring it out both for your benefit and his, whereas I cannot stay at home. I must be away the greater part of the time about my business, and at my place he would be left with my wife or hired men and small children. If I was to be at home, I would not part with him even to yourself."

Peter could restrain himself no longer, but climbing upon the curbing of the millstone near which his father stood, flung his arms around his parent's neck, exclaiming,—

"Oh, father, do take him! I'll go without my new shoes; Maria says she will go without her new bonnet and shawl, and Bertie will go without his new suit, if you will only take him. Grandpa wants you to take him, and so does mother, though they didn't like to say so. I can tell by mother's looks when she wants anything."

Peter burst into a flood of real heartfelt tears, that would have satisfied both his brother and sister had they witnessed it.

"Be quiet, my son; I'll see about it."

Wilson then handed him a certificate from the parish authorities, in which they declared: "That the boy James Renfew had been under their charge since he was three years of age, and that he was in every respect of the best moral character."

After reading this document Whitman said: "This is a strange story, yet I see no reason to doubt it; neither do I doubt it, nor wonder that you took the boy."

"If you had been in my place, and seen and heard what I did, you would have taken him in a moment. Those workhouse brats all have their friends, and enjoy themselves in their way together. But because this boy would not do as they did, they hated him and called him a fool, till I believe he thought he was a fool; and I don't know where they would have stopped, short of murder, had it not been for one thing."

"What was that?"

"The authorities told me that it was possible by long tormenting to get his temper up, and then he was like a tiger, and so strong that they were all afraid

33

of him, and glad to let him alone. He seemed to me (so innocent among those villains) like a pond lily that I have often wondered to see growing in stagnant water, its roots in the mud and its flower white as snow spread out on that black surface. He was, poor fellow, shut out from all decent society because he was a workhouse boy; and from all bad because he was a good boy. No wonder he looks forlorn."

"Can he do any kind of work?"

"I will call him and ask him."

"No matter now. What do you want for your interest in this boy?"

"The passage-money, eight pounds."

"But you have a percentage for your labor, and you were at expense keeping him at a public house, and after he was lame had to carry him in a wagon."

"My usual fees and the expenses would be about ten dollars. I will make him over to you (as he is a boy and has about everything to learn before he can be of much use) for four years for eight pounds. And if at the end of a year you are dissatisfied, you may pay me the ten dollars, and I will take him off your hands and agree in writing to pay you back the eight pounds, in order that you may see that I do not want to put the boy on you, just to be rid of him.

"I will take him, and if he runs away, let him run; I shall not follow him."

"Run?" said the miller; "when you have had him a fortnight, you could not set dogs enough on him to drive him off."

"I shall not take him but with his free consent, and not till the matter is fully explained to him, Mr. Wilson."

"Explained, you *can't* explain it to him; why he's as ignorant as one of your oxen."

"So much the more necessary that the attempt should be made. I never will buy a fellow-creature as I would buy a "shote" out of a drove."

"You are not buying, you are hiring him."

"Nor hire him of somebody else without his free consent."

The boy was now called and Wilson said to him,—

"Jim, will you go to live with that man," pointing to Mr. Whitman, "for four years?"

"He my master?" said the boy, pointing in his turn to Mr. Whitman.

"Yes. He'll give you enough to eat every-day, and good clothes to keep you warm."

"I'll go, have plenty to eat, warm place to sleep, clothes keep me warm."

"You are to work for this man, do everything he tells you."

"I love to work," replied the boy with a faint smile.

"Tell him about the length of time," said Whitman.

"You are to stay with him four years."

"Don't know."

"He don't know how long a year is," said the miller.

"You are to stay four summers."

"I know, till wheat ripe, get reaped, put in the stack four times?" counting on his fingers.

"That is it."

"Yes I go, I stay."

"What can you do James?" said Mr. Whitman.

"I can break stones for the road, and pick oakum, and sort hairs for brushmakers, and make skewers for butchers."

"What else can you do?"

"I can drive horses to plough."

"That indeed! what else my lad?"

"I can milk cows, and reap grain, and thrash wheat, and break flax."

"What else?"

"I can hoe turnips, mow grass, and stook up grain."

"That is a great deal more than I expected," said Whitman.

The money was paid, and the writings drawn, at the miller's desk who was a justice. James made his mark at the bottom of the articles of agreement, and Mr. Whitman gave an agreement to him, after reading and explaining it to him.

When they left the mill three barrels of flour were lying at the tail of Mr. Whitman's wagon.

"Jim," said Wilson, "put those barrels into that cart."

He took hold of the barrels and pitched them one after another into the cart, without bringing a flush to his pale cheek, though it burst open the tight fitting jacket across the shoulders,—while Peter clapped his hands in mingled pleasure and wonder.

"You won't find many boys, Mr. Whitman, who can do that, and there are twenty *men* who can't do it, where there is one who can. He'll break pitchfork handles for you, when he gets his hand in, and his belly full of Pennsylvania bread and beef."

Mr. Whitman did not take advantage of the self-denying offer of his children, who had volunteered to give up their new clothes as an inducement to their father to take the boy, but procured them all as he had at first intended.

After calling at the public house to get James' bundle, they turned the heads of the horses homeward; refreshed by provender and a long rest, and relieved of their load, they whirled the heavy wagon along at a spanking trot. Peter in great spirits kept chattering incessantly, but James sat silent and stoical as an Indian at the stake, apparently no more affected by the change of masters than a stone.

Wilson compromised with his conscience by putting the boy into a good family, and consulted his interest by putting the eight pounds in his own pocket,—since the workhouse authorities had paid the passage-money to the captain of the brig Betsy,—which he probably felt justified in doing, as he had agreed and was holden to take the boy back if Whitman at the end of a year required. He really meant to do it and keep the boy himself, and do well by him, for like most men he acted from mixed motives. It is easy to see, however, that he was not so thoroughly upright as Bradford Whitman.

Thus was the *unseen hand*, spoken of by Alice Whitman, guiding both the soul-driver and the Pennsylvania farmer, though they knew it not, and in accordance with the prayers of that Christian mother whose last thought was for her child.

CHAPTER VI.
"THERE'S LIFE IN HIM YET."

In due time it appeared that this silent boy had been taking careful note of the household arrangements and the routine of work. James had hitherto slept till called to breakfast, but one morning Mr. Whitman at rising found the fire built, the teakettle on, the horses fed, and James up and dressed. As they were about to go to milking he took the pail from Mrs. Whitman and said he would milk.

"You may take this pail, James, and I'll take another; the sooner the cows are out the better. Sometime when I'm in a hurry, or when it rains, you can milk my cows."

After breakfast James, without being told, began to clean the horses. They were harvesting the last of the potato crop, and Mr. Whitman, wishing to ascertain how much the boy really knew in regard to handling horses, asked him if he could put the horses on the cart and bring it out at night to haul in the potatoes as they sorted them on the ground. James replied that the harnesses were not like those to which he had been accustomed, but thought he could get them on. At the time he came with the cart, it was evident that he was no novice in handling horses, and that the animals knew it as he backed up his load to the cellar door in a workmanlike manner.

Mr. Whitman expressed his approbation very decidedly, and Peter said afterwards,—

"Father, he was ever so much pleased that you told him to bring out the cart, and that you liked what he did."

"How do you know that? What did he say?"

"He didn't *say* anything, but I have got so that I can tell when he is pleased."

Saturday evening came, work was cleared up early, and preparation made for the Sabbath in accordance with the custom of our forefathers.

"This boy, husband, must not grow up among us like a heathen. He must go to meeting, and I must make him a good suit of clothes to go with."

"He is farther removed from being a heathen if, as is reported of him, he will neither swear, lie nor steal, than some among ourselves who go to meeting every Sabbath and yet are guilty of all three. I intend that he shall not only go to meeting but to school as well."

"I thought the only thing that made you ever think of getting a boy at all, was to have his help in the short days of winter, as the children have not time to do the chores before they go, and after they get home, from school."

"True, but since I have learned that he is ignorant of everything that he ought to know, except what he learned by rote from the lips of that minister, I feel that it becomes my duty to send him to school. A boy who has made so good use of what he does know, in spite of poverty and persecution, certainly deserves to be further instructed."

"Then I must teach him his letters. I never would send one of my own children to school till they knew their letters; I won't him."

"How will you ever get the time with all you have to do?"

"I'll take the time, and Bertie can help me."

"I'll help you, mother. I'm going to teach him to tell the time of day by the clock. I asked him if he would like to have me teach him, and he said he would. He can swim and fire a gun first rate. I got him to talk a little yesterday; he said he worked with a farmer who gave him powder and small shot and kept him shooting sparrows that eat up the grain. And after that he was all summer with the gamekeeper on a nobleman's place, and used to shoot hawks and owls; he says they call 'em vermin there; and he used to drive horses for weeks together."

There were no Sabbath-schools in those days, but after meeting on Sabbath afternoon Mr. Whitman catechized his children. They were all assembled in the kitchen, and he put to Peter the first question:

"What is the chief end of man?" Peter replied,—

"To glorify God and enjoy him forever;" when James exclaimed abruptly,—

"I know that man."

"What man?"

"God. Mr. Holmes used to tell me about him; and he's a Lord, too,—he made the Lord's prayer and the Bible, and made me, and every kind of a thing that ever was, or ever will be."

"Mercy sakes, James!" cried Mrs. Whitman, holding up both her hands in horror; "God is not a man."

"I thought he was a great big man, bigger than kings or queens; and I heard a minister what came to the workhouse read in the Bible, 'The Lord is a man of war.'"

"He is indeed greater than all other beings; but he is not a man, but a spirit, and they that worship him, must worship him in spirit and in truth."

"What is a spirit?"

"Don't you know what a spirit is, what your own spirit is?"

"No."

"Oh, dear! What shall we do with him, Mr. Whitman? We shall be accountable for him; we must get the minister to come and talk with him."

"Tut, the minister would not do any better with him than yourself, not as well. Wait till he goes to school, and when he comes to obtain knowledge in general, he'll find out the distinction between flesh and spirit. All will come about in proper time and place, as it has with our children—they had to learn it, and so will he."

"What else did Mr. Holmes tell you?" said Mrs. Whitman.

"He told me the prayer and said God made it, said you must remember the Sabbath day to keep it holy. Mustn't work that day nor play; that you mustn't lie nor steal nor swear for God didn't like it, and if you did he wouldn't like you. He told me the commandments. Then I promised him I would say the prayer every night and morning, and I have. I promised him I would never lie nor steal nor swear, and I never did. I would be cut in pieces first."

"Where do you think you will go to when you die?"

"I shall go to heaven. Mr. Holmes said he expected to go there, and if I did as he told me, I would go there and be with him. I want to go there to see him. He'll take me on his knees and kiss me just as he used to do; nobody ever loved me only Mr. Holmes, and I never loved anybody else only him."

"Didn't he never tell you about your mother?"

"Yes, and said she died praying for me; and gave me a bible that was my mother's, her name is in it, but I can't read it, though I know where it is."

He drew a bible from his breast pocket and pointed with his finger to the flyleaf, on which was written "Estelle Whitneys, her book, bought while at service at Bolton Le Moors."

Bertie, who had become intensely interested in this narration, entreated that he might have the sole care of instructing James, and as the evenings were now quite long, the time after supper was devoted to that purpose. As they took supper at an early hour this afforded them a good opportunity, James being excused from milking and all other work at that hour. James stipulated that he should first of all be taught to tell the time by the clock. He was soon able to tell the hours and half hours and quarters, and by the next Sabbath had mastered the minutes and seconds.

It was the intention of Mr. Whitman to ascertain and bring out the capabilities of the boy by leaving him as much as possible to his own direction, hoping in that way to stimulate thought, and cultivate a spirit of self-reliance. He had engaged to haul another load of wheat to the miller, and also wanted to have some corn (that the old grandfather had shelled) ground, and the horses required shoeing, and as James had recovered from his lameness, and was able to carry the bags of grain into the mill, resolved to entrust him with the errand.

Mrs. Whitman demurred at this, saying that the horses had not done much work of late, and were full of life; that he did not know anything about James, whether he was capable of driving a team with a valuable load on a long hilly road or not. Besides he knew neither the way to the mill, nor to the smith's shop.

"I've watched his movements with the horses, and I'll risk him. He is altogether different from one of our boys, who are quite likely to undertake more than they can perform, and will hesitate at nothing. I'll ask him, and if he is willing to do it, I'll let him go, and send Bert with him to show him the way, and tell the miller and blacksmith what I want done."

"Why don't you send Peter with him, and then all will go right?"

"That would be just to take the business out of his hands and spoil the whole thing; whereas I want to put it into his hands and give him the sole management of the team."

James professing his readiness to go, the pair set out taking their dinner with them. Bertie was heard chattering, expatiating upon the good qualities of the horses, and telling James their names, ages, and pedigree, till his voice became inaudible in the distance.

"If he rides eight miles with Bert and don't talk any, he will do more than I think he can," said Mr. Whitman, as he looked after them, not without a shade of anxiety upon his face as he remarked the rate at which the spirited team whirled the heavy load down a long reach of descending ground, snorting as they travelled. It passed off however, as he saw that James had them well in hand, and stopped them to breathe at the foot of the first sharp rise. They returned, having accomplished their errand, and after James had eaten his supper and retired, Mr. Whitman said to Bertie,—

"I did not expect you for an hour and a half, as you had to get a grist ground, and the horses shod, and one of them shod all round."

"Everything worked just as well as it could. There was no grist in the mill, and Mr. Lunt turned our corn right up. I took the horses right to the blacksmith's and found Joe Bemis sitting on the anvil smoking his pipe. Wasn't I glad! So he went right at the horses. When I got back James had carried in every bag of the wheat, and the grist was in the wagon, and all we had to do was to feed the horses, eat ourselves, and start. Mother Whitman, we found the prettiest place to eat! a little cleft in the rocks, a birch tree growing out of it. Father, a bag of wheat is just nothing to James, he's awful strong."

"What did Mr. Lunt say to him?"

"Don't you think he didn't know him?"

"Didn't know him?"

"No, sir; and asked me who that man was with the team; and when I told him it was the redemptioner you had of Mr. Wilson he wouldn't believe it for ever so long, and said he didn't look like the same man. No, he don't father; he gets up and sits down quicker, and he was just pale, but now there's a little red spot in the middle of each cheek. His cheeks were hollow and the skin was drawn tight over the bone, and looked all glossy, same as the bark on a young apple-tree where the sheep rub against it in the spring. He looked kinder,— what is it you call it mother, when you talk about sick folks?"

"Emaciated?"

"That's it; he looked emaciated but he don't now."

"How did you find the road?"

"They have been working on the road in the Showdy district, and it was very bad, and the worst hills are there, too.

"If I had known that, I would not have put on so much load. Did you have any trouble? Did James have to strike the horses, or did he get stuck?"

"He never struck them nor spoke to them, only chirruped, 'cept once, and that was on Shurtleffs hill. The nigh wheel sunk into a hole into which they had hauled soft mud, and he said 'Lift again Frank!' Then old Frank straightened himself, and took it out with a great snort, and when he stopped him on top of the hill I could see the muscles on the old fellow's shoulder twitch and quiver."

"Did he talk with you any, going to the mills?" said the mother.

"Never opened his mouth from the time we started till we got there, but once; when he said it was a noble span of horses."

"Then you think it is safe to send him with a team?"

"Safe, mother? he knows all about it. How to guide four horses or six, and the horses know it, and do what he asks 'em to. Frank thinks he knows, and Dick does just as Frank tells him, for Dick hasn't any mind of his own."

"How do you know what Frank thinks?"

"Mother, you may laugh, but I know what Frank thinks just as well as I know what our Maria thinks. And he likes James, too; for when he hears his step he'll begin to look, and when James pats him he'll bend his neck and put his nose on his shoulder. Frank wouldn't do that to anybody he didn't like."

"Shouldn't think," said Peter, "he'd be very good company on the road if he wouldn't say anything."

"When he sat down to eat he talked a lot. Said he never saw an ox yoked in England,—that they did all their work with horses; called 'em bullocks and killed 'em for beef; said they didn't have any of our kind of corn there, and the farmers gave their horses beans for provender, and only a few oats, and that they fatted their hogs on peas and barley. He said the beans they gave their horses were larger than ours. That they had no woods, only scattering trees in the hedges, and all their land, except where it was too rocky to plough, was just like our fields. They would plough and plant and sow it ever so long, and then make pasture of it and plough up what was pasture before, and keep twice as many cattle on the same ground as we do."

"I never thought," said Mrs. Whitman, "that he would talk so much as that; or that he knew so much about any kind of business."

"Why mother, he knows more than I do, if I am his teacher."

"I asked him why he, and the men who came over in the vessel with him, couldn't work in England and get their living, instead of going to the poorhouse, or selling themselves to come over and work."

"What did he say to that?" inquired the father.

"He said there were so many folks wanted to work, there was no work for them, and because there were so many, the farmers would only give those they did hire just enough to keep alive; and if they were taken sick, or lame, or had no work, they must go to the workhouse.

"He said they used to send him away to farmers, and they would keep him all summer, make him work very hard, and not give him half so much to eat as he had at the workhouse, and after they got their harvest all in, carry him back and say he was good for nothing, so as not to keep him in the winter.

"I asked him if the workhouse folks ever drove him off, he said no, but it seemed so much like begging to ask them, that rather than do it he had gone three days without anything but water and a little milk.

"I asked him how he came to think of coming here. He said he knew winter was coming on, he had no work, no clothes, and not a friend in the world, and one day after the rest of the boys had been abusing him and calling him a fool, and showing him things they had stolen, he put some stones in his pocket and went down to the water to kill himself, but something told him not to, and he flung 'em away. And the next day Mr. Wilson came along and asked him to go to America, and he thought he couldn't be in any worse place, and couldn't suffer any more so he came."

"What did you say to that?"

"Father, I'd rather not tell."

"You cried," said Maria, "I know he did, father, he's most crying now."

"I couldn't help it May, and I guess you couldn't have helped it neither, if you had only seen how pitiful he looked, and how sad his voice sounded."

"What did he say when he found you cried?"

"He put his arm round me and said 'don't cry Bertie,' and said he was sorry he made me feel bad. I tell you, all of you, I love him, I know he's good as he can be, and I knew he was from the first, 'cause I saw Frank loved him. Frank knows I tell you."

"I suppose Frank will love anybody who'll feed and make much of him."

"No he won't father, because there was Mike Walsh who stole your coat, and ran off after you overpaid him, would feed him and try every way to get the right side of him, but he couldn't, and Frank would bite him whenever he could get a chance; and you know father he couldn't catch him in the pasture."

"Did he talk with you on the way home?"

"Never opened his mouth only to say 'yes,' or 'no,' or 'don't know.'"

"I shouldn't think you'd like him so much as though he talked more, I shouldn't," said Maria.

"Who wants anybody all the time a gabbing just like Matt Saunders when she comes here to help mother draw a web into the loom, her tongue going all the time like a pullet when she's laid her first egg. I've heard mother say it was just like the letting out of water, but when James says anything there's some sense to it," retorted Bertie resolved in the enthusiasm of friendship that no fault should be found in his *protégé*.

"Ain't you glad you took him, father?"

"I took him because I thought it to be my duty, and I think we always feel best when we have done our duty," replied the cautious parent.

"I am!" exclaimed the grandparent, "what a sin and a shame it would have been for a young able-bodied man like that to have remained starving in rags, scorned by the sweepings of a workhouse, because he could find no work by which to earn his bread, had too much pride of character to beg, and too much principle to steal."

"Aye," said Alice Whitman, "and suppose he had been driven by misery to take his own life. But now he is in a fair way to make a good and useful member of society. As far as I am concerned, he shall have as kind usage as any child of mine, for I believe he was sent to us."

"The prayers of good persons are always heard, but are not always answered at once; and I have no doubt it was the prayer of that Christian mother that stood in the way to stay his hand when he thought to commit murder upon himself."

"You need not be afraid, Jonathan Whitman, to do for and trust that lad. His father was a hard working Christian man, and his mother a hard working Christian woman. There's no vile blood in his veins, he was born where the birds sang, and the grass grew around the door-step, if he did find shelter in a workhouse. You'll honor yourself and bring a blessing upon your own hearthstone by caring for him."

"Amen," exclaimed the grandparent, laying his great wrinkled hand in benediction upon the head of his son's wife.

In making such minute inquiries of Albert in respect to the conversation between himself and James, Mr. Whitman was influenced by a stronger motive than mere curiosity. He knew, for he was a keen observer, that James would unbosom himself to this innocent, enthusiastic and artless boy in a manner that he would not to any other; and he wanted to get at his inward life that he might thoroughly know, and thus understandingly, guide and benefit him.

Reflecting upon what he had heard, he drew from it this inference, and said within himself, "There's life in him yet."

CHAPTER VII.
NOBLE CONDUCT OF BERTIE.

The next day proved rainy, but Mrs. Whitman perceived that—notwithstanding the lack of enthusiasm manifested by her husband the evening before,—though there was much work under cover that was quite necessary to be done, he did not set James about it; but told Bertie that he and James might take the day to study, after doing the chores, and, taking Peter, went to the barn to thresh beans.

"Father, can I teach James to write, too?"

"You have no writing-book."

"I have one I didn't quite finish last winter, and so has Maria."

"There's not a quill in the house, and but one pen that has been mended till there's not much of it left, and I can't spare that."

"We can pull some out of the old gander."

"They will be too soft."

"Mother says she can bake 'em in the oven."

"Well, fix it to suit yourselves."

One obstacle surmounted, another arose.

"Mother, I can't find my plummet, and there's not a mite of lead in the house; what shall I do to rule the writing-book?"

"Ask grandfather to give you a bullet; he's never without bullets."

When grandfather was appealed to, he said, "I have but one, Bertie; and that's in my rifle. I loaded her for an owl that's been round trying to kill a goose, but I will lend it to you to rule your book."

He took down the rifle into which Bertie had seen him drive the bullet, wrapped in a greased patch. "Grandpa, you never can get it out."

"Go up stairs and get a bag of wool that is right at the head of the stairs."

When Bertie brought the wool, grandfather made a circle on the bag with a smut coal, and a cross in the middle of it.

"Now, Bertie, take that bag out of doors and set it up where I tell you. I'm going to put a bullet into the middle of that cross."

After placing the bag at the distance pointed out, he said, "Where shall I stand, grandpa?"

"Wherever you like, 'cept betwixt me and that cross."

"Why, grandfather, what are you thinking of? Come right into the house, Bertie," cried Mrs. Whitman, "your grandfather's going to shoot."

"What if I am," replied the old man testily, "I'm not going to shoot all over the country. His father would hold the bag in his hand, as he has done smaller things, a hundred times."

"I know it, grandpa; but you must remember that you are an old man now, and of course can't see as well as you could once, and your hand cannot be so steady."

"I can see well enough to thread your needle when you can't, and well enough to hit a squirrel's eye within thirty yards."

The old gentleman fired, the bag fell over and Bertie cried,—

"There's a hole right in the middle of the cross, as you said, grandpa."

"Indeed! I wonder at that. Wonder the bullet hadn't gone up into the air, or into the ground, or killed your father or Peter in the barn, or into the pasture and killed one of the horses," replied he, entirely unable to digest the suspicion that his powers were waning, implied in the caution of Mrs. Whitman to Bertie.

The bullet was found in the wool, having penetrated a few inches. After hammering the bullet into the shape of a plummet on the andiron, he gave it to Bertie, saying,—

"When you are done with it give it back to me, and I will run it into a bullet again, for I want to kill that owl. It's all I'm fit for now; to kill vermin, some people think. I expect I'm in the way."

Mrs. Whitman never noticed any little testiness that occasionally clouded the spirit of the genial sunny-tempered old gentleman, who, though he would sometimes say that he was growing old, could seldom without disturbance brook the remark or even suspicion, from another.

He had been celebrated for strength and activity, and with the exception of a stiffness in his legs, the result of toils and exposures in early life, was still strong. It was surprising to see what a pile of wood he would cut in an hour. He used no glasses, had every tooth he ever possessed, his mind was clear, his judgment good, his health firm, and his disposition such as made every one happy around him. Any labor that admitted of standing still or moving slowly he could still perform; could reap, hoe, chop wood, took entire charge of the garden, and could work at a bench with tools, and nothing seemed to disturb the serenity of his mind, save the suspicion that he was superannuated. No one could equal him in putting an edge on a scythe, and he ground all the scythes in haying time, the grindstone being placed under the old chestnut, and fitted with a seat for his convenience.

Alice Whitman soon restored the old gentleman's good humor by showing him the pattern of a new spread for his bed that she was then drawing in the loom to weave; she then wheeled his great chair to the fire, flung on some cobs to make a cheerful blaze, and grandfather, restored to his composure, began to chat and tell of the birch-bark writing-books they had in his school days.

Thus did Bradford Whitman and his wife unite in smoothing the declivity of age to one who had fought and won life's battle; made many blades of grass to grow where there were none before; reared a large family in habits of industry and virtue; had fought with the savage in defence of his own hearthstone; bore the scars of wounds received in the service of his country, and having made his peace with God, resembled an old ship just returned from a long and tempestuous voyage—her sails thread-bare, her rigging chafed and stranded, her bulwarks streaked with iron-rust—riding quietly at anchor in the outer harbor, waiting for the tug to tow her to the pierhead.

The example of the parents infected the children, and they vied with one another in attention to their grandfather and in obedience and affection to their parents. Thus were Jonathan Whitman and his wife reaping as they had sown, and daily receiving the blessing promised to filial obedience.

Provided at last with quill and writing-book and plummet, the boys spent the entire day in alternate exercises of teaching and learning the letters of the alphabet, and to make straight marks.

When the boys had gone to bed, Mr. Whitman and his wife were looking at the writing and the latter said,—

"The last of James' straight marks are a good deal better than the copy Bertie set for him."

The old gentleman, after looking at it, said, "That boy will make a good penman. You can see that he improves, as he goes on; his marks are square and clean cut at top and bottom. I think, for a boy that never had a pen in his hand before, he has done remarkably well."

"Husband, what are you going to set James about to-morrow?"

"Driving horses to plough. Why?"

"We want some wood cut; and I don't think your father ought to cut so much as he does. The weather is getting cooler, and we burn a good deal more, but I am afraid it will hurt his feelings if anybody else cuts wood for the fire, as he considers that his work."

"I can arrange that. I'll tell him in the morning that I want James to learn to handle an axe; that he undertook at Hanscom's tavern to cut some wood and stuck the whole bitt of the axe in his leg the second clip, and ask him if he won't grind an axe for him and take him to the wood-pile with him, and teach him, and see that he does not cut himself."

The old gentleman was well pleased with the idea of teaching James an art in which he was so competent to instruct, not in the least suspecting that it was thought he could not supply the fire without doing more than he was able.

No sooner was breakfast despatched than, having ground an axe, he proceeded with James to the wood-pile.

The old gentleman set his chopping-block on end near a pile of oak and maple limbs cut eight feet in length, and said to his pupil,—

"Now, Jeames (he held on to the old pronunciation) I'll hold these sticks on the block and I want you to strike just there," pointing with his finger, "where they bear on the log, because if you don't, you'll jar my hands."

Not, however, reposing much confidence in his assistant, he had taken the precaution to put on a very thick patched mitten to deaden the jar.

James began to strike, the blows were forcible but most of them misspent. Whenever he struck fair on a stick he cut it off as though it had been a rush. But many times he struck over, and as many more fell short, so that only the corner of the axe hit the stick, and sometimes missed it altogether and drove the axe into the block with such force that it was hard work to pull it out.

It was by no means the old chopper's purpose to find fault, he praised the vigor with which James struck and protected his own fingers from the jar of the random blows as well as he could. In the course of an hour James improved very sensibly; perceiving this, Mr. Whitman began to point out some of his errors and said: "You must look at the place where you mean to hit and not at your axe, and you must let your left hand slip up and down on the axe-handle and guide your axe a good deal with your right hand, whereas you keep a fast grip with both hands on the axe-handle, just as a woman does when she undertakes to cut wood."

James blushed and replied,—

"If I should do that way I don't think I could strike as fair as I do now."

"You won't at first, but after a while you will. You may cut off small limbs on a block in your fashion, but you could not work to any purpose in cutting large wood on the ground. I'll cut a while and you may hold on, and you'll see how I cut."

The blows of the senior were delivered with the precision of a machine.

James took the axe again, and though, at first, he seemed to retrograde, it was not long before he became accustomed to the new method. The old gentleman now began to put on the block sticks that were so large that it required two or three blows to sever them when the blows were delivered with precision, but it required seven or eight of James'. For instance, if it was a stick that might be cut at two blows, he would deliver one and cut it half off, and then, instead of striking in the same scarf and severing it he would strike a little on one side or the other and the blow went for nothing. He now saw that it was necessary to strike fair, for by striking once in a place he could never cut a stick of any size off, and feeling that when he did strike into the same place it was more by chance than skill, began to be somewhat discouraged.

The senior noticed this and said,—

"Let me cut a spell, you are tired and will strike better after resting a while."

James could not but admire the precision and ease with which he lopped the sticks, so true were the blows that when he took and looked at the ends they seemed to have been cut at one blow, whereas the ends of his sticks looked like a pair of stairs and the bark was in shreds.

When at the expiration of an hour the old gentleman gave him the axe, and he saw what a pile of wood the former had cut, James could not help saying,—

"I don't believe I shall ever strike true."

"Indeed you will; it's all in practice. You mustn't be discouraged if you should find that little Bertie can strike truer than you can now, for the boys here begin to chop as soon as they can lift an axe, whereas it is a new thing to you."

The next morning his instructor set James to cutting large logs, showed him how to cut his scarfs and told him to strike slow, and as fair as possible, for every miss clip was so much time and strength laid out for nothing, and thinking it would only discourage James if he should go to cutting logs with him, employed himself in splitting.

It was now an entirely different thing with James. He was stiff and sore, but after he got warmed up, he found that he could strike a great deal better. The old gentleman praised his work and told him he had a mechanical eye and he knew it by his writing, and with practice he would handle any kind of a tool.

The hands of James were now blistered, and Mr. Whitman, who had a large breadth of ground to plough for spring wheat, made out two teams,—Bertie driving John and Charlie for Peter, and James driving Frank and Dick for him.

James proved an excellent driver, and Mr. Whitman was so much gratified, that at night he said to his wife,—

"I believe, after all, that boy is going to make most excellent help, he handles horses as well as anybody, young or old, that I ever had on the place."

"He has a great memory, and if he learns other things as fast as he learns to read and write, you'll never regret that you took him."

"James," said Mr. Whitman, as they were at work together the next day, "did you ever hold plough?"

"I never was anything but a ploughboy. In England the ploughman does nothing but plough, and in many places drives and holds both, but I have held plough a few hours, and sometimes half a day, when the ploughman was sick or away."

"Well, take hold of the handles."

Mr. Whitman took the reins, and James held so well, that his master kept him at it till noon. Peter and Bertie were ploughing in the same field, and they could not help going into the house for a drink, and telling their grandfather that James was holding plough, and their father driving the horses.

While matters were thus pleasantly going on among the Whitmans, the most contradictory stories were circulated in the neighborhood in respect to James.

Those who obtained their information from the landlord of the public-house where Wilson put up, having James with him, averred that Jonathan Whitman had got awfully cheated in a redemptioner; that he was lame and underwitted; a great scrawny, loutish boy, and no life in him, and had such a down look that many people reckoned he might be a thief, most likely he was, for Wilson got him out of a parish workhouse.

Others were of opinion that the next time Wilson came that way he should be treated to a coat of tar and feathers for putting such a creature on to so good a man as Mr. Jonathan Whitman; still others said there could be no doubt of it, for Blaisdell, Mr. Wood's redemptioner, who came over in the same vessel, said he thought he was underwitted or crazy, for he never heard him speak, nor saw him talk with any of the passengers.

While this talk was going on in the bar-room, a shoemaker came in, who said that Lunt the miller told him that the week before the redemptioner was at his mill with Whitman's youngest boy, and he never saw a man handle a span of horses or bags of wheat better, and that he would pitch a barrel of flour into a wagon as easily as a cat would lick her ear.

James Stone the peddler then said that the last time he was there, the redemptioner was sitting in the sun on the wood-pile, while Whitman and Peter were threshing in the barn with all their might, and the redemptioner had been there a week then.

At that moment a drover, a joking, good-natured fellow, came into the bar-room and said he was over in Whitman's neighborhood that very forenoon, and when he went by there about eleven o'clock, the redemptioner was holding plough, and Whitman was driving, and the horses were stepping mighty quick too.

This occasioned a great laugh, and the subject was dropped. The verdict, however, remained unfavorable to James, as Eustis the shoemaker was not considered very reliable, and Sam Dorset the drover was so given to joking, that though a truthful man, everyone supposed he then spoke in jest.

James now went again to the wood-pile with the old gentleman, and chopped for four days in succession, the former cutting till he was tired, and then going into the house or piling up the wood.

The weather was fast growing cooler, and it was the custom of Mr. Whitman to cut and haul a large quantity of wood to last over the wet weather in the fall and till snow came. He also wished to haul wheat to the mill himself, and wanted Peter to go with him, going two turns in a day. He therefore asked his father if he felt able to go into the woods with James and Bertie, and show James how to fell a tree, and see that he didn't fell one on himself or Bertie.

The old gentleman said he could go as well as not, that he could ride back and forth in the cart, chop as much as he liked, and then make up a fire, and sit by it, and see to them, and he thought it would do him good to be in the woods.

The old gentleman selected a tree and cut it down, while James who had never seen a tree cut down in his life, looked on; he then selected another and told him to chop into it. James did so, though he found it a little more difficult to strike fair into the side of a tree, than into a log lying on the ground. When it was more than half off his instructor told him where to cut on the other side.

James walked round the tree and stood by the lower side of his scarf, and was about to strike.

"You mustn't stand there; turn round and put your left shoulder to the tree, and your left hand on the lower end of the axe-handle, now strike."

"I can't cut so, it don't come right, I ain't lefthanded."

"That indeed! but all good choppers, when they fell a tree, learn to chop either hand forward; you must put your right hand forward."

"I couldn't guide the axe with my right hand forward; I never could cut a tree down in that way. I should only hack it off."

"Well, hack it then, you must creep afore you can walk, it comes just as unhandy to everybody at first."

He then took James to a ravine, the sides of which were quite perpendicular and the edges covered with large trees, and said,—

"Now, suppose you wanted to cut one of those trees, you couldn't stand on the lower side to cut, but must either cut them off all on one side, or chop right hand forward. Besides, there is often another tree in the way and you would have to cut both, to cut one."

CHAPTER VIII.
INFLUENCE OF HOPE.

As the old gentleman ended, James heard the crash of a falling tree, and saw that Bertie had just dropped a much larger tree than the senior had given to him, and had also cut it right hand forward; this determined him, and he began to chop into the side of another tree while his instructor, feeling that James would rather not have his eye upon him, went to help Bertie.

James took very good care to cut the tree almost off in his usual way, in order that he might be compelled to chop as little as possible in the new fashion (that is, new to him); he however found that little sufficiently puzzling. Two only out of five blows that struck upon the upper slanting side of his kerf took effect in the same place, but when he came to strike in square across on the lower side, the first blow hit the root of the tree, and the edge of the axe came within a hair's breadth of a stone; the next struck about half way between the root and the spot aimed at, and the third alone reached the right place. James sweat, grew red in the face, and showered blows at random, very few of which effected anything, and when at length the tree came down the stump looked as if it had been gnawed by rats. In cutting up the tree, James recovered his equanimity, his nervous spasm passed off, and, resolved to conquer, he cut the next only half way off in his usual manner, and when he turned to the other side, succeeded so much better as to feel somewhat encouraged, especially as he was assured by Bertie that it was long before he learned to chop right hand forward, and that in his opinion James was getting along remarkably fast, and would soon be able to chop as easily with his right hand forward as with the left.

They had brought their dinners with them, and besides a jug of hot coffee wrapped in a blanket to keep it warm. Bertie had also brought a gun, and while James was making a great fire against a ledge of rocks he shot a wild turkey, a great gobbler, and they roasted it before the fire, and also roasted potatoes in the ashes, and set the coffee jug in the hot ashes till the contents fairly boiled. They now made a soft seat for grandfather with bushes, on which they spread their jackets, and he sat with his back against the ledge that was warmed from the heat of the fire, while the sun shone bright upon his person, and then they fell to, with appetites sharpened by labor and the breath of the woods, and had a great feast, drinking their coffee out of birch-bark cups that the grandfather made and put together with the spike of a thorn-bush for a pin.

This, which was but an ordinary affair to Bertie and his grandfather, opened a new world to James. It was the first time in his experience that pleasure was ever connected with labor. Hitherto labor with him recalled no pleasant associations; it was hard, grinding toil, performed to obtain bread, and under the eye of a task-master, and dinner was for the most part a little bread and cheese, eaten under a hedge, or rick of grain, with a mug of beer to wash down the bread, made largely of peas,—with the dark background of the past and a hopeless future,—but now every moment and every morsel was full of enjoyment. The good old man, refreshed by rest and a hearty meal, breathing once more the air of the woods where he loved to be, and exhilarated by old and pleasant associations, was in a most jovial mood, that infected his companions; and when Bertie, in response to some humorous remark of his grandfather, broke out in a ringing laugh, James joined heartily in it. The surprise of Bertie at such a development can only be imagined, not described. His features expressed wonder, mingled with surprise, in so ludicrous a manner as to provoke another peal of laughter from James, who from that moment became a different boy. The fetters that had bound him to despondency as with gyves of steel were loosened. A ray of sunlight darted athwart the gloom, hope was born, and a dim consciousness of something higher and nobler began to dawn upon him. He stretched himself on the ground beside the fire, and lay looking up into the sky in a perfect dream of happiness. Rousing himself at length, he asked the old gentleman who planted all the trees on that land.

"The Lord planted them; they've always been here; as fast as one dies or is cut down another comes up. We don't plant trees here, except fruit trees; we cut 'em down. When I came on to this farm it was all forest, and no neighbor within nine miles."

"It must be some great duke or earl who owns this land. I shouldn't think he'd let you cut down so many trees. In England, if you cut a little tree as big as a ramrod you'd be sent to jail, and I don't know but be hung."

"Dukes or earls! We don't have any such vermin here; but my father came from England, and we've heard him say that there a few great proprietors own all the land, and the farmers are mostly tenants and pay rent. Thank God, any man who has his health and is sober and industrious can own land here."

"Does Bertie's father own all this land?"

"Yes, it was mine; I gave it to him."

"You can own a piece of land, James," said Bertie; "I am saving my money to buy a piece of land. I've got twenty dollars now, and a yoke of steers that I am going to sell. I mean to have a farm of my own, and raise lots of wheat, just as grandfather did, and then when I'm old I can tell what I did, just as he does; and I hope there will be a war, so that I can fight, and have it to tell of, and be made much of, just as he is."

"Such as me have a farm!" and James smiled incredulously.

"Sartain you can," replied the senior; "if you are steady and industrious and learn to work, when you have done here you can obtain all the work you want at good wages. It takes but little money to buy wild land. You can go where land is cheap and begin as I did."

This was an idea too large for James to grasp, and seemed, though magnificent, altogether fantastic. He again smiled incredulously, and repeated to himself in a low tone, "Such as me have a farm!"

"Why do you say such as me?" replied the senior, who overheard the remark. "If you want to be a man, and to be well thought of and respected, and to have friends, all in the world you have to do in this country is to learn to work and read and write and be honest; and nobody is going to ask or care who your father was, all they will want to be satisfied about is as to what you are. There's nothing can hinder you, nothing can keep you down.

"But there's another thing, and it is of more consequence than all the rest. If you want to feel right and prosper, fear the Lord who giveth food to man and beast.

"When I came into these woods, all I had left after paying for my land was the clothes on my back, my rifle, a few charges of powder and shot, a narrow axe and a week's provisions; all my wife had was her spinning-wheel, cards, a few pounds of wool, two pewter plates, one bottle and the clothes on her back and some blankets. I carried a pack on my back, and my axe, and hauled the other stuff on a sledge—for it was the last of March and there was plenty of snow in the woods—she carried my rifle and a bundle."

"But, Mr. Whitman," said James, "if it was all woods and nobody lived near, where were you and your wife going to stop?"

"My intention was to cut out a place to build a log-house, and I had expected to reach the spot at noon, so as to be able to make a bush camp by night to shelter us while building; but the travelling was bad, the sun was down before reaching the spot and we came into the woods by twilight.

"I built a fire after scraping away the snow with a piece of bark, and as we sat by it and listened to the sound of the wind among the trees, you don't know how solemn it seemed."

"I should have thought you would have felt afraid," said Bertie.

"I had been well instructed, and both myself and wife had professed to fear God—and did fear him—but we did not fear much else, though we had but a week's food, and were nine miles from any human being. We knelt down together and I told my Maker there and then, that my wife and I were a couple of his poor children; that she was an orphan and had been put out since she was twelve years of age and had never had any home of her own. That we had nothing but our hands, and health, and strength, and were about to begin for ourselves in His woods; and wanted to begin with His blessing. That we would try to do right, and if we found any poorer or worse off than ourselves, would help them and be content with and thankful for whatever He gave us, be it little or much.

"I then made a bed of brush for my wife, covered her with blankets, threw some light brush on them, and sat all night by the fire with my rifle in hand."

"I guess grandmother didn't sleep much?" said Bertie.

"She slept all night like one of God's lambs, as she was, though she had the courage of a lion. The next day I made a shelter of brush that kept out rain and snow, and by Saturday morning I had built a house of small-sized logs (such as your grandmother and I could roll up) with a bark roof, a stone fireplace and chimney of sticks and clay. I had also shot a buck, we brought a peck of Indian meal with us, your grandmother baked her first loaf of bread on the hearth, and we kept the Sabbath all alone in the woods with glad hearts. It is more than fifty years since I thus sought God's blessing, and during all that time I have never lacked. I have raised up a large family of children; they are all well-to-do in the world. I am still able to be of some use, and am ready whenever the Master calls.

"Jeames, my laddie, fear God, you may be tempted to think trying to do right has in the past brought you nothing but unhappiness, that you have only been scorned and flouted because you would not take His name in vain. But those bitter days will never come back. His providence has brought you to us, and should you live as long as I have, you will never regret having put your trust in Him!"

No force of learning, eloquence, or wit, could have produced so genial and abiding an impression upon James, as the words we have recorded. The character and person of the speaker himself—the very situation, beside a forest fire—all tended to heighten both the moral and physical effect of the sentiments uttered.

The elder Whitman possessed indeed a most commanding presence. His great bones and sinews, now that the body was attenuated by age, stood out in such bold relief as to challenge attention; showing the vast strength he once possessed, and that still lingered in those massive limbs, while the burden of years had neither bowed his frame, nor had age dimmed the fire of his eye.

In addition to all this, the accounts James had heard from Bertie of his encounters with the red men, and with bears, and wolves, together with the scars of wounds that he had upon his person, supplemented by the respect and affection with which he was treated by the whole household, caused James to look upon and listen to him with awe and wonder.

He could understand the plain and terse utterances of the old woodsman, and they gave a new and strong impulse to ideas and trains of thought that were now germinating within him.

The next morning, as Mr. Whitman wanted the four horses to haul wheat, he told Bertie they must take the oxen and cart with them, and bring home a load of wood both at noon and night. He also told his father that he had better not go, that two days' work in succession and the travel back and forth were too much for him. The old gentleman, however, said it was not, he could ride in the cart; and that as they were now to cut larger trees, it was not safe to leave the boys to fell them alone.

James had never seen an ox in the yoke, and he was much surprised to see with what docility the near ox came across the yard to come under the yoke, when Bertie held up the end of it and said,—

"Bright, come under."

He also observed how readily they obeyed the motion of the goad, and handled the cart just as they were directed.

"I never thought a bullock knew anything, but they seem to know as much as horses," said James.

"Yes, just as much."

Having ground their axes—with grandfather in the cart—they started, and when they came to the wood the oxen were unyoked to go where they pleased.

"Won't they run away?" said James.

"No, they saw the axes in the cart and know what we are going to do; you see they don't offer to start. The very first tree we fell, if it is hard wood or hemlock, they'll come to browse the limbs. They love to browse dearly, and all day they won't go farther than a spring there is near, to drink."

They now began to cut the trees, and the moment the cattle heard the sound of the axes they came running to the spot.

"What did I tell you?" said Bertie. "They know what the sound of an axe means, just as I know when I come home from school and see mother look into the oven, or reach her hand up on the top shelf, she's got something good laid away for me."

A road was first cleared, and then the trees were cut into lengths of sixteen feet, and rolled up in piles on the sides of the road.

"What makes your grandfather have them cut so long, they can never be put into a cart?" said James.

"This wood is for next winter, and won't be hauled till snow comes, and then it will be hauled on two sleds put one behind the other."

Mrs. Whitman insisted that grandfather should take a nap after dinner, and as Bertie had to wait to haul him out, James went to the wood-lot alone. He had felled a large hemlock and was cutting off the first log, when he observed a man on horseback attentively watching him. In a few moments the man rode up and inquired where Mr. Whitman was. James replied that he had gone to the mill with a load of wheat. He then inquired if the oxen were there, James told him they would be along in a few minutes, and as they were talking Bertie and the old gentleman came. This person was the drover who had seen James holding plough, and who occasioned so much merriment by saying so at the tavern. He felt of the cattle, took a chain from his pocket, measured them, and then told the old gentleman to inform his son to be at home the next Monday, for he was coming that way then, and wanted to trade with him for the oxen and some lambs.

When, on the next Saturday night, the usual company of idlers and hard drinkers assembled in the bar-room of the tavern, the drover added still more to the muddle of conflicting opinions in regard to James by telling the crowd that he "went through the woods to Malcom's, after lambs, and, as he returned through Whitman's woods, came across the redemptioner chopping alone. That he had just cut a big hemlock and was junking it up and handled an axe right smart. That he made some talk with him and called him a real good-looking, rugged, civil-spoken fellow," and went on to say that he "wouldn't give him for two, yes, three, of that Blaisdell, Mr. Woods had got. The boy certainly was not lame, for he stood on the tree to chop, and when he got down to speak to him didn't limp a particle, and he believed all the stories told about him were a pack of lies, got up to hurt a civil young man because he was a foreigner."

This brought out the tavern-keeper, and the dispute came near ending in a downright brawl, and was only prevented by the drover proposing to "treat all hands and drop it."

The elder Whitman was so much gratified with the progress made by James that he resolved to make him aware of it. The next day proved stormy, and after breakfast he brought out an axe that had been ground, and said,—

"James, that axe of yours is not fit to chop with. It is not the best of steel, nor is it made right to throw a chip, and the handle is too big and stiff; it's just the handle to split, not to chop with. But there's an axe Mr. Paul Rogers made for me that's made just right to work easy in the wood, and he is the best man to temper an edge-tool I ever knew. My cutting days are about over and I'll give it to you, and make a proper chopping handle to it, and then we'll grind it and you'll have a good axe.

"I've not the least doubt you'll make a first rate chopper, and be real 'sleighty' with an axe. This is a heavier tool than I care to use now, but you've got the strength, and practice will give you the sleight."

James, stimulated by finding that he had finally mastered the difficulty, and delighted with the kindly interest manifested by the old gentleman, gave his whole soul to work; and by the time the winter's wood was cut could chop faster than either of the boys, and could drive the oxen well enough for most purposes.

A variety of circumstances conspired not only thereby to develop the ability of James, but also to prove that he was by no means untouched by the kindness with which he was treated.

Mr. Whitman, having sold his large oxen to the drover, to be delivered in a week, desired, before parting with them, to break up a piece of rough land with them and the steers, and also to plough a piece of old ground that had been planted with corn that year, and that two horses could plough. All this work must be done speedily, as the ground was likely to shut up.

In the evening the family were seated around the fire, Bertie superintending James who was writing, when Mr. Whitman said,—

"Father, I don't see but I must hire a hand. I want to plough a piece of corn-ground for wheat, and I want very much to break up that rough piece before I give up the old oxen. By hiring some one to drive for James to plough for wheat I could accomplish it. After the land was struck out, Bertie could drive the oxen and Peter tend the plough for me."

"Peter is not strong enough to tend the plough in that ground. There will be roots to cut, stumps to drag out of the way, great turfs as big as a blanket to turn over; it needs a strong man such as this poor old worn-out creature was when you was a boy. But I can drive the oxen, and then you can have both boys to tend plough."

"I never will allow that; you cannot travel over that rough ground. I can stop the team once in a while, and help Peter."

James, who had listened to this conversation, gave Bertie a hint to go into the porch, and when they were alone, said,—

"Bertie, I can take Frank and Dick, and plough that ground alone."

"You can't do that, James; nobody here ever ploughs alone with horses. They do sometimes with old steady oxen."

"Yes, I can. In England most of the ploughmen drive themselves. The corn-butts have been all taken off, and the plough won't clog much."

James resumed his writing, and Bertie soon made the matter known to his father, who said,—

"James, can you plough that corn-ground alone?"

"Yes, sir; with old Frank and Dick. I would not try it with the other horses."

The next morning the two teams started at the same time. Bertie wanted to go and see James begin, but his father told him to keep away, as he had no doubt James would prefer to be alone.

Bertie was on tenter-hooks all the forenoon to know how his *protégé* got along, and kept chattering incessantly about it.

"Father, I saw him cut four alder sprouts as much as six feet long, with a little bunch of leaves left on the end, and then he stuck 'em under the hame-straps on Frank's collar."

"That was to mark his land out. The sprouts are so limber that the horses will walk right over them without turning aside, and the tuft of leaves on top will enable him to see them between the horses' heads."

At eleven o'clock they stopped to rest the oxen, and Bertie improved the opportunity to climb a tree that he might be able to see James over the rising ground between them.

"Can you see him?" said Peter.

"I can't see him, but he's ploughing all right. Everything is going along just right."

"How do you know that, my son, if you can't see him?"

"Because, father, I can see the heads and part of the necks of the horses, and they are going round and round as regular as can be. They are stepping lively, too, and every now and then old Frank keeps flirting up his head just as he does when he feels about right and everything suits him. You know how he does?"

"No, I don't know, for I don't take so much notice of Frank's ways as you do."

When they left work at noon, and while his father and Peter were tying up the oxen, Bertie scampered off to the field where James had been at work and came back in most exuberant spirits. After dinner he could not be satisfied unless his father went out to see the ploughed ground, and to his great delight his grandfather accompanied them.

The ground was a hazel loam, free of stones, and James had turned a back furrow through the middle as straight as an arrow. The furrows were of equal width; there were no balks, and it looked like garden mould. Mr. Whitman was very much gratified, as Bertie knew by his looks, though he merely observed,—

"That is good work."

"It is as good a piece of work as I ever saw done," said the grandfather.

When night came Bertie importuned James to tell him how he drove the horses so straight the first time going round, when they had no furrow to guide them and held the plough at the same time.

James, in ridicule of Bertie, who was so fond of imputing human intelligence to Frank, and with a sly humor, of which he had never manifested a trace before, said,—

"I told old Frank I had never tried to plough alone before, and wanted to plough a straight furrow, and I asked him if he wouldn't go just as straight for the marks as he could, and so he did."

"Oh, now you're fooling; come tell me."

"I stuck up my marks, and then I drove the horses twice back and forth over the ground, before I put the plough to 'em. Don't you know that when a horse goes over ground the second time he always wants to step in the same tracks?"

"No."

"Well, he does, and if another horse has been along, to step in his tracks. Did you never notice in the lanes and wood roads, how true the lines of grass are each side of the horse?"

"Yes."

"They wouldn't be, if horses didn't want to go in the same track. The horses could see their tracks in the soft ground, and when I came to put the plough to 'em, knew what I wanted, and that helped me to guide 'em. Horses go in the main road because in the first place folks make 'em go there, and when the ruts get worn, the carriage keeps them there, and it is easier than to cross the ruts. But in the pastures the horses and cattle always have their beaten paths, and nobody makes 'em go in them, yet they always go in them,—and all go in them,—they wouldn't be horses if they didn't."

"What did you do with the reins?"

"Flung 'em over my neck."

CHAPTER IX.
THE REDEMPTIONER AT MEETING.

While James was thus giving new proofs of capacity for usefulness, Mrs. Whitman had woven a web of cloth, sent it to the mill where it was colored and pressed, and had made James a suit of clothes for meeting, and a thick winter overcoat, and Mr. Whitman had bought him a hat.

Sunday morning came, Mrs. Whitman gave the clothes to James and told him to go up stairs and put them on, that she might see how they fitted. While the children, enjoying his dazed looks, were bursting with repressed glee, Bertie capered around the room at such a rate that Peter said he acted like a fool.

"Isn't he stuck up?" said Peter.

"I mean to peek and see how he acts when he gets by himself," said Bertie with his foot on the lower stair.

"Don't do that, Bertie; mother, don't let him," said Peter.

His mother called him back, and he reluctantly sat down to await the conclusion.

At last they heard James, with a slow, hesitating step, descending the stairs. He paused long in the entry, and at length opening the door as cautiously as would a thief, crossed the room, and with a scared, troubled look, went and stood by the window with his back to all the inmates of the room, looking directly into the main road.

Mrs. Whitman found it somewhat difficult to compose her features as she said,—

"Come here, James, and let me see how they set; they may need some little alteration."

When he turned, Mr. Whitman was looking straight at the crane, Peter was buried in the catechism which he held up to his face, while Bertie and Maria ran out to the barn and there vented their long suppressed feelings in peals of laughter, till they had obtained sufficient command of themselves to return to the house.

What unalloyed satisfaction, resulting from contributing to the happiness of others, predominated in the breasts of that household, as Mrs. Whitman turned James round and round, and invited the criticism of her husband as to the set of the garments. The grave features of Jonathan betokened a strong disposition to smile as he said,—

"I think they set well, and don't see how you can alter them for the better."

"They are a trifle long, husband, and a little large, but I can turn up a seam and it will do to let out again, for he's growing."

"Not one mite too large, wife, he's at least forty pounds heavier than he was when he came here."

The children now came around him with the charitable desire of relieving his embarrassment, and began to talk to him.

"What nice pockets!" said Bertie, thrusting his hands alternately into those of the waistcoat, and into the breast-pockets of the coat. Maria took hold of his hand and stood looking at the buttons of the coat, and Peter, passing his hands over the shoulders of James, admired the fit of the coat.

Mrs. Whitman now brought out the overcoat and put it on him, the children assisting, and thrusting his arms through the sleeves.

James knew that Mrs. Whitman was making him a suit of clothes, because she had taken his measure. But he did not know that she was making him an overcoat, and that at the same time she measured him for the coat and pants and waistcoat, had also measured him for that garment; neither did she intend he should. The surprise therefore was as great as she could have wished.

During all this time James stood like a statue, staring into vacancy, while the children made their comments and handled his limp form as they pleased. Mrs. Whitman, in the meantime, buttoned up the garment, pulled it down behind and before, manipulated it in various ways, finally pronouncing it as good a fit as could be made, concluding with the declaration that James had a good form to fit clothes to.

"Ain't they handsome? Don't you like 'em?" said Bertie, putting his arms around the passive recipient of all these favors.

Instead of replying, this apparently insensible being burst into tears. Peter and Maria drew back amazed. Bertie's eyes moistened with sympathetic feeling, and the situation was becoming sufficiently embarrassing to all, when Mr. Whitman said,—

"James, put Frank and Dick into the wagon; it's getting towards meeting time, but go upstairs first, and take off your clothes."

Thankful for the interruption, James quickly left the room.

"What made him cry, father?" said Peter. "Didn't he like the clothes?"

"Yes, tickled to death with them."

"Then what made him cry?"

"He cried for joy."

"I didn't know anybody ever cried because they were glad."

"Some folks do; your mother burst out a crying when she stood up to be married to me, and there never was a gladder woman."

"I guess somebody who didn't cry was just as glad," retorted Mrs. Whitman.

"That's a fact, Alice; and has been glad ever since. Boys, run out and help James water, clean, and harness the horses, because he has got to shift his clothes again. Tell him he is going to meeting with us, and that I want him to drive."

The great bulk of the people, in that day, rode on horseback, the women on pillions behind their husbands. They had the heavy Conestoga wagons, for six, four, or two horses, to haul wheat to market, and for farm work, but Whitman and a few of his neighbors had covered riding wagons.

As they neared the meeting-house Mr. Whitman told James to rein up, and pointed out to him the horse block. This was a large stick of timber placed near the main entrance of the church, one end of which rested upon the ground, while the other was raised so as to be on a level with the stirrup of the tallest horse. This arrangement accommodated everybody; the elderly people rode to the upper end, where they could dismount on a level, and where was a little platform, and a pair of steps with a railing, by which they could descend from the timber, while the others dismounted lower down. Many of the young gallants, however, disdained to make use of the horse-block at all.

Great was the wonderment when James drove up to the block in such a manner that the old grandfather could step out on the platform; and then drove to the hitching-place under a great locust tree, in the branches of which was hung the sweep of a well that furnished the people and animals with water, as there was no house in the vicinity, and most of the congregation came long distances to meeting.

From one to another the whispered inquiries and comments went around.

"Who is that driving the Whitmans?" said Joe Dinsmore to Daniel Brackett.

"That's Whitman's redemptioner."

"Pshaw! what are you talking about, most likely it's some relation of theirs from Lancaster. A mighty good-looking fellow he is, too; and has seen a horse afore to-day."

"I tell you it's his redemptioner."

"And I tell you I know better. Why, man alive, do you think a redemptioner who's a half fool, as everybody knows his redemptioner is, and was took out of a workhouse, would look, and act, and handle horses as that chap does?"

"Well, there's Sam Dorset, the drover, knows him, and has spoken to him; I'll leave it to him."

Beckoning to Dorset, who was sitting on the horse-block, to come near; Brackett asked, —

"Who is that young fellow who drove Whitman's folks up to the block just now?"

"Jim Renfew, his redemptioner."

"You are such a joker that it's hard to tell how to take you. Be you joking, or not? The story round our way is, and came pretty straight too, for it came from the tavern-keeper with whom Wilson always puts up, that Wilson took him out of a workhouse and that he's underwitted."

"I don't know what he was took out of, but I know this much, that I was by Whitman's, saw him holding plough and Whitman driving. I was there again, and came across him chopping in the woods and making the chips fly right smart, and last week I went there after lambs, and saw him ploughing by himself with the horses; and I venture to say there's not a man of all who run him down can draw so straight a furrow as that fellow drew. I reckon Whitman has just got a treasure in that redemptioner, and I, for one, am glad of it. Jonathan Whitman is a man who is willing that others should live as well as himself, and uses everybody and everything well, from the cattle in his pastures to the hired hands in his field. And his wife is just like him, and so are the whole breed of 'em; strong enough to tear anybody to pieces and not half try, and wouldn't hurt a fly except they are provoked out of all reason, *then* stand from under."

When the morning service was ended, Mrs. Whitman produced a basket of eatables of which they all partook, after which Mr. Whitman went into the porch.

It was not long before John and Will Edibean came into the pew and were introduced to James. John was about the age, and a great friend, of Peter, and Will of Bertie.

"Come," said Bert, "let's go sit in the carriage and talk till meeting begins."

The boys turned the front seat round, so that they faced each other, and conversed, James putting in a word at times when drawn out by some question from Peter, and while they were thus engaged Sam Dorset sauntered along and shook hands with James.

In the porch Mr. Whitman encountered his neighbor Wood, who after greeting said,—

"Jonathan, you was dead set against having a redemptioner, allers said all you could agin the whole thing; now you've got one, how do you like him?"

"I despise the whole thing as much as ever, but I like the redemptioner well enough thus far; the old saying is 'you must summer and winter a man to find him out,' and I have not done either yet."

"If you haven't changed your mind and still despise the whole thing, what made you take this redemptioner?"

"I got kind of inveigled into it. Had he been grown man, such as most any one would have been glad to have, I would have had nothing to do with it, but when I came to look at the poor lad, lame, with scarcely a rag to his back, without friends or money, and in a strange land, when I found that he came out of a workhouse, and naturally thought he could do no farm work, and noticed how kind of pitiful he looked, you don't know how it made me feel. I knew in reason that boy would be like to suffer, because well-to-do people would not have him, and he would be almost certain to fall into the hands of those who would abuse him."

"I see it worked on your feelings."

"More than that, it worked upon my conscience. I knew I was able to protect that boy; something seemed to say to me, 'Jonathan Whitman, you won't sell an old horse that has served you well, lest he should fall into bad hands; are you going to turn your back upon a friendless boy, made in the image of God who has blessed you in your basket and your store?' Still I could hardly bring myself to take a boy who had been born, as it were, brought up, at least, in a workhouse, and thought to give him a ten-dollar bill and get off in that way."

"You didn't want to take him into the family with your own children?"

"You've hit the nail on the head. As I said at first, I got inveigled into it and took him; but if it was to be done over again I would do it. Now that you have wormed all this out of me, I am going to measure you in your own bushel. For these six years past you've been aching to take a redemptioner, and importuning me to take one, now that you've got one, how do you like him?"

"Not over and above, and I don't mean to do much in the way of clothing him, or keeping him, till I find him out. When I come to see how much less he does than a man I could hire; and feel that I must keep and board him all winter when he won't earn his board; must run the chance of his being taken sick or getting hurt, I find that it is not, after all, such cheap labor as I at first imagined,—let alone the risk of his running away after he finds out what wages he can get elsewhere. I am going to find out what's in him before I throw away any more money on him. By the way, don't you think you're beginning rather strong with your redemptioner? You take a boy right out of the workhouse, who, by all accounts, has been hardly used and kept down, bring him into your family, dress him up and treat him just like one of your own children; don't you think he'll be like to get above himself and you too, and give you trouble?"

"I don't calculate to make him my heir, or indulge him to his injury; but I mean that he shall have the privilege of going to meeting and to school as my children do."

"To *school*! What, send a redemptioner to *school*?"

"Yes, I am after the same thing that you are; you are trying to find out what is in your redemptioner, and I in mine."

"That's a queer way to find out."

"It is somewhat different from yours, but suppose you had a colt and wanted to bring out his real disposition, which would be the surest way, to keep him short, work him hard, give him a cold stable, never bed or curry him, or to give him plenty of provender, a warm blanket, a good bed, and dress him down every day?"

"I suppose if there was any spirit or any ugliness in him, the good keeping would bring it out."

"I think so, and if my man is of that nature that he can't bear nor respond to good treatment I don't want him."

"But you are taking a very costly way to get information; and if, after all your expense of sending him to school, clothing, and buying books for him, he gives you the slip, you have failed of your object, which was to get cheap labor, and lost much money. While I, if my man proves worthless, have only lost a portion of the passage money."

"I shall not have failed of my object, since it was not my intention in taking this lad to obtain cheap labor, or to make money out of him."

"I should like to know what you did take him for? You're a sharper man than

I am, can make two dollars where I make one, and calculate to get labor as cheap as any body."

"I took him because I thought it my duty to befriend a friendless boy. His being a redemptioner had nothing to do with it; but his youth, his misery, and his liability to be abused had. I don't believe in cheap labor, which means dear labor in the end. I don't believe in losing fifty bushels of wheat for the sake of saving two shillings on a man's wages in harvest. Thus I shall not fail of my object if the boy does not turn out well, because I shall have discharged my duty. It seems to me, neighbor, that upon your principle of not risking anything, not trusting anybody, nor letting the laboring man have a fair chance, lest he should take advantage of it, that business could not go on, or if it could, that the relish would be all taken out of life."

The conversation was interrupted by the arrival of the hour for afternoon meeting.

Sam Dorset invited James to sit with him, he was about to decline but Bertie gave him a punch in the ribs, and volunteered to go with them, John and Willie Edibean taking their places in his father's pew. It was the design of Bertie to secure a friend for James who had some influence among people in general, for the drover was a frank, good-natured fellow, whom few could talk down and very few indeed dared to provoke, and whose occupation gave him a large acquaintance.

We shall watch with interest the different methods pursued by these very different farmers with their redemptioners.

In the course of the evening, Mrs. Whitman asked James how he liked the minister.

"I liked to hear him talk; I knew who he meant by that man he talked about in the afternoon, it was Mr. Holmes."

"No, James, that was the Lord Jesus Christ."

"I know he called him so, but that was who he meant, for he said he was just as good as he could be, and went about doing good, and that's just what Mr. Holmes was, and just the way he did. I suppose he was afraid Mr. Holmes wouldn't like it if he knew he called him by name."

"But, dear child, Mr. Holmes was nothing but a man, and the Lord Jesus Christ is God."

"The minister said he was a man and had feelings just like anybody. He said he was born at a place called Bethlehem (if he was born he must be a man) and told how he grew up, and said when a friend of his, a Mr. Lazarus, died, he felt so bad he wept, and after that he died himself; and now you say he was God, but one Sunday a good while ago when I said God was a man, you said he wasn't, he was a spirit."

"You had better drop the subject there, wife. And you will understand it better by and by, James, when you have heard more," said Mr. Whitman, "and when you can read the scriptures for yourself."

This incident, however trifling in itself, gave token that new ideas had begun to stir in that hitherto vacant mind, and to shape themselves into processes of connected thought. It, at the same time, served to confirm in the minds of his friends the belief already cherished, that he possessed a most retentive memory; as they found that as far as he could understand what he had listened to, he could repeat the most of both sermons, and had committed the questions and answers in the catechism by hearing Mr. Whitman ask them and the boys reply. The result of which was that when they came to go through the catechism again, he could get along as well without the book as the others could by its aid, and could repeat what he was unable to read.

CHAPTER X.
THE REDEMPTIONER AT SCHOOL.

The great chestnut was the favorite resort of the boys and their mates for planning all sorts of enterprises. In the hollow of it they kept their bows and arrows, fishing-poles and bats. It was so large that a little closet was made in one side, where they put foot-balls, fish-hooks, skates, powder-horns, shot, bullet-moulds and anything they wished to keep safe and dry. But in the winter they met for consultation in a little room over the workshop, which was used to keep bundles of flax in. And being on the south side of the barn, and three of its sides and the space overhead filled with hay,—while the chimney of the workshop ran through it,—was warm enough for them. When there was a fire in the workshop they sat on bundles of flax with their backs against the chimney; when there was not they burrowed in the hay and kept warm by contact, or wrapped themselves in skins. The great object of Peter and Bertie in introducing James to the Edibean boys, was that when he should go to school he might have some companions beside themselves. They had succeeded in inspiring them with the like interest for the welfare of James, and many and grave were the consultations held under the great tree, as the time for school to commence drew near.

In pursuance of a settled plan, the Edibeans began to come to Mr. Whitman's in the evenings. James was unwilling to spell or read before them, or even to write, lest they should look over, and wanted Bertie to go up stairs with him.

It was, however, no part of the boys' plan to permit this, for their design in inviting the Edibeans was to bring James to recite before them, and thus to moderate the shock to his extreme diffidence that they foresaw would occur when he should be compelled to recite before the whole school; and Bertie, excessively proud of his pupil's progress, longed to exhibit him to his friends. So he hit upon this plan,—Willie Edibean was a poor writer, but an excellent scholar in other respects. Bertie borrowed his writing-book, and showing it to James and the family, said,—

"There, James, only see how much better your writing is than Willie Edibean's. Isn't it, father? Isn't it, mother? See, gran'pa."

"It is a great deal better," said Mr. Whitman, taking both the books in his hand and comparing them, and then handing them to his father.

"James," said the latter, "you need not be afraid to show that writing-book to anybody."

"May I show it to the boys, James, next time they come?" said Bertie.

"When are they coming?"

"Day after to-morrow night."

"I don't want them to see this old book that I began in, but I've written it full, and to-night I'm going to begin the new one your father brought me. I will write in that to-night and to-morrow night instead of reading and spelling, and then you can let 'em see that."

When the evening came and Bertie produced the writing-book, James' face was redder than a fire coal. The boys lavished their praises upon the writing, in which all the family joined. Indeed they laid it "on with a trowel."

To relieve the embarrassment of James, and prevent the boys from increasing it by their questions, Mrs. Whitman placed a bowl of butternuts and chestnuts upon the table. But the old grandfather changed the subject much more effectually by saying,—

"Fifty years ago this morning, about day-break I shot a Seneca Indian behind the tree these butternuts grew on, with that rifle that hangs over the fireplace, buried him under it, and his bones are there now."

No more was thought of writing, reading, or spelling, that evening, and for half an hour the nuts were untasted.

James soon became so accustomed to the Edibeans, that he did not hesitate to write when they were present, and John Edibean proposed that they should have a reading-lesson together, and also a writing-lesson, after which they should spell together, the whole family taking part, which was done.

James could now read short sentences and spell most words of two syllables, and could make a better pen than any of them; the boys soon ascertained this and got him to make their pens. So little a matter as this tended very much to inspire him with confidence, and help him overcome the shrinking sensitiveness and self-deprecation when contrasting himself with others, and which he ever manifested in the expression, "such as me or the likes of me."

When they were about to write, it was quite ludicrous to hear Bertie sinking the master in the pupil, and with much effort to keep a sober countenance, saying,—

"Master, please mend my pen."

Jonathan Whitman had a good set of carpenter's tools, made all his farm implements that were constructed of wood, and repaired his buildings. This tendency he inherited from his father, who, according to the son, possessed much more mechanical ability and ingenuity than himself, though the stern struggles and exigencies of his early life left scant opportunity for the practice of it. But now in his old age he spent much time in the shop, repaired all the farming tools, and was considered the best man to make a wheel or stock a rifle in the whole county.

One day he was making a gate, and having lined some boards, set James to split them up with a ripping saw, and after he had finished, said,—

"You have split those boards as true as I could have split them, and cut the chalk mark right out. If I had set either of our boys to splitting them, the line would have been left sometimes on one side and sometimes on the other, and they'd have been sawed bevelling, and wider on one side than the other."

He then laid out some mortises, and set James to boring and beating them out with mallet and chisel, and then to planing the slats, after which he said,
—"James, I see you have a mechanical eye and a natural turn to handle tools. I knew that before by your chopping. I advise you to cultivate it, because it will give you a means to earn your bread. I'm most always here stormy days in the winter, come in and practise with the tools, and I'll show you. If, as I trust you will, you should have a piece of land, it will be a great thing in a new settlement to be able to handle tools."

Scarcely had the old gentleman and James left the shop, than Peter, Bertie, and the Edibeans came in, replenished the fire to heat the chimney, and taking some skins from the wagon, ascended to the loft above, and seated themselves for consultation, evidently with something of great weight upon their minds.

"The fact is," said Peter, "school begins in two days. James is going, father says so. How he'll look, great big creature, bigger than the master,—yes, he could take the master and fling him over his head,—standing up to read and spell with little tots not up to his knees. I don't believe he'll be able to get a word out."

"That's not the worst of it," said John Edibean, "perhaps some of 'em will laugh because he's a *redemptioner*, Sammy Parsons called Mr. Wood's man an old redemptioner, and the man flung a stone at him and hurt him awfully."

The master, Walter Conly, was a farmer's son, living two miles distant, and the boys knew him well, as he had kept the school the winter previous.

"Let us do this," said Willie, "Walter Conly is a nice man; we'll go over there this evening, tell him all about James, how fast he learns and how hard we've been trying to help him, and ask him if he won't hear him read by himself, and not put him in a class with little children."

"So we will," said Bertie, "he's going to board round, and I'll ask father to tell him to come to our house first and get him to send a note by me, and then James will get acquainted with him. We'll call you the minute we get our supper."

Mr. Conly, a young man of nineteen, who labored on his father's farm in the summer and taught school in the winter, and under the instruction of the minister was fitting for college, received this deputation of his best scholars with great cordiality. He listened to their story with great interest, and expressed his gratification at the spirit they had manifested, and the efforts they had put forth to benefit James, but told them that he would improve much faster to be in a class than to recite by himself, as there would be more stimulus, though he might be subjected to some mortification at first.

"If," said he, "James has so good a memory, and is as willing to apply himself as you have represented, he will very soon begin to excel his mates, because the mind of a boy of that age is more mature than the mind of a child, and he is capable of more application. He will outstrip them, that will encourage him. I will then put him into a class with older scholars, which will stimulate him still more. I shall put him to nothing but reading, writing, and spelling, for the first two months, but at home you can teach him the multiplication table, and then give him some sums to do in his head, and thus prepare him to cipher the last part of the school term."

Bertie was a beautiful boy, with a face that expressed every emotion of his heart, and Mr. Conly, observing a shade of disappointment upon his handsome features, said,—"Boys, you have manifested such a noble spirit in regard to James, that I would not, for any consideration, that you should feel hurt or be in any way discouraged. On the other hand, I want you to feel satisfied and happy, and if you are not content with my method I will hear him by himself."

The boys, after talking the matter over among themselves, concluded the master's plan was the best.

"I see what troubles you in particular. You fear that as he has never been at school, coming on the floor to spell, and standing before me a stranger, will so confuse him that he will not be able to spell perhaps at all; certainly not to do himself justice. I think, however, we can get over that. The school was so large last winter that I was compelled to make use of some of the older scholars as assistants. It will be larger this winter, as the two districts are to be put together and the term lengthened. I will appoint you, Albert, to hear the class that I put James in, and that will go a good way towards giving him confidence."

"O, sir, I thank you."

"We all thank you," said John Edibean.

"That will make all the difference in the world," said Peter. "You see, sir, what makes him so sensitive is that in England they picked upon him and called him 'workhouse,' and in the vessel coming over, the rest of the redemptioners and the sailors did so. Mr. Wilson told my father, after he came here, a good many mean fellows at the public-house made fun of him and called him a redemptioner. He told me that a good many people who came to look at and see if they would take him, called him hard names. One man told Mr. Wilson he was a chowder-head; wasn't worth his salt, and the best thing he could do would be to put a good stone to his neck and drop him into the mill-pond. And another man asked Wilson whose cornfield he robbed to get that scarecrow."

"He was lame then, sir," said Bertie, "'cause he had cut himself and had on the worst-looking old clothes, and such a downcast look. But now he has good clothes; is not lame, has got red cheeks, and we think is real handsome."

"So he is, Bertie," said Mrs. Conly, the master's mother. "I saw him in your pew Sunday, and told husband when we came home I guessed that young man was some of your mother's relations from Lancaster."

When the boys reached home, Bertie noticed that James seemed a good deal disturbed about something, and very sad, and in a few moments went to bed.

"What is the matter with James, mother? What makes him look so downcast?" said Bertie.

"Your father has told him he must go to school, and he feels bad about it, I suppose."

Bertie ran up stairs and told James not to feel bad about going to school, for the master was a real kind man, and he was going to hear him recite there just as he did at home. James' ideas of school were very vague; he only knew that he was going among a crowd of strange boys to be exposed to criticism, and put under a new master, but much comforted by what Bertie told him, he composed himself and went to sleep.

The morning school was to begin, the boys took an early start, thus giving James an opportunity to view the schoolhouse. It was a log building of the rudest kind, and nearly a hundred years old. It had remained without alteration, except receiving a shingle roof and glazed windows. The walls were chestnut logs of the largest size, save a few near the top, and the crevices between them were stuffed with clay, and moss and hemlock brush had been recently piled to the windows around the whole building, for the sake of warmth. The door was of plank with wooden hinges and latch.

It was situated in a singularly wild and rugged spot, on a high ridge of broken land, over the surface of which huge boulders and precipices alternated with abrupt hills and swales of moderate extent, the whole region heavily timbered with oak, chestnut, and beech.

The ancient building seemed to have appropriated to itself the only level spot in the vicinity, a little green plot, though of small extent.

It was bounded on the northwest by a precipice that rose perpendicularly above the roof of the schoolhouse that was built within a few feet of it. On the summit of this cliff were large beeches that thrust their gnarled roots into the interstices of the rock, and flung their branches over the ancient building. The main road was through a natural break in the ridge of rock, and beside it a pure spring of water supplied the wants of the school, and the necessities of travellers.

There lay in the mind of this apparently stolid lad, whose life hitherto had known neither childhood nor joyous youth, a keen susceptibility to impressions of the beautiful and majestic in nature. Through all those years of misery it had lain dormant and undeveloped, but of late the woods and fields had begun to have a strange fascination for him, he knew not why, and his happiest hours were spent while laboring alone in the forest. He had as yet seen nothing to compare in rugged grandeur and beauty with this, and the old schoolhouse was in such perfect keeping with its wild surroundings that it seemed to have grown there.

"Do let me look a little longer."

This to Bertie, who was pulling him by the arm and saying,—"Come, let's go into the schoolhouse. I want you to speak to Arthur and Elmer Nevins before the rest come; they are first-rate boys and live close by here, this land is on their farm. I want you to see Edward Conly, the master's brother, too."

"In a moment."

James kept gazing, and for the first time the thought came into his mind: "Oh, that I could own land like this!" As this idea like the lightning's flash darted through his mind, and with it all the stories he had heard the old grandfather tell of persons who began with only their hands and obtained a freehold, it was with reluctance he at last permitted Bertie (who might as well have tugged at a mountain) to pull him away from the spot.

Entering the house they found the Nevins boys, Edward Conly, and a few more of both girls and boys present, with a fire sufficient to roast an ox and every window open. The boys had overdone the matter, for the schoolhouse, though old, was warm, being sheltered by the precipice and the forest from the cold winds. It had been stuffed with moss and clay that fall, and the logs, though decayed on the outside were of great size, making a very thick wall and sound at heart.

If the outside of the house had arrested the attention of James, the inside was much more calculated to do so. The fireplace was of stone. The jambs and mantel were large single stones, the back composed of single stones set edgewise upon each other. There were a large pair of shovel and tongs, but no andirons, and in their stead were two stones four feet in length, and a foot in height, to hold the wood and afford a draft beneath, and an iron bar laid across to keep the wood from rolling out.

The walls were of rough logs with the bark still adhering, except where it had been pulled off by the busy fingers of the children. There was no flooring above, all was open to the roof and the purlins were decked with swallows' nests, the birds having found admittance at some place where the clay had fallen out, and despite the noise of the children during the summer school, had reared their young and migrated at the approach of winter. Along the walls on either side were seats for single scholars, and the space between was filled up with seats that held three, and aisles between.

Arthur Nevins was nineteen, and Edward Conly eighteen, they were therefore among the largest boys, excellent scholars, of good principles and dispositions, and met James in a very kind and social manner.

"I am going to take my old seat," said Bertie, selecting one of the single seats in the back corner,—"Where are you going to have yours, James?"

"I don't know."

"Well, take the one right before me, put your books in it, and sit down, then you'll hold it."

Peter, John, and Will Edibean took the back seat next to Bertie; Arthur and Elmer Nevins, and Edward Conly the seats before them. Thus by previous arrangement among the boys, who were no novices in these matters, James had Bertie directly behind; Peter and the Edibeans, Arthur and Elmer Nevins, and Edward Conly on the side, and behind; all fast friends to each other and all friendly to him. Peter, Bertie, and the Edibean boys, had determined to make the school pleasant for James, by prejudicing the Nevins boys and

Edward Conly in his favor, and they had come to school thus early for that purpose. Let boys alone for carrying out any plan of that kind they get in their noddles. They never let the iron cool on the anvil, not they.

By the time the master came they were nearly all seated, though there was some bickering about seats, that was not settled but by an appeal to him, and some trading for seats among the boys themselves.

The majority of the boys had quills for pens, plucked from their parents' geese.

Nat Witham,—a disagreeable lad, whom the boys had nicknamed Chuck,—sat in the seat before James; his hands were covered with great seed-warts that he was always pricking, and endeavoring to put the blood on the hands of the smaller children, to make them have warts, and pulling the hair of the children before him. He got more whippings than any boy in school, and deserved more than he got.

Bertie and Arthur Nevins gave this boy a Dutch quill each, to change seats with Stillman Russell, a good scholar, and a boy whom they all liked. Having thus successfully carried out all their plans, the Whitmans and Edibeans flattered themselves that they had arranged matters satisfactorily for their own progress and comfort, and that of James during the school term, but they were destined to find that,—

> "The best-laid schemes o' mice and men
>
> Gang aft a-glee."

Great was the curiosity manifested, when the master called out the class to which James had been assigned, and told Bertie to hear them. You might have heard a pin drop. James was taller by a head than any boy in the school, and his classmates were children; they had attended a woman's school in the summer, but it was two months' previous; they had become rusty, and had to spell half their words. James, on the other hand, who had been over the lesson with Bertie the evening before and early that morning, read right along in a very low tone, but without hesitating a moment, greatly to the relief of Bertie, whose heart was in his mouth, for he was afraid James would not muster courage to hear the sound of his own voice.

It was no less a matter of surprise to the school, most of whom were ready to titter at seeing such a big fellow reading with little children.

When, in the afternoon, he came to write, and the master complimented him for the excellence of his writing, James took heart of grace and felt that the worst was over, and when he entered the house at night, Mrs. Whitman gathered from the expression of his face that all had gone well.

While Peter and James were doing up the chores at the barn, Bertie, who was bringing in the night's wood, embraced the opportunity to unbosom himself to his mother.

"Oh, mother, James did first-rate, ma'am, first-rate."

"Yes, child, I hear you."

"He's tickled to death. What do you suppose he did, mother? He didn't know anybody saw him, but I was up on the haymow; he put both arms round Frank's neck, and hugged him, and talked to him ever so long, and I expect he told Frank how glad he was that he had read and spelt, before the whole school, and got through the first day."

"What reply did Frank make?" said his mother, laughing.

"He wickered. You may laugh, mother, but he knew well enough that James was glad, and that was his way to say he was glad too."

"I suppose Frank heard you on the mow, and wickered for some hay."

"James," said Bertie, not heeding the interruption, "won't talk with other folks, but he's all the time talking to the horses when he thinks nobody hears him."

The naturally proud and sensitive nature of James shrank from familiar contact with those who had been reared under such different conditions. He was haunted with the notion that, in their secret mind they looked upon him as inferior, and notwithstanding the kindness they manifested, did in thought revert to his former condition; but in regard to the animals this feeling had no place, he lavished upon them his caresses, and understood their expressions of gratitude. To them, he well knew, the redemptioner and "work'us" was master, benefactor, friend.

Thus passed away the first week of school, to the mutual satisfaction of all concerned.

CHAPTER XI.
THE PLOT EXPOSED.

The next week the master set James copies in fine hand, and also copies of capital letters; and he began to learn at home, and recite to Bertie, the multiplication table, that was, in those days, printed on the covers of the writing-books. The next week the master gave him short sentences to copy, and wound up the week's work on Saturday, with setting him for a copy of his own name and that of his mother before her marriage. James was so much delighted with this as to overcome his usual diffidence, and show it to Mr. Whitman.

When school was half done, Mr. Conly put James into the class with Bertie, who no longer instructed James in reading, spelling, or writing at home, as the latter could read nearly as well as his former teacher; and write much better than any boy in the school, or even the master.

The afternoon of Saturday was a half-holiday and stormy; the old gentleman had a fire and was at work in the shop. Mr. Whitman having broken a whiffletree in the course of the week, laid the broken article on the bench, intending to mend it. James saw it, made a new one by it, and put the irons of the old one on the ends. About the middle of the afternoon, Mr. Whitman bethought himself of the whiffletree, and going to the shop, found the remains of it on the bench, and a new one lying beside it.

"Father, did you make this whiffletree?"

"No, Jonathan; your redemptioner made it."

Mr. Whitman made no remark, but his father noticed that afterwards, on stormy days, he but seldom gave James any indoor work, but seemed well content to have him work in the shop with his father, who in the course of the winter and spring taught him to dovetail, hew with a broad axe, and saw with a whipsaw.

Although Peter, Bertie, and their friends, had taken such unwearied pains, and exhausted their ingenuity, to render the position of James at school both pleasant and profitable, circumstances conspired to render their efforts, to a great extent, and for some time, abortive.

Children hear all that is said in the family, and often much more than it is meant, or desirable, they should.

Many of the boys at the other extremity of the district, had seen James while Wilson had him at the tavern. They had many of them heard disparaging remarks made by their parents and brothers at home. Some of them had listened to the talk in the public-house by their elders respecting him, and imbibed the tone of feeling in the neighborhood that was in general hostile to redemptioners, and were thus prejudiced against him, even before he came to school. The parents of some of the largest scholars were, in politics, the opposite of the Whitmans, and they had heard their parents say that no doubt Jonathan Whitman took that ragamuffin to train him up to vote as he wanted him to, and then would get him naturalized. This feeling of prejudice would have probably worn off, if James had been less reserved, and had joined with the rest in the horse-plays that were ever going on at recess and between schools.

James, however, did not know how to play; sport and amusement were to him terms without signification. The only things he could do that boys generally practise were to shoot, swim, and throw stones. He could shoot indifferently well, swim like a fish, and could kill a bird or a squirrel with a stone.

His sensitiveness made him believe the boys would not care to associate with him, and his whole mind was given to his books, for he had begun to appreciate the value of knowledge, and desired to make the most of the present opportunity, for he did not expect to have another.

When the other boys were at play during noon and recess, he was in his seat getting his lessons, and never spoke unless he was spoken to.

This gave occasion to those who had come prepared to dislike him to say that he was stuck up; that the Whitmans and Edibeans, Nevins and Conlys, had made too much of him; that he was getting too large for his trousers, and should be taken down, and they were the boys to take him down; that he put on great airs for a redemptioner, just out of the workhouse.

Some were nettled because he, in so short a time, distanced them in study, and in spelling went above them, and kept above.

The master one day gave mortal offence to William Morse, because, being busy setting copies, he told him to go to James to mend his pen.

Some who disliked the Whitmans and Edibeans, because they were better scholars than themselves, and their parents were better off, were willing to see James annoyed, because they knew it would annoy them.

Chuck Witham felt aggrieved because he had sold his seat so cheap, and wanted Bertie and Arthur Nevins to give him two more quills; but they told him a bargain was a bargain, that they gave him all he asked; and being possessed of a sullen, vindictive temper, he likewise was on the watch to annoy them through James.

This hostile spirit had been long fermenting in the breasts of a portion of the scholars, and was only prevented from breaking out in offensive acts from wholesome fear of the strength of James, and uncertainty in regard to the temper of one so reserved.

The boys were constantly pitting themselves against each other, and testing their strength and activity by wrestling, jumping and lifting rocks and logs.

James never manifested the least interest in their sport, not even enough to look on. Thus they could find no opportunity to form any estimate of his strength, or disposition. His whole bearing, however, was indicative both of strength and activity, for he had lost the low, creeping gait he once had, and the despondent look. In addition to this, two of their number, Ike Whitcomb and John Dennet, were fishing for eels in the mill-pond the day Wilson brought James to Mr. Whitman, and told the others that they saw him pitch the barrels of flour into the wagon as though they had been full only of apples. This information tended also to inspire caution.

There was still another sedative, and by no means the least influential. There was a circle of friends around James, not merely those we have named, but several others from both districts, of like sympathies and principles; and though far inferior in numbers, they comprised the best minds and the most energetic persons of the whole school, and were actuated by a sentiment of chivalry, taking the part of the oppressed, that made them doubly formidable.

Arthur Nevins was in his twentieth year; the most, athletic boy in the school, the leader in all exercises that tested strength and endurance, and resolute as a lion. There was no doubt which side he would take, in any affair that Peter or Bertie Whitman were concerned in.

As, however, this feeling of enmity increased, and grew all the faster from being causeless, and open rupture being considered imprudent,—it found vent at first in ill-natured remarks, slurs and gibes, as, for instance: "There goes the redemptioner." "Here comes 'work'us;' got any cold vittles?" "Any old clo'es?"

At noon, when James was in the schoolhouse, and his enemies outside, one boy would shout to another so as to be heard all over the schoolhouse,—"I say, John Edmands, do you know how to pick oakum?"

"No."

"Well, then ask Redemptioner. He learned the trade in the work'us, and he's a superior workman."

Did James leave the schoolroom at recess, half a dozen snowballs flung by nobody would hit him. When at night he had his books under his arm going home a volley of balls would cover his books with snow.

James endured all this in silence, and without manifesting the least resentment, which only served to encourage imposition. Not so, however the Whitmans, and the Nevins boys, and the Valentines; when either of those caught a boy flinging a snowball at James, they returned it with interest, and Arthur Nevins generally had an icy one at hand.

This brought on a general snowball fight, under cover of which James, as his enemies said, "meeched" off.

It was now the turn of James to build the fire. Orcutt, who built it the morning previous, had put on a very large rock-maple log, which, being but half burnt out, gave promise of a noble bed of coals for James to kindle his fire with in the morning.

After school at night, the three boys cut up and carried into the schoolhouse a large quantity of wood to build the morning fire, but when James reached the schoolhouse in the morning, there was not a coal on the hearth, the fireplace was full of half-melted snow, and not a single stick of all the wood carried in the night before was to be found anywhere.

James had his axe on his shoulder, and was equal to the occasion; he cut a log, back-stick, fore-stick, and small wood, went into the woods and split kindling from a pine stump, then went to Mr. Nevins' for fire. Arthur and Elmer instantly came with him; Elmer with a firebrand, and Arthur hauling a load of dry wood on a hand-sled, which, in addition to what James had already prepared, made one of the hottest fires of the season, and soon dried up the snow-water that flooded the hearth, and the floor around it that was smeared with ashes. They cut some hemlock-brush, made a broom, and soon restored things to their pristine order.

"Now," said Arthur, "whoever did this thing thought that James, not being used to wood fires, would not be able to make one; the master and scholars would get here, find no fire, and he would appear like a fool, and be blamed. James, don't you lisp a word of it, and we won't; if it comes out, the one who did it will have to tell of it himself, and then we shall find out who did it."

The perpetrators of the trick did not know that James had built the fire every morning at Mr. Whitman's for two months.

Just as the school was called to order, Arthur and Elmer came in, and stood so long with their backs to the fire, that the master at last said,—

"Boys, are you not sufficiently warm?"

They were by no means suffering from cold, but as they stood thus, facing the whole school, they took careful note of the surprise depicted on several faces at finding a good fire, and everything as usual, likewise of sundry nods, winks, and whispers; sometimes saw something written on a slate, and the slate held up for some one in another seat to read the message. When the two brothers came to compare notes that night, after returning home, they were not in much doubt as to the perpetrators of this low trick.

The Nevins boys held themselves in readiness to assist James, if needful, the next morning, who came early but found everything as usual.

"Their gun has missed fire," said Arthur to James.

"Elmer, you and I must be all eyes and ears, for we shall certainly hear about it to-day. They'll get no fun out of it, unless it comes out."

It was not long after school began, before there took place an unusual movement all over the room. Every one seemed to be excited in regard to something, but in a very different way; some very much pleased, but by far the larger number indignant. Presently a slate was passed to Arthur, on which was written, "There is a story going, that night before last the fireplace was filled with snow, and all the wood we cut was carried off; but it is a lie, for if it had been so, James would have told us of it," signed "Albert."

The slate was passed back with the question, "Who told?"

Soon the answer was returned,—

"Chuck Witham started it."

At recess the affair became a matter of discussion, but it was almost universally condemned. Even most of those who were prejudiced against James and the Whitmans revolted at the low character of this act.

The girls came out *en masse* in favor of James, avowing it was the meanest and most dastardly thing they ever had heard of; that there was not a more obliging or better behaved boy in the school than James, and if they knew who the fellows that did it were they would never speak to them again.

The girls had ascertained the willingness of James to oblige; for, noticing that he always made and mended pens for Bertie Whitman, they got Maria to carry their pens and quills to him, and as they became better acquainted, went to him themselves.

Arthur Nevins said very little, but taking Chuck aside said,—

"Who told you all that news?"

"Sam Topliff."

He went to Sam, and found that Will Orcutt told him. Going to Orcutt he inquired,—

"Who told you about what was done in the schoolhouse, night before last?"

"None of your business."

"Say that again, I'll shake your teeth out of your head; you were one of them."

"No, I wasn't one of them, neither."

"Ay, my fine fellow, you may think it a good joke, but I can tell you it may prove a sore joke to you. Every decent boy, and all the girls in school, are down on you; and if it gets to the ears of the master and the school-committee, you'll see trouble, for it was not merely a trick upon a boy, but it was trespass, breaking into the schoolhouse in the night. You broke a lock, you villain. Mr. Jonathan Whitman is one of the school-committee, and is not a man to be trifled with; you had better think about it."

He then left him, but when Arthur started for home at night, Will Orcutt followed him and said,—

"I wasn't one of them, and you needn't think, nor say, I was."

"Then why won't you tell who told you?"

Orcutt made no reply.

"If you'll tell me the names of all who were in it, I'll give you a pistareen, and if you won't, I'll tell Mr. Whitman you was one of them."

"I'm afraid to; they'll lick me to death."

"I never will tell who told me."

"But they'll know, because they know I am the only one, except themselves, who knows who did it."

"If I guess whom they were, will you tell me if I guess right?"

"If, instead of the pistareen, you'll give me a quarter, and keep it to yourself till day after to-morrow noon, I'll tell you."

"Why don't you want me to keep it to myself any longer than till day after to-morrow noon?"

"Because to-morrow is my last day of school, and I am going off the next morning to Reading, to learn a trade, and I know you won't tell a lie."

"I'll give you the quarter, and promise to keep it till then."

"Then go into the schoolhouse with me. I'll show you on the fire-list."

The fire-list was a paper fastened to the master's desk, on which were the names of all the boys who were expected to take their turns in making the fires, and Orcutt pricked with a pin the names of William Morse, David Riggs, George Orcutt.

"Two of them are the very fellows I had picked out, the other was Sam Dinsmore. I never should have thought your brother George would have been in it."

After this matter came out, the boys told James that he was able to take his own part, and ought not to tamely submit to anymore abuse; for still the petty insults from small boys, set on by the larger ones, continued.

Peter Whitman told the others, that there were only four or five large boys who set the rest on, and they ought to pitch into them, give them a good beating, and protect James.

"I don't feel like going into a fight," said Arthur, "to protect a fellow who is better able to protect us than we are him, and could thrash the whole of 'em with one hand tied behind him; they are a set of cowards, and would be quiet enough if they once saw in him any inclination to resist."

"I think as Arthur does," said Elmer.

The Edibean boys were of the same mind.

"But he won't resist. He'll only say, 'It is not for such as me to be making a disturbance,'" said Bertie, sorely puzzled.

"Do you think he's afraid of 'em, Bertie? Don't he know we'll back him up?"

"I don't believe he cares a straw for them, or cares whether anybody backs him up, or not; but it seems as if he thinks, because he came out of a workhouse, that he was made for other people to wipe their feet on."

"Let's go at him," said Stillman Russell; "and tell him that he must stick up to them, and thrash the next one who insults him, and we'll back him up. But if he don't, we shan't care anything about him and shall be ashamed of him."

"That's it; only leave the last part out, for that would break his heart, and it would be a falsehood for me to say I would not care anything about him," said Bertie; "and let us also do another thing. James thinks everything of my grandfather; they talk together a great deal, when they are at work in the shop, and grandfather never will tell anything if you ask him not to. We'll tell grandfather the whole story, and get him to stir James up. If grandfather tells James to defend himself, he'll think it's right, and he will, but as for us, we are but boys like himself."

"It is not for such as me to make any disturbance. I didn't go to school to make a disturbance. I went to learn," was the reply of James to his aged adviser.

"*Such as me,*" replied the irate grandfather; "don't ever use that phrase again. Haven't I told you, time and again, that in this country, one man's as good as another, provided he behaves as well; and if he don't he is not. It's the character, and not the nation, the blood, nor money, that makes a man here."

"The boys in the school don't seem to think so."

"The most of 'em do, and their parents do, and the most of their parents wouldn't uphold 'em in anything else. It is only a few rapscallions who are at the bottom of the whole thing. They are keeping the whole school in confusion, and taking the attention of the scholars off their lessons; and you are helping to keep it along by putting up with it. If they insult you without provocation, knock 'em over, and they will be quiet as frogs, when a stone is flung into the pond."

"It is not my place to strike and hurt boys whose fathers own land, when my father hadn't any land; my mother went out to service and died in the workhouse, and was buried by the parish. If I was in England they would all call me a workhouse brat. Old Janet, my nurse, when she got mad used to say to me,—

"'My grandfather was a hieland lord and my father was a hieland gentleman; but your mither was a servant girl, and your father was a hedger and ditcher, and out of nothing comes nothing, ye feckless bairn.'"

"Pshaw, it's no fault of yours that your parents were poor and that you was born in a workhouse, nor disgrace neither; and it's no merit of theirs that their fathers own land. It came about in the providence of God, who is no respecter of persons."

"Is not a man who owns land, better than one who don't?"

"No; he may be a great deal worse; owning land don't make a man any better in the sight of God, and it ought not to in the sight of men."

"I always thought that anybody who owned land was next to the quality; ain't the quality better?"

"No."

87

"I always thought they were kind of little kings."

"Kings are no better."

"O, yes, grandfather, kings must be better, because the Bible tells about 'em; and Mr. Holmes always used to say, his most sacred majesty."

"All moonshine; half of 'em are great rascals. Being a king don't make a man better or worse any more than owning land does. It only gives them a better chance to act out their true characters."

"If a king was no more and no better than a man, how could he cure the king's evil?"

"No king ever did cure it, and it's my opinion it never was cured."

"O, yes, there was Farmer Vinal's son, whose father I worked for, had a great swelling on his neck, and his father carried him into the procession when the king went to the tower, and the king touched it and it went away."

"I've no doubt it went away," replied the sturdy republican; "but if the king had never been born, it would have gone away all the same. It's a disorder that once in the blood is always there, and goes and comes. Medicine will appear to cure it, and drive it from one part of the body to another, and just as like as not, it went away on account of some medicine the child had been taking. You'd better put all such nonsense out of your head; it is not worth bringing over the water. If those boys impose upon you, defend yourself; you are big enough. Give no offence and take none; the whole district will uphold you in it."

CHAPTER XII.
STUNG TO THE QUICK.

James could be neither goaded to retaliation by the provocation of his persecutors, nor stimulated to self-defence by the arguments and persuasions of his friends, so thoroughly had the bitter lesson of submission to superiors been impressed by the iron fingers of stern necessity; but an event now occurred, which, placing the matter before him in a new light, removed his scruples in a moment.

The persons who had put the snow in the fireplace were well known to James, for Arthur had not scrupled to expose them after the time had elapsed during which he had promised to keep the secret. James also knew that they still continued to instigate Chuck Witham and other boys to annoy and insult him. He occupied a side seat near one of the back corners of the schoolhouse, and his head, when bent over his book, was on a level with a crevice between two logs, that was stuffed with clay and moss. One night after school, Chuck Witham bored a small hole through this clay, and filled the hole with cotton, for fear James would feel the draft and observe it. The next day he brought to school, half an ox-goad, with a long brad in it, made of a saddler's awl.

The day was warm for the season; there was quite a large fire, and at recess time, the master opened a window on each side of the fire to create a draft, and ventilate and cool the room.

James was in his seat writing, when he suddenly sprang to his feet, upsetting his inkstand, and throwing all his books to the floor. The master was walking back and forth on the floor, and seeing him put his hand to his head, looked out of the window and saw Chuck running from the hole, for the woods. He instantly pursued and caught him, with the goad in his hand, called the scholars in and gave him a severe whipping. Witham, with the expectation of mitigating his punishment, declared that he was persuaded to it by Morse, Riggs, and Orcutt, and that Will Morse gave him a two-bladed knife to do this and other things he had done to James. This declaration was made before the whole school, and Peter and Arthur Nevins now recollected that William Morse stayed in during recess, a thing he had never been known to do before, and it was evident to all that he had stayed in to gloat over the torture about to be inflicted upon one who had never injured, or even spoken to him.

The brad was long, and entered deep, for the stab was given with good-will, and the blood flowed freely.

At noontime the boys and girls collected together in knots, commenting upon the affair, when Chuck Witham, still writhing under the effects of the castigation, for it was most severe, made some disparaging remark about redemptioners, in a tone loud enough for James to hear, as he was passing by on his way to the spring, to wash off the blood that had dried on his neck, upon which William Morse laughed heartily, in which he was joined by Riggs and Orcutt.

Perfectly willing to pick a quarrel, Bert replied,—"Morse, you should have had that licking yourself; for you set Chuck on, and have been at the bottom of all the mean tricks that have been done, and that you had not courage to do yourself."

This brought a sharp rejoinder from Morse. Riggs and Orcutt sided with Morse, and the debate became so warm that just as James came along on his return from the spring, Morse, feeling he was getting the worst of the argument, caught a stick from the wood-pile and felled Bertie to the ground. James saw the blow fall on the head of the boy whom he loved better than himself,—yea, almost worshipped,—his scruples vanished in a moment. It was no longer the workhouse boy against the landed gentry; but, forgetting all that, he dealt Morse a blow that cut through his upper lip, knocked out a tooth, flattened his nose, and sent him backward over the wood-pile. Riggs turned to run, but came in contact with the broad shoulders of Arthur Nevins, who was purposely in the way, and before he could recover himself, James, seizing him behind, flung him to the ground, and catching up the stick that fell from the hand of Morse, beat him till he cried murder. While this was going on George Orcutt would have made his escape, but Stillman Russell, the most retiring boy in school, and so diffident that he would blush if you spoke to him, put out his foot and tripped him up. Before he could rise, Arthur Nevins put his foot on him, but James went into the schoolhouse, and resumed his studies.

"Now for Chuck Witham," shouted Will Edibean. Chuck took to his heels with three boys after him, but Edward Conly cried,—"He's had enough; he's only an understrapper," and they came back.

The boys had formed a ring round Orcutt, and whenever he would attempt to break through, one would trip him, another pull him over backwards, and while on his back others would pelt him with great chunks of snow and crust, or push three or more smaller boys on top of him; and even the girls took part and flung snowballs, so much was his conduct detested. In the morning before school, it being a thaw, the smaller boys had rolled up several great balls of snow, meaning at noon to make a fort. With these they buried him, and stuck up over him, this inscription, printed with a smut coal on a piece of fence-board,

"JUSTICE.

Administered by the Scholars of District No. 2."

They next formed a cordon around him, snowballs in their hands, and the moment he attempted to move pelted him anew, and kept watch till the master was so near that he could not but notice the inscription, and then all went into the schoolhouse and were seated when he entered.

Morse having washed himself at the spring, came in late, in company with Riggs, while George Orcutt crawled out of his prison, and sneaked home.

The face of Morse was discolored, and his lips swollen, and Riggs exhibited two red stripes on the back of both hands, and one across his face, extending from the roots of the hair across the forehead and face to the lower jaw. They tried to attract the attention of the master. Morse displayed a bloody handkerchief, and Riggs snivelled occasionally, but the master was too much occupied to notice them, and asked no questions. As for James, he was commended by nearly the whole school.

"Is he not a noble, manly fellow," said Emily Conly, "to bear so much from those mean creatures, while he might at any time have done what he has done to-day?"

"Yes," said Mary Nevins, "and when at last he did turn upon them, it was not upon his own account, but Albert Whitman's, and our Arthur and Elmer both say they don't believe he would have touched them, let them have done what they might to him, if William Morse had not struck Albert."

"What a different spirit he manifested," said Emily, "from Morse, who after hiring Witham to stick the awl into James, stayed in at recess to see and enjoy it, but Renfew didn't stop and look on when the other scholars were punishing George Orcutt, but went right back to his books. Oh, I do like him." Then feeling she had gone too far, and seeing the rest of the girls begin to titter, she blushed to the roots of her hair, and stopped short.

"Never mind, Emily," said Jane Gifford; "we all like him; all of the girls are on the side of the redemptioner."

"My brother Stillman thinks the reason he learns so fast, is because he is so old, and sees the need of it, and makes a business of learning, as a young boy wouldn't; and not knowing anybody, and being so by himself, has nothing to take off his attention. Still. says if he knew all the boys and girls, and had brothers and sisters, and went with them, to bees and apple-parings, and singing schools, and parties, and spelling schools, he wouldn't learn half so fast; but now he'll learn as much and more this winter, than a small boy would in three years," said Eliza Russell.

The friends of James could hardly contain themselves till school was out. Arthur Nevins had invited Peter, Bertie, the Edibeans, and Ned Conly, to take supper with him, and have a real "howl of triumph," and had sent Elmer home at recess to tell his mother she would have seven hungry school boys at supper time. After a bountiful supper, they sat down to eat nuts and apples, and to congratulate each other upon the success of all their plans.

"The master," said Ned Conly, "is going to put James into arithmetic soon."

"He's got all the multiplication by heart now," said Bertie, "and every night after supper, father and grandpa give him sums to do in his head, and he can add, and subtract, and multiply, and divide, and makes handsome figures. When he first came to our house he didn't know how long a year was, but called four years four times reaping wheat, and couldn't tell the clock; but now he can tell how many months there are in a year, and how many days in a year, and how many hours in a day, and minutes in an hour, and all about it. I think that's a good deal for a boy to do in one fall and winter, starting from nothing. He is fast learning to handle tools, too, and can dovetail, and plane and saw and handle a broad axe."

The first question asked by Bert when he reached home, was,—"Mother, where is James?"

"Gone to bed."

"And grandfather, too?"

"Yes, James said the whole of his multiplication table, and didn't miss a figure, and then your father and grandfather gave him sums to do in his head."

"Did he tell you what happened at school to-day?"

"He didn't tell us anything."

"Just like him. Didn't he tell you there had been a real sisemarara—an eruption, an earthquake—there to-day. Didn't you see the blood on his shirt collar? Don't you see that bunch on top of my skull?" displaying a swelling the size of a hen's egg. "Oh, he's done it; he's done it up to the handle." And Bert went capering about the room, and slapping his sides with his hands.

"Tell us what you mean, if you mean anything, Albert," said his father, "or else sit down and let Peter."

"Tell, Pete, tell 'em regular, and I'll put in the side windows, the filagree work."

Peter rehearsed the whole matter to his parents, by virtue of keeping his hand part of the time on Bert's mouth.

"Why didn't you tell your father or me what was going on, and ask your father's advice?"

"Because," said Peter, "James begged us not to; said he didn't want to make a disturbance, and the boys would get ashamed of their tricks after a while, and leave off. James said we might tell grandfather if he would promise not to tell, and he did, and so we told him."

"What did your grandfather say?"

"He had a long talk with James, and told him he had borne enough; to give no offence and take none; but if they continued to insult him, knock 'em over."

"Well, I don't know about such doings; husband, what do you think of it?"

Jonathan Whitman, who had listened all this time without question, replied, —"I think father gave good advice, and James did well to take it."

There the matter dropped. Morse, Riggs, and Orcutt were so ashamed, and so well convinced that nearly all the members of the school heartily despised them, and that if they made complaint at home the master and scholars would inform their parents of the provocation James had received, that they lied to account for their bruises, and made no complaint at home.

Jonathan Whitman and his next neighbor, Mr. Wood, were great friends, and had been from boyhood, though about as unlike as men could well be, and though, when his boys told him of the doings at school, Mr. Wood fell in with the general verdict of the district, "served them right," he could but feel a little sore, that his neighbor should be so much more fortunate in his choice of a redemptioner than himself.

The first time they met he could not forbear remarking, —

"Jonathan, they say that you are finding out what's in your redemptioner pretty fast; that he begins to feel his oats, and is showing a clean pair of heels. How do you like him now, neighbor?"

"Better and better. Old Frank is the best horse I ever had, and a little child might safely crawl between his legs; Bert has done it many a time, but a man would run the risk of his life who should abuse him."

These apparently untoward events accomplished what nothing else could have done, and which all the efforts of his friends had utterly failed to effect, they broke the crust and shattered the reserve, hitherto impenetrable, that isolated him, and furnished a stimulant that urged him onward in a course of more rapid development.

Before the boys separated on the evening which they spent together at Mr. Nevins', they were closeted an hour in Arthur's bedroom. What grave consultations were held, and what profound ideas were originated in their teeming noddles, will probably never be fully known, save that as they parted, Bertie shouted back: "Good night; now we've got him a-going, let's keep him a-going."

CHAPTER XIII.
THE SCHOLARS SUSTAIN JAMES.

The next morning Peter, Bertie, John, and Will Edibean, the Nevins boys, and Edward Conly, by pure accident, entered the schoolroom at the same moment with James, and some little time before the master came.

James, as usual, made directly for his seat; but they all surrounded and crowded him along to the fireplace, and instantly the Wood boys, the Kingsburys, the Kendricks, Stillman Russell, and all the girls, got round him, shook hands with him, told him he did just right, the day before, that those boys had always domineered over the smaller scholars, set them on to mischief, and made trouble in school, and with the master when they could. James, to his amazement, found himself the centre of an admiring crowd; he blushed and fidgeted, stood first upon one foot, then upon the other, and rolled up his eyes, till Bertie, fearing he would burst into tears, as he did when he received his new clothes, took him by the hand, and said,—

"Come, James, let us look over the reading-lesson before the master gets here."

When recess came, Peter and Bertie went to his seat, and asked James to go out and play with them. This, to use a homely phrase, "struck him all of a heap."

"How can I go? I don't know how to play any of your plays."

"We are not going to play plays or wrestle, but fire snowballs at a mark, and you are first-rate at that," said Peter.

James still declined; but Bertie stuck to him like bird-lime, and so did Peter, who called Ned Conly, whom James particularly liked, to aid them; but all in vain, till at length Bertie said,—

"Come, James, if you don't want to go upon your own account, go to please me; this is the first thing I ever asked you to do for me."

James rose directly; and Bertie, taking him by the hand, led him out of the house in triumph. The windows of the school were furnished with board shutters, and the boys had utilized one of them for a target by propping it with stones, and making three circles on it, and a bull's eye in the centre. The boys, having heard how well James could throw stones, stipulated that he should stand six paces farther from the target than the rest, otherwise, they said, "there would be no chance for them."

As James wanted the sport to go on to please Bert, he assented to this. Bert threw the first ball, hitting just outside the centre ring.

"I can beat that," said John Kendrick, and hit within the second ring.

Arthur Nevins hit right on the third ring. None of them, however, struck the bull's eye. It was now the turn of James. His first ball struck within the innermost circle, and about half-way from that to the bull's eye; and the second he planted directly in the central dot, and covered it all over. They all shouted,—

"You can't do that again."

Upon which he plumped another on the second. None of the boys except James hit the centre, but very few within the second ring; and they were blowing their fingers, and beginning to tire of the sport, when Sam Kingsbury, pointing upwards, shouted,—

"Only look there!"

Following the direction of his finger, they saw an owl of the largest size (that had been overtaken by daylight before he could reach his roosting-place) sitting upon the branch of a large oak, motionless, and apparently lost in meditation, and entirely regardless of the uproar beneath.

"If anybody had a gun," said Arthur Nevins. "I wonder if there's time to run home and get mine before school begins."

"No," said Peter, "and if you should, perhaps you'd miss him; but I'll bet James'll take him with a snowball."

"I could with a good stone, but I don't think I can with a snowball; for I never threw a snowball in my life before to-day."

James searched the stone wall of the pasture, but could find no stone to suit him, and urged by the boys to try, made three snowballs as hard as he could, with a small stone in the centre of each. The first ball brushed the feathers of the philosophical bird, and broke the thread of his meditations; but as he was gathering himself up to fly, a second struck him with such force under the wing as to bring him down half stunned into the snow, and before he could recover himself Ned Conly flung his cap over his head and caught him.

"Give him to me, will you, Ned?" said Bertie.

"I will, if you and Peter and James will come over to my house to supper to-morrow night and spend the evening."

James objected decidedly to this arrangement.

"Well, he can't have the owl unless you come."

"Come, James, do go, because I want it ever so much to put it in a cage. I never had an owl in my life. I have had crows, and eagles, and bluejays, and robins, and coons, and foxes, and gray squirrels. I've got a nice cage that my bob-o-link was in."

James was sorely pressed. He liked Ned Conly, for Ned and Stillman Russell were the only boys with whom he had any intercourse approaching to intimacy. Ned Conly in school sat next beside and Stillman Russell before him; he also could not bear to prevent Bertie from getting the bird that he saw he wanted. The perspiration fairly stood in drops on his forehead. At length he said,—

"I cannot go to supper, for then there would be nobody to do the chores, and it would not look well to leave Mr. Whitman to do them, but I'll come after supper."

They, therefore compromised on that ground.

"The master's coming; how shall we keep him till school's done?" said Bert.

"Cut his head off," said James.

This was the first time that James had ever volunteered a remark, or been guilty of an approach to a witticism, and Peter stared at him astonished.

"I've got a skate-strap; you may have that," said Chuck Witham, who was aching to be once more noticed, for no one spoke to him now.

"Thank you," said Bert, though not very cordially, and took it, and with this they fastened the owl in the entry of the schoolhouse.

"Is not Ned Conly as quick as lightning?" said Arthur Nevins to Elmer; "who but he would have thought of that way to get James over there; he might have invited him till Doomsday to no purpose, but when James found Bertie couldn't have the owl unless he went, that brought him. Only think how long we've been trying to get him to come to our house."

97

JAMES BRINGS DOWN AN OWL.
Page 175.

"What shall we do with James, mother?" said Peter, as he and Bertie were preparing to go to Mr. Conly's. "What shall we do with him when he comes? We don't want him to sit all the evening and look straight into the fire, and never open his mouth, and Ned won't either, and he'll be frightened half to death."

"I'll tell you what to do," said the grandfather; "ask him questions that he cannot answer by yes and no; he'll have to answer them, and after he hears the sound of his own voice a few times he'll gain courage."

"What shall we ask him?"

"Ask him about the manner in which they do farming work in the old country, and if you can get him started, he will, I have no doubt, tell a great many things that Mr. Conly's folks would like to know, for he never learned to reap, and mow, and break flax, and swingle it, and handle horses as he does, without working on the land a good deal. He talks when he is in the shop with me."

The boys set out, leaving Maria to come with James, in order that he might not be obliged to come in alone.

The Conly family consisted of Emily, Edward, and Walter the schoolmaster, who was then boarding at the Edibeans.

After James and Maria came in, the first greetings were over, and the usual remarks in regard to the weather and the school had been made, and something said about a spelling school that was to come off in the near future. James merely listening, the conversation began to lag. Bertie grew desperate, and as was his wont resolved to make or mar, began to tell Mr. Conly about James hitting the owl, and about the accuracy with which he could throw stones, and then turned to James and asked,—

"James, how did you learn to throw stones almost as true as folks fire bullets?"

"I learned by throwing road metal when working on the roads. In England they keep a good many parish poor at work breaking stones for the roads; every man has a pile of stones before him, a hammer and a ring, he breaks a stone till it is small enough to go through the ring and then throws it on the pile."

"What does he put it through a ring for?"

"Because the rings are all of a size, and that makes the stones all of a size, then they haul these stones and spread 'em very thick on the roads, and spread coarse gravel on them, and roll the whole down with a great iron roller that it takes four and sometimes six horses to haul, and roll it down so hard that a wheel won't dent it."

"It must make a nice road," said Mr. Conly.

"Yes, sir, one horse would haul as much on that kind of a road as two, yes, as three, on the roads we have here. I was set at work on the roads, and we didn't work half the time and used to practise throwing stones. There was one fellow, Tom Lockland, could beat me,—and but one,—I knew how to break a stone to make it go true."

"Where did you learn to drive horses? They say when you first came here you knew how to drive horses," said Ned Conly, who perceived what Bert would be after.

"The governor at the workhouse used to hire me out to drive the teams to haul these stones. I drove one horse first, and then two, and then four, and sometimes six to draw the great roller."

"Why, then," said Mr. Conly, "couldn't you go and work for yourself and support yourself?"

"Because there's no work to be had. Why, sir, there are five men to do one man's work. People are so plenty a man can only get a day's work once in a while, and get so little for it that it will barely keep him alive, and when there's no work he must fall back upon the parish or starve. The farmers don't generally like to hire the parish poor, and then the settlement hurts poor people."

"What's that?"

"If a man gets a settlement in a parish, and can't maintain himself, that parish must help maintain him."

"How does he get a settlement?"

"If a man was born in any parish, his settlement is there. If he is bound for an apprentice forty days in a parish, his settlement is there. If he has been hired for a year and a day, he gains a settlement. If he has rented a house that is valued at ten pounds a year he gains a settlement."

"I understand; it's something like what we call gaining a residence."

"Well, sir, the settlement act works very badly for a poor laboring man. Some of the parishes are quite small, and if in the parish where a poor person belongs, and has got his settlement, there is no work he can't go into the next parish and get work, though there may be plenty of work there."

"Why can't he go?"

"He can go, sir, but he will get no work, for nobody will hire him for fear he will get out of work or fall sick, and stay long enough to gain a settlement; they will say: 'Get you back to where you came from,' and hustle him right out. Sometimes the farmers will hire a man for a few days short of a year, lest he should gain a settlement. They will take a boy out of the workhouse, keep him all summer till after harvest, and then quarrel with him and drive him off."

"Can't they be obliged to take an apprentice?"

"Yes, sir, or pay a fine; but the fine is so light they had sometimes rather pay the fine."

Bertie found that by thus drawing a "bow at a venture," he had struck upon a fruitful theme, and the evening passed so rapidly that it was nine o'clock before they thought it was eight, and when at last they came to separate, Mr. Conly made James promise that he would come again with Peter and Bertie. So much had his feelings and temper become modified by the discipline to which these high-minded boys, guided solely by their own instincts, had subjected him, that as Bertie told his mother when they got home, "James didn't hang back at all when Mr. Conly asked him to come again with us, but said he would like to."

"So that is the young man," said Mr. Conly, to his family after the boys had gone, "that some of the scholars took a miff at as a redemptioner, and outlandish, and all that. I for one have got a good deal of information this evening, and I doubt very much if William Morse, or Riggs, or George Orcutt, could give so good an account of the methods of work here."

"Father," said Peter, "the master says James had better begin arithmetic at school."

"I am going to the village to-morrow, and will get him a slate and a book."

"There's a slate in the house, only it has no frame, but make that do, and instead of a slate get him a large book to set down his sums in. He writes so well and makes such handsome figures, he will make it look nice to show at the committee examination."

When Peter told James, the latter said he could make a slate frame himself, and did, of curled maple. Fondness for mechanical work grew upon James daily, and engrossed a portion of the time that had before been devoted to study. Peter had mechanical ability, and could make whatever he fancied. Not so, however, with Bertie, and thus an abundant opportunity was furnished to James to supply his friend. James made for him a sled, a crossbow, and a wheelbarrow, grandfather making the wheel; but James could hit nearer the mark with a stone, than Bertie could with his crossbow.

James now mingled freely with the other boys in their amusements at recess, and between schools; that is, he did not thus do every day. For some days he would not leave his seat, being inclined to study, but mingled with them sufficiently to produce the best of feeling, and distanced them all in lifting or pitching quoits, but in regard to wrestling,—a sport of which they never seemed to tire or get enough,—he was merely an interested spectator. One Saturday afternoon Peter said to him,—

"James, you do everything else us boys do, why don't you wrestle?"

"Because I don't know how."

"Well, learn then, we all had to."

"It seems to me I have got enough to learn that is of more value than wrestling, besides I am the largest boy in school. How it would look to have some little fellow like George Wood, or Chuck Witham, lay me on my back, and what a row it would make; if some of the larger boys did it that would be another thing."

"Why not do as you have done in respect to reading, writing and spelling, learn at home, wrestle with me and Bertie? We are not much, to be sure, but I can throw most of the boys, and you can learn the locks and trips, and how to guard and handle yourself, and then when you come to wrestle at school you won't be ashamed. If grandfather was not so stiff in his legs of late years he'd take delight in learning you."

"Your grandfather?"

"To be sure. Grandfather has been an awful wrestler in his time. I can just remember when he wrestled. After you practise with us we can get Ned Conly and Arthur Nevins to come over here and wrestle. They are capable wrestlers, and father would wrestle with you."

"Does your father wrestle?"

"I guess he does; there's nobody can throw him, and he never was thrown. He won't go into a ring to wrestle at a raising or at a town meeting now, because my mother don't want him to, but grandfather told me that was not all the reason, because mother was never willing he should go into a ring, but he always would. Grandfather says it is because he feels he's getting a little old, and is afraid some young man would get the better of him, and that he don't blame him for not running that risk, after he had held the ring for years against three towns, fetch on who they would."

"Does everybody wrestle here?"

"Everybody who thinks anything of themselves; everybody but the women and the minister, and they look on. They say the minister is a first-rate wrestler, and sometimes tries a fall in his back yard with friends who come to see him. A man who can't wrestle, is thought very little of in these parts."

"Is that so?"

"Yes, ask grandfather, or ask the schoolmaster. He's a good wrestler. Come, I'll get Bertie, and we'll begin to-night."

"I can't begin to-night."

"Why not?"

"Because it's most night now and the chores are to be done."

"I'll call Bertie, and we'll soon do 'em."

"Then I can't, because it is Saturday night, and I want to look over the lesson for Monday morning and get my catechism."

"Will you Monday night?"

"Yes, if your father don't want me to do something."

The boys took very good care that their father should not set James to doing anything, and after the chores were done they went into the barn floor.

James took hold of Bertie first, but he was so strong and his arms were so long, that Bertie could not get near enough to trip or move him in the least, James stiffening his arms and holding him off while Bertie twisted and wriggled like an eel on the end of a spear.

On the other hand James could not throw Bertie, because he was afraid of hurting him, else he might have either twitched him down or have lifted him bodily from the floor and taken his feet from under him at any moment.

"That's no way to wrestle, you great giant," cried Bertie.

"I told you I didn't know how."

"But you must slack up your arms and give me some chance. How do you think I am ever going to throw you if you won't let me get near you?"

"I don't mean you shall; folks don't wrestle to get thrown, do they? Your grandfather didn't."

"But you must give me some chance to get at you or you'll never learn. How could two men wrestle if one was in the barn and the other in the house; or one here, and the other in Philadelphia? We might as well be."

Peter flinging himself upon the hay, rolled over and over convulsed with laughter, crying,—

"I'll bet on James, he'll hold the ring I'll be bound, I mean to call grandfather to see the fun."

"If you do I'll not try to wrestle again," said James.

James gradually yielded to the exhortations of Bertie, and permitted him to come near enough to push him over the floor, and it was not long after the wily boy got him to lift his feet till he tripped and threw him.

"There, you see how I did that, now do the same by me."

"I shall hurt you."

"That's my look-out."

It was not long before James got thrown again, but he was all the while gaining knowledge and watching the operations of his opponent, and at last gave Bertie a fair fall. James was evidently much pleased, and Bertie not less so. The former who at first had been dragged into the sport by the influence of his friends, began to take great interest in it, mastered the trips, and locks, and feints, without resorting to main strength, and at length made such progress that Bertie could no longer throw him.

He now began to wrestle with Peter, when he passed through the same experience, being thrown at first, but kept improving till at length Peter could but seldom get him down. Edward Conly and the Nevins boys now came over, and he wrestled with them, beginning now to wrestle at the back, in which mode of wrestling he excelled them all, as in that practice strength, a stiff back and capacity to endure punishment, avail more than agility and sleight.

A small plot of level ground before the schoolhouse, free from stones, and covered with long moss, where the boys were wont to wrestle, was now bare of snow. A wrestling match was got up, and had not been long in progress before Bertie persuaded James to enter the ring. The instant he entered, William Morse stepped in as his antagonist.

The castigation administered by James had never ceased to rankle, and he had not the least doubt but the opportunity had come for revenge, or at least to mortify his enemy before the whole school.

"Won't he get terribly mistaken?" whispered Bertie to Arthur Nevins.

"He thinks he's taking hold of a green redemptioner."

They had scarcely placed themselves in position, till he was thrown. Red as a fire brick, and burning with shame,—for a great shout greeted the victory of James,—he took hold only to be again thrown. David Riggs then stepped in with the same result.

The boys then clamored to Orcutt to take his turn, but he declined. Edward Conly came in and was thrown, and after him Arthur Nevins, who threw James after a short struggle. James was now as eager to wrestle as he had been backward before, and wrestled every day till there were but two, Edward Conly and Arthur Nevins, who could throw him at arm's length, and no one could throw him at the back. It was quite wonderful to notice the change imparted to his whole bearing by these exercises; before he was stiff and awkward in all his movements, but now he was lithe, graceful, his step was lighter and more elastic, and smiles had taken the place of the despondent look he formerly wore, insomuch that it was a matter of common remark in the neighborhood.

CHAPTER XIV.
RESENTING A BASE PROPOSAL.

The ground was now getting bare fast, and baseball began to be in order, and James must learn that. Peter brought a ball to school and James soon mastered the game in the simple method in which it was then played, and bore no more honorable appellation than that of "knock-up and catch."

"How many things a boy has to learn," said Bertie to Peter as they were going home from school after playing ball for the first time. "I didn't think a boy had so many things to learn till we began to teach James."

"Because we had to teach James right along, but we were years about it ourselves. We spread it all over."

"There's only one more thing I want James to do, then I shall be satisfied. Ned Conly says master is going to have a spelling school and invite scholars from the other districts, and I want to persuade James to spell, and if he'll only spell more words than William Morse, Orcutt and Dave Riggs, I shall sit down contented and perfectly happy, and let things take their course."

"You are a revengeful little viper, brother of mine, did you know it? You can't forget the blow on the head Morse gave you."

"It is not that. I wouldn't have you think it is that, but I want James to beat those three boys who have done all they could to injure him, and out of pure malice because that seems what ought to take place."

"Well, I shouldn't wonder if he did, for they are three about as poor spellers of their age as there are in school."

Mr. Whitman bought James a large blank book, and in it he set down his sums and printed with a pen headings beginning with capitals at the top of the pages, and took great pains with the writing and the forms of the figures. In addition to this he took some brass mountings from the stock of an old fowling-piece, put them in a vice and filed them all away, and sprinkled the filings over the headings of his pages before the ink was dry, having also put glue in the ink to make the brass dust adhere. On the last day of school the master passed this and the books of several other boys around among the school committee as examples of proficiency.

On the evening of examination day they had the spelling school, and James out-spelled Morse, Riggs and Orcutt. Peter was fully occupied during the spelling holding his hand over Bertie's mouth to keep him from saying "good" at every success of his pupil and loud enough for everybody to hear.

Mr. Whitman and his wife, and even grandfather attended both the examination and the spelling school. To go out in the evening except to a religious meeting was something that the old gentleman of late years never had done.

The family went home rejoicing in the success of their endeavors, and experiencing that unalloyed happiness, the result of benefiting others; and the term which had opened so gloomily for James, closed in triumph.

Mr. Whitman lived some distance from the saw mill, and accordingly had a sawpit in the door-yard where he often sawed small quantities of stuff for wheels, harrows and other uses, and in the course of the fall and winter the old gentleman had, when he wished to saw anything, taken James to help him, and thus the latter had obtained considerable practice in working with that implement.

Mr. Whitman had in the winter, cut and hewn out some rock-maple logs, to saw into plank for mill-wheels, and cogs, which required to be sawed very accurately; he also had cut some red-oak for common uses, in respect to which he was not so particular; he therefore resolved to saw the red-oak first, and, if James proved equal to the work, to cut out the mill-stuff afterwards. The two had worked ten days with the whipsaw, when Mrs. Whitman said to her husband,—

"How do you get along, sawing your stuff with James?"

"We get along well. It has always been my way, since father has been so lame, when I had timber of any great amount to saw, to hire Mr. John Dunbar, give him nine shillings or two dollars sometimes a day, and board him; but I thought as James seemed to take to handling tools, and was a strong, tough boy, and I was going to have him for some years, I would try and teach him, and in two days more we shall cut all the stuff, and it will be done as well as though I had hired Dunbar, though it has taken much longer, and made harder work for myself, and after haying I mean to learn him to saw on top."

"A good whip-sawyer, husband, always commands good wages, and it will be fitting James to get his living when he leaves you."

"I intend to do more for him, and must, to carry out the idea I started with, which was to treat him, as far as fitting him to make his way in the world is concerned, as I do my own boys; not only teach him all I can about labor, but also give him some ideas about property, and the value of a dollar, for a man may work his fingers off to no purpose, if he don't know how to take care of what he gets.

"I have got some clear boards in the workshop, and I think I shall let him make himself a chest of them, and give him a lock and hinges, and handles, and paint to paint it, and then he will have something, and some place that he can call his own."

"But what is the use of talking to a person about saving who has nothing to save, and no way of getting anything; the principle can't grow much without the practice, and he has nothing to practice with. It seems to me very much as if grandfather had sat in his arm-chair, and tried to teach James to fell trees by telling him how, and James contented himself with listening. What is the use of giving him a chest with a lock, when, as Bertie says, all in the world he has got to lock up is his mother's Bible, and one sheet of paper, with the agreement you made with him, written on it?"

"Very well, let him put them in, and his school-books, and his Sunday clothes; then make him up some shirts, and knit him a good lot of stockings. There is something, not much to be sure, but enough to give the idea of ownership. There is something of his own that he can take with him, something quite different from the state of a workhouse boy."

"But you gave Peter a pair of calves; he raised them, and sold them; Bertie has a pair of steers now, and Maria a pair of sheep. I think it has a good effect upon them, and I don't see why it should not upon James."

Jonathan Whitman, who was never in haste to decide, and very seldom announced his intention to do anything till his mind was fully made up, changed the subject of conversation, and there the matter rested for that time.

It was not late enough to work upon the ground, and Mr. Whitman gave the boards to James, and the old gentleman after he had cut and planed them, assisted him in laying out his dove-tails, and by a little instruction from him, James succeeded in making a handsome chest, and was evidently highly gratified, although he was so reticent and singularly constituted, that he never manifested either pleasure or gratitude, as do more impulsive persons. George Wood was at Mr. Whitman's just as James was putting the last coat of paint on his chest, and James lifted the cover and let him look inside. The boy went home and told his folks about James' chest.

"Ay," said Mr. Wood, "Jonathan puts too much confidence in that redemptioner altogether, and now has given him a chest; no wonder the fellow is tickled with it, for he has got something to carry his clothes in when he gets ready to run off."

An event now occurred that placed the character of James in a very strong light, and completely justified the good opinion Mr. Whitman had formed in regard to him.

They had just finished sowing wheat, and James, having worked very hard till after sundown, had put up the horses and sat down upon the ground to cool off and rest, with his back against the underpinning of the barn, which, as the ground fell off, was raised up several feet on the back side. Into the space thus left the hens were wont to crawl, lay, and sometimes hatch.

"Bertie," said Mr. Whitman, "we don't get near the eggs we should this time of year. I don't believe but the hens lay under the barn; why won't you look?"

Bertie took up a short plank in the barn floor, crawled under and crawled about; he drove one hen that was sitting from her nest; found several nests with eggs in them, and was searching for others, when he heard the sound of voices outside, and recognized that of James. Looking through a hole in the rocks he saw Daniel Blaisdell, Mr. Wood's redemptioner, in earnest and even passionate dispute with James. Prompted by curiosity, he crept near enough to hear the conversation, the nature of which made him an eager listener.

Bertie inferred from what he heard, that they had been talking some time; that Blaisdell wanted to leave his employer by stealth, as he could obtain plenty of work at good wages, for the next six or eight months, whereas, at his present place, he should get only his board and clothes, and "very mean board and beggar's rags at that," and wanted James to go with him, which it seemed the former had bluntly refused to do, as in reply to some remark of James, that Bertie was not then near enough to hear, Blaisdell said,—

"If you are fool enough to work for nothing, when you can get high wages by going after them, I am not."

"Do you think I have no more principle, or good feeling, than to leave a man who has treated me better than many of the people in England, I have worked for, treat their own children; and that, too, just when he wants me the most; who has put me in the way of learning to read, write, and cipher, which of itself, is worth more to me, than four years' labor at the highest wages?"

"He had selfish ends in it, because he thought it would pay in the long run. It didn't cost him much to send you to school in the winter, when there was not much to do; and he knew it would make you smart, and contented to work for nothing, four years."

"You agreed, Mr. Blaisdell, before you left England, if Mr. Wood would pay your passage, to work on his farm three years; you have only worked about eight months, and you want to leave him, without his knowledge, and at the busiest time of year. Do you consider that right, Mr. Blaisdell?"

"Do I consider it right? To be sure I do. He knew what labor was worth over here; I didn't. He knew, too, that I, and hundreds like me, were starving on the other side, and took advantage of our necessity to get his work done for nothing. He has tried to get ahead of me all he could, but he got hold of the wrong man. I don't say but it would have been different had he fed me well, clothed me decently, and showed some consideration; but he has taken all the advantage he could of my necessity, and now I'll take all I can of his. There's no law in this country against begging, and no hanging for stealing. I'll leave him, and you had better go with me. Come on."

Bertie was so anxious to hear the answer James would make, that in his efforts to get nearer, he displaced a stone of the wall that fell outward, but the parties were too much occupied to notice it. The opening, however, permitted a glance at the features of James, and Bertie could perceive that he was both excited and irritated. At length he said,—

"I have nothing to complain of; but every thing to be thankful for. I shall stay with Mr. Whitman the four years, and do all that I can; and if after that, he should be taken sick, and become poor, and need my help, I'll stay with him, and try to do by him, as he has done by me."

"Then you must be a fool. They all said on board ship coming over, that you was a fool, and didn't know enough to take care of yourself, and now I believe it. It cost Whitman about forty dollars to get you over here, and you are going to work four years for him for that. It wouldn't be four coppers a day, while you can get a dollar a day now, and nine shillings in harvest. As for your board, he won't miss that, nor your clothes, for they will all be made in the house."

Bertie saw that James was growing more and more angry every moment, but he kept his temper down admirably, and merely said,—

"If I were under no obligation to Mr. Whitman, I have pledged my word to stay with him for four years. To break it would be a lie: I have never told a lie, and I never shall."

"Don't tell me that; a man must lie once in a while, especially a poor man. There ain't a man in the world but has lied, and you are lying when you say that."

Scarcely had the words left his lips than he received a blow that sent him headlong across the back of an ox, that lay chewing his cud near by. An ox always rises first behind, and the startled animal jumping up, flung Blaisdell on to his neck, and still more frightened, rising forward, flung him from his horns, to which he clung, to the dung-heap; and the terror of the ox communicating itself to the rest of the cattle in the yard, they began to snort and curvet around the prostrate intruder.

"Be off with you, or I'll break every bone in your carcass. It is you, and the likes of you, who have given redemptioners a bad name, and taken the bread out of a great many honest people's mouths on the other side, who might have found good homes in this country."

Blaisdell was a burly fellow, and ugly enough, but he had seen somewhat of James' strength on the passage over, and had received unmistakable evidence that he was no longer the discouraged being who could be abused with impunity.

Oblivious of eggs, sitting hens, and leaving his hat full of eggs behind him, Bertie rushed into the house, seized his father and mother, hurried them into the parlor, and shutting the door, told them every word he had heard, and all he had witnessed.

"Well," said Mrs. Whitman, turning to her husband, "you have got to the bottom now; you have found out what is in your redemptioner, and also in neighbor Wood's."

"Now, my son," said the father, "you must not mention this to Peter, Maria, your grandfather, nor any one, and by all means not to James. Will you remember what I say?"

"Yes, father, I will; for I never had a secret to keep before, except some boy's nonsense."

"Well, then, remember you are trusted, and don't get Will Edibean to help you keep it."

"But, husband, ought you not to tell neighbor Wood?"

"No; if the man means to run off, he'll run. He can't watch him all the time."

"But he could lock him up nights."

"He would break out, or set the house on fire."

"But, perhaps if he knew, he would treat him better. You think he don't treat him very kindly?"

"That wouldn't keep him. He wants money every Saturday night to get liquor with. I am not going to be mixed up with it, nor have James mixed up with it. I'll warrant you'll not hear a lisp from him."

The next morning, about ten o'clock, Mr. Wood came in, much excited,

saying,—

"Good morning, Jonathan. I've found out what's in my redemptioner. He's run off, and stolen one of my horses, and the other horse is lame, and I want one of yours to go after him. I'm glad now I didn't lay out any more on him."

"You are welcome to the horse, and I'll go with you, if you wish; but, he's not worth his board. If I could get the horse, I would let the man go about his business."

"I won't. I'll get a writ for him, and give him his choice, to go back to work, or go to jail. I want to punish him, and I want you to go with me."

The second day of the quest they found the horse feeding beside the road, with the bridle under his feet, but could get no trace of the man.

It was near planting time. Mr. Whitman, the previous fall, had ploughed under a heavy crop of clover, and in the spring sowed the ground to wheat, with the exception of a quarter of an acre, that he had reserved to plant.

He then said to James,—

"SCARCELY HAD THE WORDS
LEFT HIS LIPS THAN HE RECEIVED
A BLOW THAT SENT HIM
HEADLONG ACROSS THE BACK OF
AN OX." Page <u>198</u>.

"I'll give you the use of this land. You may take the team; haul all the dressing on it that is necessary, and plant it with potatoes; take care of them through the summer, dig them in the fall, sell them, and have the money; but you must pay me for the seed, or return me in the fall as many potatoes as you plant. When you come to hoe them, you can have the horse to plough amongst them. You must keep the ground clear of weeds; if you do not, I shall hoe the potatoes, and then you will lose the crop. You may plant them, and put on the dressing, in my time, but you must hoe them at odd chances that you will find plenty of before breakfast, while the horses are eating, at noon, and after supper, and father will instruct you about planting them."

By the old gentleman's direction he put on a large quantity of dressing, and then advised him, as the land was in such good heart, and abundantly dressed beside, to plant his potatoes in drills, as he would thus get more seed on the ground. When he began to plant, Maria insisted upon dropping the seed for him.

Peter and Bertie had each of them a corn patch of his own, and they hoed the three pieces in company. Sometimes James would be up at three o'clock in the morning, to hoe among his potatoes, or in Bertie or Peter's corn patch, just which needed hoeing the most.

The boys had considerable time at their disposal, some before breakfast, some at noon while the horses were eating and resting, and also after supper, which they had at five o'clock, as not much work was done after that except in haying, or wheat harvest.

This was the time chosen by grandfather to instruct James in shooting with the rifle. James at first only manifested that fondness for a gun common to most young people, but he soon began to feel the hidden motion of that strange passion which throbs in the very marrow of the hunter, and became as enthusiastic as his preceptor, who before the summer was out, had taught him to shoot at flying game.

Mr. Whitman, while Walter Conly was boarding at his house, had engaged him to help him, from hoeing time till after wheat harvest, and to his great surprise, James, after a few days' practice, did nearly as much as Conly; after the first two days he kept up with them both, hoed as many hills, and as well as they did. In mowing, he could not get along as fast, but cut his grass *well*, but after he had pitched hay three days, he could put more hay on the cart or the mow by one half, than Conly could, and do his best.

The most importance was attached to the wheat harvest. There were no reaping machines then; all was done with the sickle and cradle, and in reaping, James distanced the whole of them, for in that work he was at home.

Mr. Whitman and Conly were tying up some grain, beside a piece of potatoes, when the schoolmaster observed,—

"I never in my life saw so handsome a piece of potatoes as that."

"Those are not my potatoes. I have none half as good as them."

"Whose are they?"

"They belong to James. I told him he might have all he could raise on that piece of ground. He had my father for counsellor, both in respect to the quantity of dressing, and the method of planting, and by the looks, I think he could not have had a better one. In that respect James is different from any boy I ever saw; he has not a particle of conceit about him; is always willing to take advice, and generally asks it."

"There is not much danger of your redemptioner's leaving you, at least not till after the potatoes are dug, and they are never known to leave in the fall, as then they begin to think of winter quarters."

"I took the boy, not to benefit myself, but to help him, and I am willing he should go when he can do better; but I know very well that he is better with me than he can be away from me, and therefore I try to make him contented and happy. I gave him the use of this land because I have noticed that since he has obtained some notion of time, knows how many days there are in a month, and how many months in a year, that he will sometimes say: 'A year is a good while,' and perhaps when he remembers that he has agreed to stay here four years, it seems to him like being bound for a life-time. But now when he has a crop in the ground to take up his attention all summer, the proceeds in the fall, to put in his chest, and look at in the winter, and another crop to look forward to in the spring, it will shorten time up wonderfully. He'll forget all about being a redemptioner; won't feel that he is working just to pay up old scores, and he'll be more contented. I know I should; besides it will teach him to lay up, and put life right into him."

"I think it has put life into him, for he works just as though he was working on a wager all the time."

CHAPTER XV.
SOMETHING TO PUT IN THE CHEST.

That night as Mr. Whitman, accompanied by Peter and Bertie, reached the door-step, they were met by George Wood who said their mare had broken her leg, and they were going to kill her, that she had a colt four days old, and his father would sell it for a dollar.

"Father," shouted Bertie, "won't you let James have it, and keep it for him till it is grown up? You know Peter and I have each of us a yoke of steers, and James ought to have something. Will you, father?"

"James has no dollar to pay for a colt."

"I'll lend it to him, and he can pay me when he sells his potatoes."

"But how do you know he wants a colt? Perhaps he had rather have the dollar."

"Oh! I know he does, of course he does; you know how much he thinks of a horse, father, there's nothing he loves like a horse. He's got no father nor mother, nor brother nor sister, and it will be something for him to love just like a brother. He's out to the barn, I'll ask him, and if he says he wants him will you let him keep him?"

"He won't say so, if he wants him ever so much, but you have a sort of freemasonry by which you reach each other's thoughts, and if you think he would like very much to have him and pay a dollar for him, you may get him."

It is to be presumed that James wanted the colt; for when work was done, Peter, Bertie and Maria all got into the wagon that was half filled with straw, and in the edge of the evening brought home the colt.

James watched his opportunity, and taking Mrs. Whitman aside, said,—

"I don't think Mr. Whitman ought to keep this colt for me, it is doing too much for such as me. It takes a good deal to keep a horse."

"That don't amount to anything, James; we've hay enough, and pasture enough; there's no market here for hay and we want to eat it up on the place, and we never shall miss what that little creature eats."

"But by-and-by he will eat as much as the other horses."

"Then you can sell him or let us use him, it will be handy to have a spare horse to use when the others are at work, and to go to market or to mill with."

"I am afraid Mr. Whitman will think I asked for him, and can never be satisfied. I was out to the barn, when Bertie came running, and asked me if I should like such a little thing to make a pet of, and I said 'I am sure I should,' and away he went; he didn't tell me he had asked his father to keep it for me, and the next thing I knew they came with the colt, and said it was mine and that their father would keep it for me."

"Husband wanted you to have it, he knew just what Bertie would do when he went to the barn; you have never had any home, and we want you to feel that this is your home. Husband wants you to have this little colt because he thinks it will make you happy, and by-and-by it will be worth considerable to you, and you can see it grow, and we shall never feel the difference."

"It will make me happy, for I do love horses, I think they are nearer to us than other creatures, and I shall love this little fellow like a brother, but I want you to tell Peter and Bertie not to ask their father for any more things for me. I am afraid Mr. Whitman will think I put 'em up to ask."

"Why, James, he loves to give you things. They did not ask him to send you to school, nor to give you boards to make your chest, nor to let you have that piece of ground to plant, it came out of his own head and heart; he is just the best man that ever was in this world, and the children take after him, and he takes after his father. Grandfather is getting a little childish sometimes now, but he is the best old gentleman that ever was, and a real treasure."

It was so dark when the boys got the colt home, that they could not have a fair view of him, but the next morning the children were all at the barn by sunrise, and their mother with them, to give him his breakfast.

"Isn't he a beauty?" said Bertie. "Mr. Wood says, when he comes to his color he'll be a chestnut, same as Frank, mother. He's a real good breed, Mr. Wood and I traced it out; he's half-brother to Frank and perhaps he'll be just like Frank."

The mother had been injured four days, and the Wood boys had taught the colt to drink milk by putting a finger in his mouth and his mouth in the milk.

"Mother," said Peter, "Mr. Wood has brought up a great many colts by hand, and he said that they ought to be fed a little at a time and often, to do right well. James nor we can't come from the field to feed him, Maria can't do it because she's at school all day. What shall we do?"

"I'll feed him twice in the forenoon and twice in the afternoon, a little at a time and often is the way, and then you and James can feed him morning, noon and night."

After a few days' feeding with her fingers, Mrs. Whitman nailed a teat made of rags and leather to the bottom of the trough, and the colt would suck that. All she had to do then was to pour the milk into the trough.

No one could have witnessed without emotion the wealth of affection lavished upon that colt by James. Much as he loved the children there was always a little feeling of restraint, and a little distance pervading their intercourse on his part. Bertie and Maria would put their arms around his neck and hug him, but he never returned their caresses.

Not so, however, in regard to the colt, the only pet he ever had, the only live thing that had ever called out the childhood feelings and sympathies of his nature so long dormant, and which they now fastened upon and clung to in their entire strength and freshness.

In the morning, before the rest were stirring, he would fondle and talk to it by the half hour. As the little creature grew stronger and playful, and could lick meal and eat potatoes and bread, James would put bread in his waistcoat pocket and lie down on the barn floor, sometimes he would put there maple sugar, then the colt, smelling the delicacies, would root them out with his nose, and as he became earnest get down on his knees and lick the lining of the pocket, and turn it out to get the sugar.

Just back of the house was a piece of grass ground extremely fertile, with a great willow in the centre of it. An acre of this was fenced and reserved for a pasture in which to turn the horses to bait when work pressed, and it was important to have them near at hand. In this pasture James put the colt when he was old enough to feed, and there he would frisk and caper and roll and try to act out the horse, and when tired lie under the great willow, stretched out at full length as though he was dead or sound asleep. Whenever James came in sight he would cry for him, and when the other horses came in from work there would be a vocal concert vigorously sustained on both sides.

"Poor little thing," said Bert, "he's lonesome, why don't you turn him into the pasture with the other horses? He wants somebody to talk with him that can understand his language. I would, James."

"I'm afraid to, he won't know any better than to run right up to them, and they will bite or kick him; perhaps they'll all take after him, get him into a ring and pen him in the corner of the fence and kill him."

"Put one of 'em in his place, and let us see what they will do."

They turned old Frank in, the colt ran right up and began to smell of him. Frank smelt of the colt, seemed glad to meet, and did not offer to bite or kick him. Frank was just from work, hungry and wanted to feed, but the colt wouldn't let him, kept thrusting his nose in Frank's face and bothering him, when the old horse gave him a nip, taking the larger portion of the colt's neck into his great mouth. The little creature screamed with pain and ran off, but soon came back and began feeding close by, just as Frank did, the latter taking no further notice of him.

"They'll do well enough," said Mr. Whitman, who was looking on. "Frank won't hurt him, he was only teaching him manners, you can leave 'em together."

They eventually became great friends, and after they had fed to the full would stand in the corner of the fence or under the willows, the colt nestled under Frank's breast, and the latter with his head over the colt's back.

The colt would follow James like a dog; and sometimes when Frank would take a notion not to be caught James would call the colt to him and start for the barn, and the old horse would follow them right into the stable.

Mr. Whitman had an offer for wheat at a high price, and kept Mr. Conly and hired another man (as he had two barn floors) to help thresh, threshing being then all done with the flail, or else the grain was trampled out by cattle. The evenings were now getting to be quite long. James therefore began to study, and Mr. Conly assisted him and heard him recite. This was a golden opportunity for James, and he made the most of it. While devoting every leisure moment to study, James was not unmindful of his crop, there was not a weed to be seen among his potatoes, and I should not dare to say how many times the fingers of James and Bertie and Maria had been thrust into the hills on a voyage of discovery, and their conclusions, as reported by Maria to her mother, were most satisfactory. The soil indeed was full of great cracks, caused by the growth and crowding of the potatoes.

When Mr. Whitman found that Mr. Conly was disposed to assist James, and that James fully appreciated the privilege, he so arranged his work as to afford him every possible opportunity, and the boys were ever ready to take an additional burden upon themselves for the same purpose. One evening Arthur Nevins came in to see the boys, and said he had been to the mill that day and saw a notice posted up that Calvin Barker was buying potatoes for a starch mill, and would pay cash and a fair price for first-rate potatoes sound and sorted, no cut ones. Potatoes were cheap, there was not much of a market for them, and the traders would pay but part cash and the rest in goods.

"Now is your chance, James," said the grandfather, "you want the money and don't want goods."

They brought only seventeen cents per bushel, but there were one hundred and sixteen bushels and a half, and after returning a bushel and one half to Mr. Whitman to replace the seed received of him, and paying Bertie for the colt, James had eighteen dollars and fifty cents left. In addition to this were several bushels of small and cut potatoes that he put in the cellar to give the colt.

Barker paid James in silver, and after reaching home he piled the coins up on the table and gazed at them with a sort of stupid wonder. Never before had he at one time possessed more than two shillings, seldom that,—more frequently a few pennies for holding a horse, opening a gate, or doing some errand for the men in the glass-house, and he counted them over and over.

James now knew the value of a dollar in theory, how many cents there were in a dollar, and how many mills in a cent; and yet he had little more conception of its practical value than a red Indian, for he had not received any wages nor bought anything above the value of a penny loaf or a bit of cheese. At length, looking up wistfully in the face of Mr. Whitman, he asked,—

"How much would all these dollars buy?"

"According to what you might buy. They would buy a good deal of some articles and not much of others; they would buy about twenty-four bushels of wheat and thirty of corn, but they would not buy a great deal of coffee, or indigo, or broadcloth, or silk."

"I'd buy a gun and lots of powder and shot," said Bertie.

"Would it buy any land, Mr. Whitman?"

"Yes."

"How much?"

"That would depend upon circumstances. In the western part of Ohio, of wild land, one hundred and eighty acres—more than half as much as I have got here."

"O my! how much is an acre? I know what the arithmetic says, one hundred and sixty square poles. But how big a piece is it?"

"That little pasture where the colt is measures about an acre. One of those dollars would buy ten pieces of land as big as that pasture out there; but you must recollect it is wild land, all woods, no house, no road: you have to cut the trees down before you can grow anything on it."

"I know grandfather has told me 'twas just so once where this house stands.

But would it buy any land here?"

"Yes, it will buy an acre, buy two, perhaps three of some land; of most land it would not buy one."

"It would buy a yoke of little steers, and quite a lot of sheep."

"But why don't you buy a gun? You love to shoot," said Bertie.

"I mean to save my money to buy land."

"That's right, James," said grandfather, "then you will have something under your feet that will last as long as you will, and longer, too. Not that I would say that it don't pay a man who can shoot to buy a gun; but every thing in its place."

James had now something to put in his chest, and went up stairs to deposit the money there. When he came back Mr. Conly explained to him the source of values, and told him that land became valuable by being settled, made accessible by roads, productive of crops and cattle, and by mills being built to grind the grain and manufacture the timber.

"When I go trading, James, I'll take you with me, and then you will learn the prices of things, and after a while I'll send you to trade as I often do Peter and Bertie," said Mr. Whitman.

Mr. Whitman now said to James and his sons,—

"I think I shall turn out about two acres of the field to pasture, and take in as much more of woodland. I can get the land cleared and fenced with logs by giving the first crop; but if you three boys wish to take the job, I'll give you the crop for three years; but you must keep the sprouts down and the fire-weed and pigeon-weed, and you may keep the ground you now have the use of two years more."

They all said they would do it.

"That," said Peter, "will be to become backwoodsmen, and do just what grandfather did, and we'll make a chopping bee."

"No, we won't; we'll do it ourselves. If we are to be beholden to the neighbors, I won't have anything to do with it. I should be ashamed if we three could not do what your grandfather when he was young would have done alone, and not thought it a hard task either," said James.

"So I say," replied Bertie, "do it ourselves."

"But how shall we find out how to do it quickest, and to the best advantage?" said James.

"Father will show us," said Peter.

"Here sits a venerable gentleman," said Bertie, making a magnificent gesture in the direction of his grandparent, "who can show us better than father."

Bertie was prone to be grandiloquent at times, and he had just been reading Patrick Henry's celebrated speech, and committing it to memory. He then asked his grandfather what time of the year was the best to do it.

"The best time to do it is in June, because then the stumps will bleed freely and be less likely to sprout, and the leaves will draw the sap out of the bodies of the trees and dry them, so that they will burn better, and the leaves will dry and help to burn them; but you can't do it then, because it will be right in hoeing time; you will have to do it after harvest, and let it lie over till the next summer."

"Then," said James, "we shall not get any crop, not even the second year."

"You will get a crop into the ground the second year, and harvest it the third, though you may get a crop the second year, but in the meantime you will keep the ground you have now and be getting something from that. If it should prove a dry summer you could burn it in June of the second year, and sow it with spring rye or barley, and if you get a good burn, an extra burn, you might venture to put in corn, for a crop comes along master fast on a burn, the hot ashes start it right along."

"I don't think," said James, "we had better try to burn it till after wheat harvest, as we shall have the other pieces, and it would interfere so seriously with Mr. Whitman's work, that if he was willing I shouldn't be."

The old gentleman now told James there was another way in which he might earn something for himself; he might shoot the coons that would be getting into the corn in the moonlight nights, and when there was no moon he might tree them with the dog, and shoot them by torchlight, and the hatters at the village would buy the skins. There was a pond in the pasture where there were plenty of muskrats.

"How do you get the muskrats?"

"This time of year set traps in the edge of the water for them; in the winter they make houses among the flags at the edge of the pond and go to sleep like flies, then you can catch 'em in their houses. You can now shoot very well with a rifle, and if it was not for going to school you might in the winter get a wolf or a bear; a wolf's pelt would bring two dollars, but a good bearskin would bring twenty, more than all the potatoes you worked so hard to raise. But no doubt you might trap a fox or two, and their skins bring a good price."

"But where should I get a trap?"

"Come along with me."

The old gentleman took James into the chamber over the workshop and opened a chest, in which were traps of all sizes and adapted to catch different animals, from a mink to a wolf or bears; there were but two of the latter but great numbers of the others, all clean and oiled, and in excellent order. He then opened a closet in which were chains to fasten the traps to prevent the animals from taking them away, and clogs, and broad chisels on long handles. The latter, the old gentleman told him, were ice chisels to cut ice around the beaver lodges in the winter.

"When I was younger, I used to leave Jonathan and the other boys to take care at home in the winter, and I and old Vincent Maddox used to take a hoss each, and traps, and rifles, and go over the Ohio river and trap and hunt sometimes till planting time, and sometimes I took one of my own boys. It's a kind of pleasure to me to clean up the old traps, and repair 'em, and look 'em over, brings back old times, though I never expect to use 'em much more 'cept perhaps to take a fox or an otter."

"Did Mr. Whitman use to go with you?"

"No, Jonathan never took much to such things. He's all for farming, but my William, who's settled in the wilderness on the Monongahela, was full of it from the crown of his head to the sole of his foot. He's a chip of the old block. But Jonathan is right, farming pays the best now; but in those days if you raised anything there was no market for what you could not eat, and trapping and hunting, and killing Indians for the bounty on their scalps were all the ways to get a dollar."

Peter and Bertie liked well enough to watch for and kill coons in the corn or on the trees for a few hours in pleasant moonlight nights, but did not possess that innate hunter's spirit that reconciled them patiently to bear hunger, cold and watching to circumvent their game; but James did, and his former life of poverty, hunger and outdoor exposure with but scanty clothing had rendered him almost insensible to cold and wet, and he embraced every opportunity that was offered him to shoot or trap. Besides coons and muskrats, he shot, on the bait afforded by a dead sheep, two silver-gray foxes, and caught one cross fox and two silver-grays in traps that the old gentleman told him how to set. His greatest exploit and one that elicited the praises of grandfather, was in the latter part of winter, trapping an otter, that brought him twelve dollars.

The elder Whitman instructed him in the right methods of stretching and curing the skins, and sent them to Philadelphia to a fur dealer with whom he had dealt a great many years, and James received for what he took alone, and half of those he obtained in company with Peter and Bertie, sixty-eight dollars.

CHAPTER XVI.
A YEAR OF HAPPINESS.

The success of James in trapping did by no means overshadow his love for the soil, neither did it lead him to neglect his studies, nor cool his affection for the colt. A quart of oats every night, and potatoes, Sunday morning, with plenty of hay, made the animal grow finely.

This winter James so excelled in writing that the master employed him to set the copies. Everything passed along pleasantly in the school; James mingled freely with the scholars in their diversions, and even Morse, Riggs, and Orcutt forgot the old grudge, or pretended they had. He likewise so far conquered his reserve as to spend a sociable evening where he was invited; went through the arithmetic, and took surveying by the advice of the old gentleman, who told him it would put many a dollar in his pocket if he could run land, and he could in no other way get it so easily, especially if he ever went into a newly settled place.

In short, it was the happiest winter James had ever passed; time seemed to take to itself wings, and he could hardly realize it was March when March came.

As the time for work upon the land drew near, James said to Mr. Whitman,—

"I don't think you need to hire a man this summer; the boys are some older. I have got the run of the work, and have learned to cradle grain as well as to reap. I think we can do the work."

"It is poor economy to have barely help enough to get along, providing the weather is just what you would wish. I shall plough less, and dress heavier than I have done; that will leave less ground to go over. I think we can get along till hay and wheat harvest, then I will hire George Kendrick; he can spread, rake, build the loads of hay, tie up grain, and reap a little; he's but a boy, and won't want much wages."

Although they could not set to work upon their new land till autumn, the boys were teasing their father to go and measure it, and their grandfather said it was a pleasant day, and he would go with them.

When the boys came to see how large a piece of land was contained in a measure of two acres, and how near together the trees were, their courage cooled a little.

"If we are to cut all these trees," said James, "snow will fly before we get half done."

"You haven't got to cut half of 'em clear off. If I was twenty years younger I could fall the whole and lop off the large limbs, and burn and pile it in eight weeks."

When the time came to clear their land, the old gentleman went with them, and spotted a great oak with long spreading limbs.

"That's the *driver*; that's not to be cut yet."

He then spotted a great number of trees in a line before it, and in a space as wide as the branches of the great tree extended. He then directed the boys to cut the tree nearest the drive-tree nearly off, and the next ones less, and the next less still, till the outside ones received only a few blows.

While the boys were at work, the old gentleman began leisurely to chop into the great tree, sitting down to rest when he liked, till he had cut it as nearly off as was safe. This occupied him the greater part of the forenoon, and, seating himself in the sun, he slept till James shouted that they had cut all the spotted trees.

"Then come here, all of you."

The great oak stood at the summit of gently descending ground. Directly before it was a clump of enormous pines, which the boys had been directed to chop into till they stood tottering to a fall, and before them were some large hemlocks and sugar-trees that had been cut half off, and below these smaller trees that had received but a few blows of the axe.

All were now assembled at the foot of the oak. A few well-directed strokes from the old gentleman's axe, it began to nod, and small, dead limbs to fall from it; then came a short, sharp crack. Slowly it toppled, and seemed but to touch the trunks of the tall pines that stood seventy feet to a limb, when down they went with a tremendous roar upon the hemlocks, and the whole avalanche, smoking and cracking, plunged right down the descent into the mixed growth below: leaves, limbs, and bark flew high into the air, a wide lane was opened through the forest, as when a discharge of grape ploughs through a column of infantry; the very earth shook with the concussion, and the sunlight broke in where it had not shone for a hundred years.

Bertie leaped upon the trunk of the great oak, and swinging his hat, shouted,

"Hoorah, grandfather, you know how to do it, don't you?"

"I should be a dull scholar if I didn't, considering how much experience and practice I've had."

Scores of trees were prostrated, some torn up by the roots, others shorn of their branches, and sure to die when scorched by the clearing fire, others broken off at various heights. The trees broken off or stripped of their branches were not cut down, as, casting no shade, they did not interfere with the crop, but were left to rot down.

Finding the labor so much less than they had anticipated, the boys set to work with resolution, and before the ground froze, cut the trees, lopped the larger branches, and cleared up the work of the season. James raised three bushels of potatoes more than the previous year, and obtained two cents a bushel more for them of the same buyer.

The Whitmans all possessed musical ability. Mr. Whitman and his wife sang in the choir till they were married; and the children, though they had received no training, and could not read music, all sang by rote; and soon after school began, Bertie made a new discovery. One of the cows that he milked had spells of holding up her milk, and caused much inconvenience.

"I'll swap cows with you, Bertie," said James; "you milk my old line-back, and I'll milk the black cow; perhaps she'll give down her milk better to me."

The black cow after this gave down her milk, which was for some time a great puzzle to Bertie and Peter, although their parents said it was because James milked faster, and it was easier to the cow.

James was the first to rise, and generally had his cows nearly milked by the time the rest got into the yard, and was ready either to work among his potatoes or to sit down to study till breakfast was ready, and the black cow was always milked before Bertie got along.

Bert imagined James had some method of charming the cow, and resolved to find out, so getting up before light he hid himself in the barn. By-and-by James came out and sitting down to the cow leaned his head against her and began to sing an old folk ditty to make a cow give down her milk, and Bertie's quick ear discovered to his astonishment that James had both an ear and most excellent voice for singing, though so great was his diffidence and power of concealment that no one of the family had ever suspected it before. Bertie told his father and mother.

"If that is so," said Mrs. Whitman, "let us get Walter Conly to keep a singing school this winter, and let James and our children go, we need better music in the church, most of the choir have sung out."

When snow came they harnessed up the colt in a most singular vehicle called a drag, made of rough poles, the shafts and runners being made of the same pole. The harness they made of straw rope, which James, who had been taught at the workhouse, showed them how to twist with an instrument that he made, called a throw-crook. It was made of a crooked piece of wood bent at one end and a swivel in the other end by which he fastened it to his waist, and turned it with one hand, while one of the boys attached the straw and walked backwards as it twisted. He told them great use was made of these ropes in England to bind loads of hay and grain, and to secure stacks of grain. They braided the straw to make the saddle, and twisted hickory withes for bit and bridle. They put Bertie and Maria on the sled and the docile creature drew them to the schoolhouse with some help; there he was fastened in the sun beneath the lee of the woods and fed.

When school was done at night the creature, colt-like, and limber as an eel, had twisted round, gnawed off the straw halter, then the shoulder-strap, which permitted the traces to fall, and then being freed from the drag he rubbed against the tree to which he had been fastened till he broke the girth and freed himself from the saddle; and ended by devouring the whole harness, except the bridle, even to the reins.

"Oh, you little monkey," cried Bertie, "if I had given you that straw at home you would have turned up your nose at it. How do you think Maria is going to get home? She won't bake you any more corn cakes nor give you any more sweet apples."

The snow was quite deep; they put Maria on the drag, James and Peter and the Wood boys hauled the drag, and Bertie led the colt after the vehicle. They made another straw harness, but took care to fasten him with a leather halter and hitch him short.

The inhabitants of the district and the scholars were so much attached to Mr. Conly that they assessed themselves to keep the school that was out in February through March, Mr. Whitman offering to board him the entire month. The days were so long that James found much time to work in the shop, both before and after school. Mr. Whitman was making a pair of wheels, tongue and axle-tree for one of his neighbors, and finding how much progress James had made in handling tools, availed himself of his help. When the job was finished, James, with some aid from Mr. Whitman, made an axle-tree, wheels and shafts, with which to break the colt. He had just put the finishing stroke to his work by boring the linchpin holes, and sitting down upon the axle-tree and contemplating it, he said,—

"There, I have done all I know how to do to those wheels; I don't know whether they'll run off or on, but I hope they will answer the purpose."

The old gentleman was in the shop making a grain cradle, he viewed the work, took off the wheels, measured the shoulder, and the taper of the ends of the axle, and said,—

"I call that a good piece of work, and I believe those wheels will run true as a die; you have learned something since Jonathan brought you to our door two years ago last fall; you couldn't have made a sled stake then and made it right."

"Indeed I have, grandfather, and I owe it to you, and I have often wondered that you should take so much pains with a strange boy, and as you may say an outcast, with neither kith nor kin."

"I have tried to teach you some things, and chiefly those that would put you in the way of getting your bread in this country, and the things that I knew by experience to be both necessary and profitable to a young man going to take up land, which is the best, safest, and in my judgment, the happiest venture here. I have spent a great many hours teaching you to handle a rifle, for though playing with a gun is just time thrown away in an old settlement where there is nothing to shoot but sparrows and robins, my family would have often gone without a meal had it not been for my rifle; and the money that bought the greater part of this farm came by trapping and hunting. If I could not have handled tools I must have gone without cart or plough or harrow, for I had no money to buy, and must have gone nine miles to borrow.

"But there is one thing more necessary for you than anything I have ever tried to teach you, and I cannot teach it, I wish I could."

"What is that, grandfather?"

"The grace of God, something that cannot be learned as you can learn to line and cut the shoulder of an axle-tree to make the wheel run true, or to work out a sum at school, and yet it is by all odds more necessary than any and all of the things you have learned here."

"But you never told me anything about this before."

"Perhaps you think it strange that when I have taken so much pains from the time you came here to teach you other things, and so many other things, that I have never said anything about that."

"Yes, grandfather, I do."

"It was because I didn't think the time had come for me to speak. I knew you were becoming acquainted with the Scriptures, that you heard the gospel faithfully preached every Sabbath, and that you would not then have understood my talk, but now you know what I mean, do you not?"

"You mean what you prayed, that Peter and Bertie and Maria and I might have, this morning at family prayers. But how can I get it? If neither the schoolmaster nor you can teach me, and I can't learn it myself, how am I going to get it?"

"Beg for it. When a man has nothing to buy bread with, and can't work, he must beg. Get it where I got mine, on your knees."

"But the minister says folks must feel that they are sinners, and confess their sins and ask forgiveness in the name of the Saviour. I don't feel that way; don't feel that I have got anything to confess."

"You don't?"

"No, sir. I can't confess that I have lied, or sworn, got drunk, or stolen, or broken the Sabbath, or cheated anybody, because I never have. I know I am not bad, like the workhouse boys I was brought up with, nor like some folks here, and I never go to bed or get up but I say the Lord's prayer."

"What makes you say in the Lord's prayer 'forgive us our sins,' if you have no sins to be forgiven; and what sense was there in putting it in the Lord's prayer, that was made for the whole world, and you among the rest, if you have no sin?"

"I don't know."

"The reason you don't feel that you have anything to confess is that you don't know what's inside of you. Everybody is the same way by nature. I used to be."

"What must I do then?"

"Ask the Lord to send His spirit to show yourself, and if He does, you will see need enough to ask pardon. I hope you'll think about it, James, for I never was so set upon anything as I am upon this. It is not an affair of the moment with me. I have had it in my mind from the first spring you were here till now, and it has grown upon me of late, because within the last six months I have begun to feel that I have not much longer to tarry here. I don't think I shall see the leaves fall again."

The tears sprang into the eyes of James. He exclaimed,—

"Grandfather, don't talk so; I can't bear to hear you talk in that way. You will live a good many years to make us all happy."

"That's impossible according to the course of nature. I have lived to see all my children settled and making a good living, and what is more, giving evidence of grace, though Jonathan and Alice have not as yet seen their way clear to come forward, and I am ready to go; but I would like to see you and Peter, Bertie and Maria, rejoicing in the Lord."

This conversation affected James as had nothing else in the course of his life. He loved and revered the old gentleman, and though he was aware of his great age yet the idea of parting with him had never crossed his mind, and when at night he repeated the Lord's prayer as usual, the words "forgive us our sins" were fraught with a new meaning. He resolved to search the scriptures and find out if he was a sinner or not.

A few days after this one half-holiday Bertie came into the shop and hung around, sat upon the bench and whittled, a thing quite unusual, as he had no desire to handle tools, and was seldom in the shop except James or Peter was making something for him, at length he said,—

"Grandpa, I want you to pray for me."

"My child, I have done that ever since you were born, but what makes you ask me now? How do you feel?"

"I don't know, I never felt as I have these last two days. I want to be good. Mother says I am a good boy and so does father and the schoolmaster, but I know I am not good the way the Bible calls good."

"My dear boy, it is the blessed spirit that is showing you your heart. We must both pray, for in these things one cannot take another's place. Tomorrow is the Sabbath day and I hope you will find pardon through the Saviour, and that it will be the happiest Sabbath you ever spent. How came you to turn your thoughts that way?"

"I was hurrying to get my part of the chores done before school time when these thoughts came into my mind just like a flash, and they won't go away."

After meeting on the next Sabbath, as the minister, Mr. Redman, came to shake hands with the old gentleman as he always did, the former said,—

"Mr. Redman, if I were you at the close of the meeting to-night I would ask any persons who felt disposed to converse on religious subjects to tarry."

"I don't believe there would a single person stop. Never during my ministry here have I seen the people as thoughtless, and Christians themselves so indifferent; it is one to his farm and another to his merchandise."

"Didn't you notice how full the meeting has been to-day and how attentive the people were?"

"The pleasant Sabbath after several stormy ones accounts for the full attendance, and our people usually give good attention. But what leads you to think there is any special interest among the people?"

"The Lord has told me so."

Mr. Redman looked anxiously into the face of his Elder, fearing that his mind was enfeebled, but in the clear eye and compressed lips and earnest expression of his features he saw nothing to confirm his suspicions, and replied,—

"Although I perceive not the least reason for doing as you desire, I will reflect upon it and if when we meet to-night you are of the same opinion, I'll certainly do it."

"Will you mix a little prayer with your reflections?"

"I will."

When Mr. Redman got home he related the affair to his wife, and inquired if she thought there was any more thoughtfulness than usual among the females of the parish.

"In my opinion there was never less, but I would do as Elder Whitman requests."

"He is a very old man and may be in his dotage. I am afraid it would seem ridiculous and do more harm than good."

"He has the clearest head of any man in this parish to-day, and is more likely to know the mind of the Lord than anybody else, and I know never would say what he did to you without a solid reason."

Mr. Redman, a nervous person, greatly puzzled and agitated by what he considered an unreasonable request, was unable to fix his mind upon any definite topic of remark, and went to the meeting with very slight preparation.

He was surprised to find the house was filled and Mr. Whitman of the same opinion, which served to increase his agitation, and after a few, as he felt, incoherent remarks threw the meeting open and sat down.

Mr. Whitman instantly got up and said,—

"I am an old man, about the oldest among you. I feel that I have been an unprofitable servant and that, profitable or unprofitable, I am almost at my journey's end, but this is no time to depart. I would not die in such a dead state of the church and people of God as this. My neighbors, you must wake up, and wake up to-night. I must go and I want to carry better tidings than it is possible to carry now. Can I face my Master, and yours, and tell him that the wise and the foolish are slumbering together, and that the seed his servant sows rots in the furrow because it is not watered with the prayers of the church, and because Christian people are more concerned to train their children to get a living than they are to save their souls?"

He went on for half an hour, and when he sat down there were three or four on their feet together, for his words went through the people like an electric shock.

At the close of the meeting Mr. Redman gave the notice and more than half of the assembly stopped. Among them was Walter Conly the schoolmaster, his brother Edward, and sister Emily; Will Orcutt who had come home from Reading on a visit, and his brother George; Arthur and Elmer Nevins, John and William Edibean, and the Wood boys, Jane Gifford, Martha Kendrick; many heads of families, Lunt the miller and Samuel Dorset the drover. Mr. Whitman and his wife, Peter and Maria, remained, but the grandfather saw Bertie and James go out. It gave the good old man a heartache, and he said within himself,—

"God's ways are not our ways, His will be done."

That night after the old gentleman had retired to rest, Bertie crept to his bedside and said,—

"Grandfather, the reason I did not stop to-night was I didn't want to talk with anybody only you, but I have prayed to God a great many times, and asked him to take me for his child, and make me just what he wants me to be, and somehow I feel as though he hears me."

"Would you be ashamed to have your father and mother know how you feel?"

"I shouldn't be ashamed to have the whole school know I am trying to be good and be a Christian."

A week passed away, and the old gentleman found no opportunity to talk with James, as he was busy out of doors, and did not come into the shop, but on Saturday evening as the former was sitting in his bedroom, James entered and said,—

"Grandfather, I have done what you wished me to, and I have been studying the New Testament to find out what sin is and whether I am a sinner."

"What did you find there?"

"I found that sin is the transgression of the law; that it is not doing this or that, but having a wrong principle, and that I had a wrong principle, and so there was not a bit of good in me. When I came to cipher the thing right out, I saw that it was not because it was a sin against God that I didn't do as the rest in the workhouse did, but because Mr. Holmes told me not to, and that Mr.

Holmes was my God all the while."

"Ah! you've got to the bottom of it now, my boy."

"But why did not Mr. Holmes tell me about my being a sinner, and about pardon through the Saviour, as you have, and as Mr. Redman does?"

"Because Mr. Holmes was not only a good man, but a man of sense, all good men don't have common sense. You were a child then, and he did not mean to burden your mind with things that, not understanding, you would forget, but he knew if he told you not to lie, steal nor swear, and taught you the commandments, that you would know what that meant, and he put the idea of God in your mind. He knew that you loved him and would do as you promised him you would, and that if you kept clear of those sins it would keep your conscience alive, and that if you said the Lord's prayer it would give you the idea of going to God, and though you might not understand it would finally have its effect, and as you grew older that influence would grow stronger."

The religious interest increased not only there, but extended to other towns in the county, and was part of that wonderful religious movement called "The Great Awakening" that pervaded Kentucky, was more or less felt in every state then in the Union, and which provided Christian pioneers for the new settlements constantly forming.

CHAPTER XVII.
REDEMPTION YEAR.

It was now planting time. James, this year, planted his patch with corn, as he had planted it with potatoes two years, and the boys planted potatoes. The weather proved very dry and so favorable for farm work that the planting and sowing were finished much earlier than usual.

"Now, boys," said Mr. Whitman, "if you handle yourselves, you can burn your lot over and plant corn before hoeing comes on: and, after harvest, you can knock the sprouts from the stumps and kill the fire-weeds."

They put in the fire, and got an excellent burn.

They now determined to make a log-rolling and invite the neighbors, far and near, to come with axes and oxen to cut and roll and twitch the unburnt logs into great piles to be set on fire and burned entirely up. The old gentleman was busily at work in the shop, when Maria came running in, and said,—

"Grandpa! George Orcutt is coming up the road, and he looks as though he was coming here."

"I hope he is; and if he turns up here, you tell him the men-folks are all in the field, except me, and that I am at work in the shop."

In a few moments George came in, and was received very cordially by the old gentleman. George said his father had broken one of the glasses in his specs, and as he was about the age of Mr. Jonathan, but some older, he might have a pair that he did not use, that he would lend him till he could get another pair. He said that William was coming, but he had an errand at Mr. Wood's, and told his folks he would do the errand.

"There are glasses enough in the house. I don't use 'em; but I have got two pair that were my father's. Jonathan has got two pair, and Alice has a pair that she don't use much of any now. I was glad to see that you stopped awhile ago after meeting. I trust you have found the hope you sought then?"

"No, Mr. Whitman, I have not; there's a thing stands right in the middle of the road, and blocks the whole road up."

"What is that?"

"You know, I suppose, what happened at school?"

"Have you any hardness against James?"

"No, sir; and I have told the Lord I am sorry, and asked his forgiveness; but that is not satisfactory, and I don't feel that it is any use for me to go to my Maker till I have forgiveness of James, but I don't know how to bring it about."

"I'll fix it for you; it is only about half an hour to supper time; you'll stop and take supper with us?"

"I dread to go into the house."

"Never be afraid to do right, because you will have help. But, before you go in, I want to show you some things James has made."

The old gentleman showed him a wheelbarrow and crossbow he had made for Bertie, and the wheels and shafts he had made to break the colt in, and told him that James had made himself a nice chest, dovetailed it together, and painted it.

"Come, let us go into the house and find the specs."

Mrs. Whitman received George in so kindly a manner that it relieved him of much of his embarrassment.

The old gentleman told Maria, when she went to call the men-folks to supper, to tell her father that George Orcutt was in the house and would stop to supper.

"Boys," said Mr. Whitman, "George Orcutt is in the house; I suppose you can guess what has brought him here. He will feel embarrassed enough, no doubt, and I want you all to shake hands with him as if you meant it, and receive him as though nothing had happened, and as you did when he used to come here."

"I am sure I will," said Bertie; and so they all said, and did accordingly; but the grandfather excelled them all, for, as soon as they had shaken hands with George and talked a little, the former said, "James, I've been showing George your cart, and have told him about your chest. Why won't you take him upstairs and let him see it?"

They went upstairs together.

"I think we had better sit down to the table," said Mr. Whitman; "they will feel better to find us eating than they will to find us all sitting here still, and have to look us in the face when they come down."

133

Before James and George came down, the boys and their father had eaten their supper and gone out, leaving James and George to eat together.

There were traces of tears on the cheeks of the latter, but he looked happy and as though a great load was lifted from his heart, and felt so much relieved that the boys persuaded him to pass the night with them. In the course of the evening he told Bertie that David Riggs and William Morse, who had also stopped at the meeting on the Sabbath succeeding the one upon which he stopped, felt as he did, and wanted to do likewise, but did not know how to bring it about. The four friends talked the matter over, and it was resolved to invite David and William to the log-rolling and the supper afterwards, and George was commissioned to invite and come with them.

The day was set, the neighbors responded to the summons, the logs were piled and burnt, and great numbers of the smaller stumps torn out by main force and flung on the piles. David, William and George were among the first on the ground, David bringing four oxen and George and William a yoke each. Before they parted harmony was restored between them and James and Peter and Bertie.

The boys were very solicitous that their grandfather should go out and look at the burn but he was not able. The good old man had been failing since the approach of hot weather and could only work a little while in the garden in the morning; and at evening and during the greater part of the time dozed in his chair. In the midst of wheat harvest there came a week of extremely sultry weather which affected him very sensibly, and as Mrs. Whitman was passing through the room where the old gentleman sat asleep in his chair, she was alarmed by the extreme paleness of his features, went to the chair and found him unconscious. She summoned her husband and children, who were near by reaping, but when they reached the house he was no more. A well-spent life had ceased without a struggle. His death, though not unexpected, threw a gloom over that happy family that not even the assurance of his preparedness could dissipate, and that yielded only to the soothing hand of time.

James, to whom he had stood in the place of a parent, was so affected that for several weeks he could speak of nothing else. Mr. Whitman now conducted family prayers as his father had done, and in a few weeks himself and wife, James and the children, united with the church. As the result of the singing school there was formed a new choir, which Peter, Bertie, and James joined, also Emily Conly, Jane Gifford, Sarah Evans, Maria Whitman, and Prudence Orcutt.

When the boys came to harvest their corn they found an opportunity to sell it in the ear to an agent who was buying corn and shelling it at the mill with a machine that was moved by water-power, and shared forty-nine dollars and fifty cents each. James also obtained eighteen dollars and some cents for that raised on the same piece that he had before planted with potatoes.

The season throughout had been dry and held so, the boys therefore took the oxen, pulled out all the roots the oxen could start by means of their help, and with the axe cut down all the stubs that had been broken off and left. There were also a great many logs that were too green to burn and had been piled up around the stumps; these they hauled together and then setting fire to the corn stubble made a clean burn of weeds, sprouts and logs, feeding the fire till the whole was consumed and a good seed bed made for another year.

Edward Conly kept the school in the winter and everything passed off pleasantly. James was now, as one of the choir, brought to the choir meetings, mingled with the girls as he had never done before, and was even induced by Bertie and Edward Conly to speak a piece and take part in a dialogue at a school exhibition.

The boys resolved this spring (as they had cleared their burn so thoroughly) to plough it a few inches deep and sow it with rye. It was hard work for the cattle, and as they stopped to breathe them, Bertie cried out, in his abrupt fashion,—

"Look here, James; by the time this grain comes off, or not long after, your time will be out, your four years."

After reflecting a moment, James replied,—

"So they will. Can it be that four years are gone already?"

"What are you going to do about the next crop after this? Father promised us three crops; I don't suppose he thought anything about the time."

"I'll give it to you and Peter."

"We'll buy it of you," said Peter.

"You are not going away," said Bertie. "What is the use to talk about that. This is your home just as much as it is ours; we won't let you go, will we, Pete?"

"Of course we won't."

"Father," said Bertie, at dinner, "do you know that James' time is out next fall?"

"Yes."

"But you said he and we might have three crops off that burn. If he goes away he'll lose his crop."

"He won't go away. I'll hire him and let him have his crop to boot. I suppose he'll work for me, won't you, James?"

"Work for you, Mr. Whitman. I'll gladly work for you a year without wages, and then I shall be altogether in your debt, for coming here has been my salvation, both for soul and body."

"You are worth more to me than any man I can hire, and I shall hire you, and pay you all you are worth. Whatever I have done for you I have received back, and more, too, in relief from the care and anxiety of looking up help at critical periods, and in having the best of help, and also in feeling that I had a man in whom I could place confidence, whom the children could love, and who would not teach them any bad habits. More especially do I think of how much father loved you, and only a few days before his death he said to me,—

"'Jonathan, James' time will be out next year; don't lose sight of him when I am gone, and be kind to him for my sake."

So far was Mr. Whitman from forgetting when James' time was out, that early in the spring he had written to his brother William, telling him about James, and how much they were all attached to him; that under the instruction of his father he had become a good shot with a rifle, had learned a little of trapping, and to travel on snow-shoes. He then asked him to take him with him a winter trapping, as he was anxious to earn money to buy land.

He received a letter from his brother saying that he would willingly take James, more especially as a Seneca Indian, with whom he had trapped two winters, was dead. That he need bring no traps, except, perhaps, a few small ones, nor lead, nor powder, as these articles could be procured at Pittsburg, nor blankets, for they had enough; and to come on horseback, as he had plenty of hay and grain, for which there was no market, and that he would meet him at Pittsburg the last week in October or the first in November.

Mr. Whitman put the letter in his pocket, and said nothing about it at the time.

When the rye came off they shared twenty dollars each, after returning two bushels to Mr. Whitman.

It was now the twenty-seventh of September, the corn and grain were harvested, and the potatoes nearly dug. It was in the evening, cool enough to render a fire comfortable, and the boys were seated around the hearth, mute, and evidently expectant.

Mr. Whitman went into his bedroom, and returning with a letter in his hand, said,—

"James, you have honorably fulfilled the agreement made with me four years ago, and are now your own man, and to-morrow we will pass receipts. Of course you now want to earn all you can. I know that the desire to own a piece of land and call it your own is eating you up. Bertie says you talk about it in your sleep, and I want to put you in the way of getting it."

He then told James of the letter he had received from his brother, and put it in his hand. When James had read the letter, he said,—

"There is nothing I so much desire as to own a piece of land. Working out by the month on a farm is a very slow way of getting money to buy it with, as in the winter a man can earn but little more than his board, and the winters are long here; in England the plough goes every month in the year. I should like very much to go."

"Trapping is a poor business to follow, but a very good resort for a young man who wants to obtain something to give him a start. You can go out there, trap till April, and if you are commonly successful can earn more than you could in a whole farming season, and get back in time for farm work, when I will hire you for the rest of the season, and you and the boys can raise another crop on your burnt land."

There was no time to be lost, as the journey was long, and James began instantly to make his preparations.

"Father," said Bertie, "the colt is too young for such a journey with a heavy load, it will spoil him. Why don't you let James take old Frank? He'll be back by the time we want to plough, and Frank is good for anything."

"I will, if you and Peter think you can part with Frank." Mr. Whitman gave his father's rifle to James, a most excellent piece. He took with him a few otter and beaver traps, pork, bread, and also a camp kettle, as he calculated to kill game, and camp where taverns were not convenient.

"Where are James and Bertie?" said Mr. Whitman, the night before James was to set out.

"They have gone over to Mr. Conly's," said Peter.

"James has been over there two evenings this week. I should think if he is going in the morning he would want to be at home this evening."

"He thinks a great deal of Edward Conly, and I believe Walter is expected home to-night."

"I guess," said Maria, "that it's not Edward nor Walter, but Emily whom he thinks the most of, for he went home from meeting with her last Sunday night, and he never went home with anybody before. I don't believe but what Bert knows."

"If he does he won't blab it all round," said Peter.

James took with him flint, steel and tinder, fish-hooks and lines, and one blanket, and provender for Frank.

He started off with the good wishes of all the household. Bertie put his arms round old Frank's neck and told him to remember that he had a character to sustain, and not to stumble on the mountains. The old roadster bent down his head, rubbed his nose on the shoulder of his young friend and seemed to signify, I will.

Uncle Nathan Kendrick, an old trapper, not far from the age of the deceased grandfather, had given James a rough draft of the roads, with the names of the streams, fords, and towns, the localities of the public houses and log taverns, and the distances, and the places where grass and water were to be found, and that were good camping grounds.

In the meanwhile the object of all this solicitude rode on, crossed the Susquehannah at Harris Ferry, and found a good tavern, where he put up. The next morning he started on, fed his horse on grass and provender, buying provender at the farm-houses for the horse and what little he required for himself, as he shot or trapped most of his provision. At night he camped early, and after he left the older settlements behind, he built a brush camp every night and put Frank into it to protect him from the wolves, building his fire in front.

He found no difficulty in regard to living. When he stopped to bait at noon on the banks of the Yellow Breeches Creek, he shot a wild turkey, and had a sumptuous dinner. At Falling Spring he caught muskrats and snared a partridge, and caught fish in the Conococheague Creek; on the top of the North Mountain he found a log tavern, where he obtained provender and camped; from thence, crossing the Alleghanies, he came to Laurel Hill and Chestnut Ridge. This ridge was covered with a heavy growth of chestnut trees, mixed with oaks, which rendered it a resort for wild turkeys, coons and deer, and in the openings was an abundance of sweet grass for the horse. Here he camped two days to rest the horse after the fatigue of climbing the mountains, and while there he shot a deer and trapped two minks.

James now found himself within about two miles of Pittsburg village, then an assemblage of log houses, having some trade in furs and by flat-boats down the river with New Orleans, Ohio and Kentucky; also some trade by pack-horses with Baltimore and by water carriage by way of the Kiskiminetas Creek and by portage.

Frank had not been in a stable since leaving Harristown. It was near sundown, the wood was too thick for grass to grow, and James resolved to put up at some farm-house and give him a good baiting of hay.

Seeing a log house, the logs of which were hewn on the sides and chinked with lime mortar, a large barn and good breadth of land cleared, he made application and received a cordial welcome from the farmer, a Scotchman. His family consisted of a wife and three children, with all the necessaries of life in abundance. When the evening meal was over, he called the family together for prayers, and, according to the Scotch custom, read a hymn, and finding that James sang, they all, even to the children, united in praising God.

James had now the opportunity to clean his horse thoroughly from dust and sweat, and feed him bountifully. Aside from his attachment to a good horse, he knew that Mr. Whitman would never have let anybody else have him, and was therefore very anxious to bring him through in good shape, and nothing could exceed the pains he had taken with him on the road, the result being that he was in excellent flesh and spirits, and showed no signs of a hard journey.

James was much disappointed next morning, when he rode into Pittsburg, at the mean appearance of the village, having heard so much of the conflicts around Duquesne. He found most of the houses built of logs, some of round logs, others two-story and the logs hewn, one brick house and a few stone, some good frame houses, and a church built of hewn timber, but plenty of public-houses.

CHAPTER XVIII.
WILLIAM WHITMAN.

James was proceeding leisurely along the street bordering on the river, called Front Street, when, as he approached a log tavern where a great number of teams were standing, his horse was suddenly caught by the bridle, and upon looking up, he was confronted by one of the finest-looking men he thought he had ever met, and who, extending his hand, exclaimed,—

"Is this James Renfew?"

James replied in the affirmative, as he clasped the offered hand of the stranger, and returned his hearty grasp.

"I am William Whitman, and I knew old Frank the instant I set eyes on him. How are you, old playmate?" patting Frank's neck. "He's just my age; twenty-five years old last April, the tenth. Frank and I are one year's children. How smooth he looks; young as a colt. You'll have a good time here, old fellow, this winter, plenty to eat and nothing to do."

"Ah! there's father's old rifle," laying his hand on the weapon, that lay across the forward part of the saddle. "Oh! what a good father he was to us, and brought us all up in the right way. I know in reason he is better off, and that we must all die, but the old rifle brings everything back,—all the old days when he used to teach me to shoot under the old chestnut. Father did not know how old that tree was. How long have you lived with my brother?"

"Four years."

"And you have lived right among them all that time, and was there when my father died?"

"Yes, sir; your father taught me to work with tools, and to shoot, and trap, and could not rest till he brought me and Peter, Bertie and Maria, to pray to God, and then he died."

"You don't know how glad I am to see you, and how glad Mary will be to see somebody right from home. I suppose you knew my wife was Bradford Conly's daughter?"

"Yes, sir; I went to school to Walter two winters; and Edward Conly was the last person except your brother's folks that I shook hands with."

William Whitman went for his horse, and they set forth; the road, very good for a few miles, soon became a mere bridle path between spotted trees. Clearings were sparse, and consisted of a few acres, the houses were built of round logs, the roofs covered with splints hollowed like a gouge, two laid hollow side up, and a rider rounded so that the edges of it turned into the hollows of the under ones, was placed on top, like the tiles of a West Indian house.

"I am taking you to a rough place by a rough road, but we shall be comfortable and find something to keep soul and body together when we get there."

They now came in sight of the Monongahela and to some high bottom land of about six acres, smooth, bare of trees and covered with a thick sward of grass, in which was a young orchard, and in the midst of the orchard stood a house built of logs, the tops and bottom hewn, and the chimney of brick laid in lime mortar, and the bottom logs of the house were underpinned with stone and the stones pointed with lime mortar. The windows were small but glazed and fitted with bullet-proof shutters, and the roof covered with pine shingles nailed. There was also a good frame barn and a corn crib of round logs. Besides this natural meadow, about ten acres had been cleared of forest, part of which had that season been planted with corn and sown with wheat, and about three acres were already green with winter rye, the remainder was in grass. The house stood at a slight elbow in the stream, and thus commanded a view of the river in both directions. Mr. Whitman told James it was about three miles to where the river Youghiogheny came in.

"We are a rough-handed people here, Mr. Renfew, have forgotten what little breeding we ever had, but we can give you a hearty welcome," said William as they dismounted, and fastening the horses, he led the way to the house.

"Mary," he said to his wife who met them at the door with a babe in her arms, "this is Jonathan's boy, James Renfew. I reckon he must think about as much of him as he does of Peter or Bertie. If he didn't, he never would have let him have Frank to come out into this wilderness."

"Now, Mr. Renfew, just sit you down and talk with the woman while I see to the horses."

James told Mrs. Whitman how lately he had parted with her parents and brothers, and as Mr. Whitman just then came in, everything in relation to the old gentleman that he thought would be interesting to them.

Suddenly Mrs. Whitman exclaimed,—

"Husband, what are we thinking about? Mr. Renfew has not had anything to eat and now it is past noon." Her husband took the child, and she soon had biscuit in the Dutch oven and slices of venison, killed the day before, broiling.

"Take a seat in my wife's rocking chair, Mr. Renfew," pointing to a singularly constructed affair in the corner; "you see it took three to make that chair. The Lord found the stuff; I did a little cabinet work, and Mary the ornamental part."

It was made by fitting a board into two-thirds of a hollow cedar log for a seat, and notching into it for the arms, and slanting the back, to the bottom, were fitted rockers. The wife had made a cushion, covered and stuffed the arms and back, and thus made a most comfortable chair.

The cradle was more remarkable still, being made of an entire hollow sycamore log; this log, after being cut off the right length, was sawed down two feet from the ends, the piece taken out leaving the rest for the top; the ends were filled with basswood bark, pressed flat and fastened with glue, made by boiling the tips of deer's horns; and rockers were put on.

It was large enough for three babies, as a large log was taken in order to get height sufficient for the top, but the space was filled with a bed and stuffing. Two pewter platters, four earthen mugs, wooden plates, spoons and bowls, all of wood, made the table furniture, and bedsteads were made of rough poles.

On the other hand there was a handsome loom with reeds and harness, all in excellent order, large and little wheels and reels and cards, and good feather beds and bedding.

"I see you are looking at my wife's cradle," said William, "it was made for the occasion, but the child is comfortable, and may be President of the United States yet."

"Did you make that loom? It is very handsome."

"Yes, I thought as it was a thing we should always need, I would take time and make it well. I could have made a cradle of boards, but we needed the boards for a roof, and nails are a scarce article here. The fact is we brought the things we most needed, and I brought my tools, because I knew I could with them hatch up something to get along with, and when I got time make something better. Now, Mr. Renfew,—"

"Call me James, if you please, I shall feel more at home."

"Now, James, if you'll take care of the beasts, I'll take my rifle and see if I can get a wild turkey, or pigeon, and then we'll have another chat; for to-morrow we must get ready for the woods."

"You may think it silly, James, but I'll go out with you, for I want to see and pet old Frank; nothing brings home so near as seeing him," said Mary.

"That's because I always rode him over to her father's when I was courting her, and she used to ride on his back, on the pillion behind me, to singing school, huskings and all sorts of doings."

Away he went, humming a merry tune. While Mrs. Whitman was talking to Frank, patting him, pulling locks of sweet hay out of the mow and giving to him, James looked after the retreating form of her husband, who was making the woods ring with his music, and said within himself,—

"What a man!—far from neighbors, with three little children, bullet-proof window shutters, five rifles and a shot-gun hanging over the fireplace, and gay as a lark. He's just like Bertie for all the world; it's just as Mrs. Whitman said, 'If you like Bertie you'll like his uncle, for they are just alike.'"

At dusk Mr. Whitman returned with a turkey and three pigeons, and after the evening meal was partaken of and the children in bed, James asked him how he came to think of settling where he was when there was plenty of wild land east of the mountains, and especially as the homes both of himself and wife were there.

"I came up here when I was seventeen years old with uncle Nathan Hendrick trapping, we trapped on this stream and on the Youghiogheny; there were beaver here then,—a few,—a good many otters and foxes, and no end to the coons; we did well and that gave me a taste for trapping.

"When I was eighteen, father gave me my time, a good rifle, and money to buy a good set of traps. I worked two summers on farms, and in the winters came up here and trapped alone. Then I had fallen head over ears in love with that girl who is jogging the cradle, and she wanted to get married and settle down awful"—upon this he received a sound box on the ear from his wife. "You see we wanted to get together, I had taken a great liking to this place, couldn't get it out of my head, used to dream about it. I hadn't much money but wanted considerable land, couldn't bear to be crowded; and this land was dog cheap. About this time I got acquainted with a half-breed Indian, who told me there was good trapping and hunting on the Big Beaver. I went and looked over this land, made up my mind just exactly as to what I could do with it, saw that I could get along faster here than anywhere else, because I could do two things as you may say at once."

"What two things?"

"I could trap and farm. I made up my mind at once and bought two hundred acres, though it took all the money I had. I went to a blacksmith in Pittsburg who I knew often saw the half-breed, and got him to ask him to trap with me the next winter, and for the smith to write me, and went home. When I got home, father had given the farm to Jonathan to take care of him and mother. I hired with Jonathan at twenty-five dollars a month. I worked till August and had a hundred dollars."

"Why didn't you work through the season?"

"Because I had received a letter from the smith saying that the half-breed would trap with me, and I knew I could trust that Indian.

"I gave forty-five dollars of my money to that woman for safe keeping (it was an awful risk, but I did it). I borrowed a mule and a pack-saddle of Mr. Nevins and put on him seventy-five steel traps, powder, lead and blankets, a few tools to make dead-falls (wooden traps) and other fixings, took old Frank, put a saddle and pillion on him and some light things, tied the mule's bridle to Frank's tail, put Bertie on the pillion, and started. The Indian had agreed to meet me at Turkey Foot."

"What is Turkey Foot?"

"Don't you remember that just after you left Somerset you crossed a creek with high banks?"

"Yes."

"Not far from that the Yo. (Youghiogheny) splits into three forks. That is the middle one, and the place where they divide is called Turkey Foot, because it looks so much like one.

"You know what that boy is; keen as a brier and smart as steel. Wasn't he tickled when he found he was going and where he was going; he hugged me, kissed me, and hardly knew which end he stood on."

"That explains something that has puzzled me. When I got near the crossing I found an Indian path, and Frank was so determined to follow it that I had to strike him several times before he would give it up. I could not imagine what it meant, for I thought I knew he had never been there before."

"When we reached Turkey Foot the Indian had been there a week, and had laid in a lot of provisions; he had the carcass of a deer hung up and had smoked and dried the best parts of several more, and had killed and dried a lot of wild pigeons."

"What did Bertie say to the Indian?"

"Made friends with him right off; stuck to him like his shadow, Bert's tongue running like a mill-clapper and the Indian grunting once in a while, but the half-breed made him a bow and arrows and a little birch, and he went back with the two horses, about the biggest-feeling boy ever you saw.

"We paddled down the Yo. into this stream, and down this to Pittsburg, got some more traps there, went down the Allegheny twenty-five miles to Big Beaver, and up that about fifteen miles; went to trapping and trapped till the middle of April. The Indian wanted to carry his furs to Canada, so we made another canoe and came to Pittsburg, where I stored my furs."

"Then I suppose you took the canoe, came to Turkey Foot, and from there home?"

"By no means. I wrote a letter, told 'em what I had done; that I was well; hoped they were the same; must excuse all mistakes; came here, and went to felling trees, till the fifteenth of May; then I went eight miles to the nearest neighbor, and got him to come with his team, and plough up an acre of the clear land; planted it with potatoes and corn, and sowed a little flax. I then cut all the grass that grew on the bottom land, and in openings in the woods, made a hand-sled, hauled it to the stack and stacked it. Then I went right into a thick place in the woods and built a log camp; it was only fourteen feet by twelve, and just high enough to get into, with a splint roof, a stone fireplace, no chimney, only a hole through the roof, and no floor, but brush laid on the ground. It had but one window, and that was made in the door; was filled with oiled paper, and had a slide for stormy weather. Then, after making a house for cattle, I went to chopping till the last of August, and then went to hunting and trapping again."

"Did you go back to the Beaver?"

"No, indeed; had hunting and trapping enough on the spot. I had built no fence because I had no cattle, and the bears, deers, and coons were determined to have my corn. Sometimes when I turned out in the morning, I would find a moose or a deer feeding on my grass, or browsing among the trees I had cut last. In a brook about a mile off there were a few otters, and many minks and foxes. I bought a lot of hens and geese, on purpose to tole the foxes, and went to trapping and shooting in good earnest. I made a log-trap for bears and wolves, and once in a while shot a moose or deer, and trapped otters and foxes. I had so much meat lying round that it toled the foxes and wolves; the wolves soon drove off the deer and moose, and then I shot the wolves on bait. Every wolf I killed I got ten shillings bounty and his skin was worth two dollars; and a bear's skin from sixteen to twenty. That's what I meant when I said that here I could do two things at the same time. I had built a house, raised corn, potatoes, flax, and hay enough to carry me through the winter, felled five acres of trees, and earned by trapping and shooting more than I had all the summer before, working for my brother, and been at work for myself most of the time. As for the deer, bears, and wolves, I didn't go after them, and it did not take much time to set the traps, and what was of no less consequence I had got a first-rate birch. There's nothing like a birch to a wild Indian, or a new settler."

"Is a birch then so valuable?"

"Next to the Bible and the narrow axe."

"I don't suppose you meant to go on to your place till spring?"

"Didn't. I pulled my flax and spread it to rot, put my pack, rifle and provisions into the birch and started up-stream. I didn't go to the Forks where I met the half-breed, but into Sewickly Creek, and paddled up it to within a rod of the road, hid the birch in the woods, took my pack and started for home."

"That was a long hard journey."

"It was all that. I told this little woman what I had done, made it as bad as I knew how; told her just what a miserable place she would have to live in, and gave her the choice to go back with me or I would go back alone, trap all winter and come for her in the spring, and before another winter build a more comfortable house; and all her folks and most of mine thought that was the best way.

"But she wouldn't hear a word of it, said if I could stand it, she could; wasn't a bit afraid, that it was the best time of the year to go because the roads were better and the streams we would have to ford were low; and that I ought to be on my land early in the spring to sow or plant the ground I had ploughed. So we got married, and then the old folks set in worse than ever for us not to go till spring, and even the neighbors took it up, but I had one on my side and he was worth all the rest."

"Who was that?"

"Father," said William, sinking his voice to a whisper.

"Yes," said Mrs. Whitman, "his opinion was worth more than all the other's opinions. A few nights before we set out, and when all the young girls, my schoolmates, were pitying me and doing all they could to make me feel worse, the good old man took me into the other room and said: 'Mary, never you mind those young people, don't let anything they say jar you a particle. Listen to the old man who has been over every inch of the road you and William are starting on. If you live to my age you'll look back and say that the days you spent in the brush camp were the happiest days, for they were full of hope; but when you have lived to my age you will have outlived all your hopes but the hope of eternal life, and that is the best of all, because the possession will be more than the expectation while everything else falls short. You have got a good husband, his heart is tender as a child's, but his mind is as firm as a piece of the nether millstone. He's a cheery lad, he'll look on the bright side, keep your heart up and his own too. You are married now and have taken the first step, don't look back, it didn't work well with Lot's wife. I never knew it to work well with anybody, look ahead; a man isn't half a man and a woman isn't half a woman who has never had any load to carry. I take it you'll work in an even yoke; you are both smart, and no doubt feel that you are equal to anything, and perhaps look down on people who have not your strength and resolution, but it is better to look up, and the first night you get into the camp I want William to take the Bible and read and pray, and I want you to ask him to.' I didn't have to ask him."

"Didn't you wish you had taken your parents' advice before you got over the mountains, and before you got through that first winter?"

"By no means. We had no table only some pieces of bark set on four stakes, driven into the ground; no bedstead, but put the beds on the brush; we had no room for furniture, because I must have room for my wool and flax wheels, to spin the flax William had raised and the wool I had brought from home."

"Were you comfortable?"

"I never saw so warm a place as that camp. William covered it all over with brush outside, and the snow drifted over it; we had plenty of bear and wolf skins, and if it had not been for the hole in the roof we should have roasted."

"How did you get the wagon here,—there was no road?"

"William got a teamster who was going to Pittsburg with four horses and a light load to take the canoe, and it arrived in Pittsburg before we did. We put our things, part of 'em, in that, and we came in; the next day he got the rest and left the wagon till winter, and then made a sled and hauled it up the river on the ice. The river makes an excellent road in winter for a sled and in summer for the canoe."

"Yes; and Providence keeps it in repair, and no road tax to work out," said her husband.

James could not have been placed in a better school to learn how to cut his way through life than with this cheerful, resolute pair in the wilderness.

The next morning they took the birch canoe from the barn; Whitman gummed the seams, and they carried it to the water. Whitman held it, told James to get in, sit down in the middle and keep still; he then got in himself, and standing up, with one stroke of the paddle, sent the light craft flying into the middle of the stream. James was delighted with the movement of the buoyant craft.

William then told him to kneel down and take the paddle while he kept the balance, and to paddle without fear, for he would keep her on her bottom.

"James, you have got to learn to use this birch. Can you swim?"

"Like a fish."

"Well then, take off part of your clothes and try it; for most likely you'll upset."

James crossed the stream, came back and attempted to go up stream; he went up a little way, but in turning to come back, the birch went out from under him, then righted, and was three times her length from him in a moment.

"You can't get into her, give her a shove to me." James gave the canoe a little push with one hand, and the light craft spun over the water to William, who held her while James swam ashore.

"What queer things they are! I was in the water before I could wink."

"Ay, they'll tip you out, and right themselves without a drop of water in 'em, and then sit and laugh at you. We must now make up our minds how many traps we can tend. How many traps did you bring?"

"Only twenty-five small ones."

"I think we ought to tend three hundred. I am going to trap on the same ground that the Indian and I trapped on last year. My traps are there hid under rocks. I shall get a few more. If you'll take care of the cattle and practise in this birch, I'll go to Pittsburg and get the traps, and leave 'em there to take when we go along, and to-morrow we'll start."

James, in the course of the day, got used to the birch, and met with no farther mishap.

Whitman got home at dusk, and called him to supper, when he found a young woman of twenty and a stout boy of eighteen by the name of Montgomery. They could neither of them read or write, and were to stay with Mrs. Whitman during the absence of her husband, and she was to teach them to read and write. Jane Montgomery was also to weave a web of cloth for her mother, as they were recent settlers and had as yet no loom. The next day was spent in preparations for departure and in putting all their things into the birch,—cooking utensils, blankets, provisions and other matters, tools to make dead falls, and repair camps, and snow shoes.

CHAPTER XIX.
TRAPPING.

They proceeded down the Monongahela to the Alleghany; down the Alleghany to the mouth of the Big Beaver, and up that about thirty miles till they came to a fork. Taking the easterly fork, they proceeded about three miles till they reached another fork. Here they found a temporary camp, which they repaired and passed the night in, collected the traps Whitman had concealed the year before, and set them as they went up the stream, till in the course of five miles they came to another temporary camp in very good repair. They went on five miles more, and found another camp that needed slight repairs. Having repaired this, they went on five miles more, and found a camp with a bark roof, stone chimney and fireplace. The roof and chimney needed some repairing. They passed the night here and found more traps, which they set, and replaced some that were worn out with new ones. They now returned, and as they went found in the traps two beavers, four minks and one otter. This put them in good spirits. They paddled rapidly down to the Fork, and ascended the other streams and began to set the new traps, as this was the ground the half-breed had trapped. In the course of five miles they came to a temporary camp and repaired it, setting traps as they went. Here they found stretchers for skins. At the distance of five miles they came to a permanent log camp with a stone fireplace, chimney, and a lug pole in the chimney to hang a kettle on. There was a window with oiled paper in it, bark shelves, backwoods stools, and a table made of cedar-splints. There were also bark dishes and wooden spoons and plates. This was the main or home camp. Here they unloaded the birch and deposited all their provisions. They made a hemlock broom, cleaned out the camp, collected small hemlock and cedar brush for beds, heated water and washed and scalded every thing that had need of washing; and cooked the tail of a beaver and roasted a fish they caught in the stream for supper.

The next morning they proceeded up stream five miles, setting traps until they reached another temporary camp, which needed much repairing, and did not reach the home camp till dark. After supper they sat some time chatting and arranging their plans for the winter.

"I can't help thinking of the Indian; there in the corner are his arrows and bow. If I could use them as well as he, we should get more deer meat this winter," said William.

"A rifle is better than a bow."

"True, but we cannot fire a rifle till the stream is frozen. The beaver is a very timid creature, and while they are running about the bank the less noise we make the better, but the bow is a silent weapon, and in an Indian's hand effective."

Such was the divergency of the creeks that when each was at the upper end of his line of traps they were ten miles apart, but every other night they met at the home camp where they did most of their cooking; the other camps were for shelter and to skin their game in and stretch and keep the skins.

Every Sunday they met at the home camp, and indulged in a pot of pork and beans, and sassafras tea and Johnny-cake, baked on a flat stone, with a slice of pork. When they had made their plans and partaken of the supper William threw himself upon the brush, wrapped the blanket around him, and was asleep in a moment.

But in respect to James the situation was too novel to permit of sleep. He went out and seated himself upon the birch, that was turned upon the bank. It was a night of stars but moonless. He was nearly three hundred miles from home, sixty from any village, and half that from any habitation; no baying of dogs, rumbling of wheels, nor any of the sounds of civilized life fell upon his ear as he reflected and listened to the moaning of the stream as it swept past, and the sounds new and inexplicable to him that came up on the night wind from the forest. A strange feeling of loneliness came over him. He felt his own nothingness as never before; the mighty forest seemed closing around and about to crush him; and commending himself to God he also wrapped himself in his blanket, and lay watching the flickering firelight till sleep and fatigue overpowered him.

Here they remained and trapped till the middle of April, and then made up their furs. Mr. Whitman took them to Philadelphia. They divided five hundred dollars between them, and James reached home the sixth of May.

The Whitmans were seated at the dinner-table. During the forenoon they had been preparing the ground to plant corn, they had been working four horses, putting James' colt in with Dick, in the absence of his mate.

"Father," said Peter, "hadn't we better plough that piece of burnt land, and not wait for James?"

Mr. Whitman was about to reply, but his voice was drowned in a loud neigh that penetrated every cranny of the dwelling, and took precedence of all other sounds, and was instantly followed by a most vigorous response from the four horses in the barn, in which the tones of Dick were the most prominent.

"It's Frank's voice, Frank and James!" shouted Bertie, running to the door, followed more leisurely by all the rest.

Great was the joy and fervent the greetings, and not less warm the welcome bestowed upon old Frank, who, after a whole winter's rest, had renewed his age.

"Take him to the stable, Bertie," said his father, "or Dick will tear the stall down, he wants to see his mate."

James was soon seated at the table, when Mr. Whitman said,—

"Do you like that part of the state better than this, James."

"No, sir, it is too near the Indians."

"But hasn't General Wayne settled them?"

"Yes, sir, for a few years, perhaps; but there are a great many of them in the country beyond the Ohio, and they will always be ready to take up the hatchet, and certainly won't lack provocation. Then there's no market but by flat boats two thousand miles down the river to New Orleans, or by pack-horses and wagons over the mountains. If you raise crops you can't sell 'em; a good cow is worth but five dollars, a horse ten; wheat thirty cents a bushel and won't bear transporting over the mountains,—nothing will but whiskey. Four bushels of grain is a load for a horse over the mountains, but he will carry twenty-four made into whiskey."

"By-and-by it will be different."

"They hope and expect it will, but it may be a long time. Why should anybody go where he can get land for nothing, and that is good for nothing to him after he has got it, as he can't sell anything from it? It is about as broad as it is long. I have no doubt there is land this side of the mountains, and wild land too, about as cheap, and where crops can be got to market."

As no one of the family thought of questioning James as to his route, naturally supposing that he came back by the same road over which he went, he did not tell them that he turned off at the foot of the north mountain, proceeded up along the west bank of the Susquehannah, crossed it at Northumberland, and travelled for two days inspecting the country, looking over the farms and clearings, inquiring the price of land improved and wild, the price of cattle, grain, and opportunities for market, and also in relation to the state of roads, and distances from markets and the means of conveyance.

"Boys," said Mr. Whitman, "you may take the harnesses off the horses, we'll have a half holiday to talk with James, and it would be too bad to put old Frank into the team the first day he came home."

It was a matter of necessity that James should (after conversing with Mr. Whitman, and telling him all the news in regard to his brother's family) go directly to Mr. Conly's, carry letters, and tell him and his wife everything in relation to their daughter, her husband and the grandchildren, interesting for them to know. It was, however, not accomplished that afternoon or even in the evening, of which it consumed a large portion, but required so many evenings that at length it began to attract attention.

"James goes to the Conlys a great deal. Do you think he has any particular reason?" said Mr. Whitman to his wife.

"I don't know. Mr. Conly's was the first place he ever went to; he and Edward are great friends; always have been. The master, you know, worked here all one summer and has always tried to help James from the start. I think it would be strange if he didn't go there a good deal, especially as he goes nowhere else."

"I know all that, but I am of the same mind still."

"Bertie knows; I mean to ask him."

Mrs. Whitman interrogated Bertie, but though generally so communicative, he was all at once very reticent.

"Bertie, your father and myself are the best friends James has in the world, and your father is able to help James if he is so minded. If there is anything in this, you know and ought to tell us, for it will go no farther."

"Well, mother, if you must know, he's dying for Emily, and she's dying for him."

"Then why don't he tell her so? There's not a better girl in the country, nor more capable."

"Because he imagines a host of things. He thinks because she and her folks know all about his coming out of a workhouse, and she knows what he was when he first came here, and how he was picked upon and scouted at school, they must kind of look down upon him; that though they might pity him, treat him as a friend and try to help him along, it would be another thing if he wanted to come into the family, and even if they didn't care they might think other people would, and throw it up at them that she was going with a *redemptioner*."

"That's all the merest nonsense, and his imagination. I go there with him, and after a little while get up to go; then up he'll jump and go with me, though they ask and urge him to stop. He'll go home from meeting with her, and sometimes I go with them on purpose, and she'll ask us to go in, I'll say I must go, and give him a punch in the ribs to go in, but no, off he comes with me. I know by what Ed. says the old folks would like it, and I tell him he can't expect her to break the ice, and would not want her to. I wish I could shut them up together, I'd starve them to it as they do a jury."

"If they like each other, and it suits all round,—I know it would suit William and his wife; he wrote a long letter to your father, and sent it by James, in which he said everything good about James that he could say, and has made him promise to trap with him next winter,—and if there is nothing in the way but James' diffidence, it will take care of itself. There never was a man yet who liked a woman and didn't find some way to let her know it."

"Yes, mother, she may know; I expect she knows it now, but how shall she know it enough?"

"There will be some way provided."

James and the boys concluded to sow their land with wheat and grass seed, as this was their last year, Mr. Whitman finding the grass seed. Matters went on in their regular course till the beginning of wheat harvest, when Mrs. Conly sent for Mrs. Whitman to come over there and spend the afternoon, and for Mr. Whitman to come to tea.

"I have had a letter from Mary," said Mrs. Conly, "and she is just crazy for me to let Emily come on with James Renfew this fall, when he goes to trap, and come back with him in the spring, she does so long to see some of us: and she can't come on account of the baby, and it's such a good chance. I thought I never could let Emily go over the mountains. I don't see how I can; and I want to talk it over with you."

After weighing the matter all round, these sage counsellors concluded that Mary Whitman ought in reason to be gratified; she was away there in the woods; and it was natural that she should want to see her sister, or some of her folks; and she was so lonely when William was away trapping. There could be no danger from Indians, since General Wayne had chastised them so severely.

"I have not said a word to Emily yet. It may be that she will be afraid to venture so far, for she never was from home a night in all her life."

"I think she'll go," said Mrs. Whitman; "she thinks so much of her sister, and these young folks are venturesome."

When the matter was broached to Emily, "though she was at first," as her mother said, "struck all up in a heap," yet she consented, *on her sister's account*, to venture.

When Mrs. Whitman, after going home, broached the matter to James, she feared, as the good woman told her husband, he would faint away; for he turned as many colors as a gobbler-turkey when a red cloth is held before him.

As for Bertie he was in raptures.

"Could anything be more nice, mother? How happened it to come just now?"

"Nothing could be more natural, Bertie; Mary Whitman has been teasing her mother ever since she was married, to let Emily come out there, and when she found James was coming again to trap, she was just furious, and there was no doing anything with her.

"You must go over there with James to-night, for Mrs. Conly will want to know about it and encourage him, for I am afraid he will appear so diffident that Mrs. Conly, and perhaps Emily too, will think he don't want her to go with him, though I know better than that."

"If he does, mother, I'll pull every spear of hair out of his head. Oh, I wish it was me instead of him, I'd make my best bow, so, mother (suiting the action to the word), and I'd say that nothing would give me greater pleasure than to enjoy the company of Miss Conly, and that I considered it a privilege to be the instrument of cheering Mrs. Whitman in her loneliness."

"Ay, you are very brave, but if it was your own case, you might, perhaps, be as bad as James."

"I don't believe that, mother, but I mean to come home early and leave James there if I can."

Bertie, however, came home before eight o'clock and with him James, who went directly to his bedroom. The moment the door closed after James, Bertie exclaimed,—

"It's all fixed, mother."

"What's fixed?"

"About her going with him. I told him what to say; he didn't say half what I told him, nor the way I told him, but it came to about the same thing."

"If he had he would have appeared ridiculous."

"Why, mother?"

"Because your manner of expressing yourself would have appeared as much out of the way from his lips as would your head on his shoulders."

"I mean to tell him that the journey is his chance, and if he don't improve it he'll never have another, and never ought to."

"You had a great deal better tell him that Emily never would have consented to go with him, and her parents would never have let her go, if both she and they had not reposed the utmost confidence in him, neither would Mary Whitman have made the request; and that will encourage him to overcome his bashfulness."

"Mother, how much better you can plan than I can."

"She has had a good deal of experience in managing men," said Mr. Whitman, who had been a silent, but by no means indifferent listener.

"Husband, do you want me to box your ears?"

CHAPTER XX.
JAMES AND EMILY.

They set forward the first week in September. James had left everything but his rifle and ammunition in the wilderness, and on his way home had stopped every night at a tavern or farm-house. He therefore had nothing to carry of any consequence, and put a pack-saddle on his colt, which Mr. Whitman had broken in the course of the winter, and in the pockets of the saddle put all Miss Conly's clothes, flint and steel, provender, pepper and salt, and mugs to drink out of, and knives and forks. Behind the saddle of Miss Conly's horse was strapped a round valise, in which she carried her needles and some clothing and light articles. When the weather was pleasant they put up only at night at the taverns, which were generally poor; halting at noon by some stream or pleasant spot that afforded grass for the horses. At such times James would often shoot game and cook it on the coals, or catch a fish in the stream, and they would lunch.

The diffidence of James gradually wore off as he became better acquainted with his companion and found how implicitly she relied upon him for care and protection, but that very fact, coupled with his high sense of honor, prevented him from giving voice to the words that were often upon his lips, because he felt that to do this when they were alone in the wilderness was taking an undue advantage and placing her in an embarrassing position,—and more terrible still, should he meet with a refusal, how awkward and constrained would be their positions going back together, as go they must in the spring.

He could not, however, endure the thought of going into the woods before the matter was settled, and remaining in a state of suspense all winter. They were now within a day's journey of Pittsburg and James had not effected the purpose nearest his heart. He now began to accuse himself for having neglected on the road opportunities that would never occur again, for at Pittsburg they would be in a crowded tavern; and at William Whitman's his stay would be brief, and there would occur no opportunities so favorable as many he had suffered to pass by unimproved.

The sun was setting as they neared the Scotch settler's, where James had before been made so welcome, and Pittsburg was but two miles away. Mr. Cameron was seated bareheaded on the door-stone with his wife, watching the children, who were frolicking with a calf they were rearing. Hearing the tread of horses, he looked up and instantly coming forward, said,—

"Gude e'en, Maister Renfew, I am blythe to see you, and to find that you like us weel eneuch to be ganging this way again."

"I never enjoyed myself better than I did last winter, and I am glad to find you and your family all in good health, for I see they are all here. This is Miss Conly, a sister to Mrs. Whitman, and is going to spend the winter with her."

"I'm right glad to see baith you and the lassie, and now light ye down and the gude wife'll gie ye some supper in the turning of a glass, and ye'll spend the Sabbath wi' us, and Monday morning ye can gang on rejoicing,"

"You are very kind, Mr. Cameron, but it is early and we can get to Pittsburg before it is very late."

"I'll niver consent to it. The horses are weary, so is the lassie; I ken it by the glance of her een. Ye'll surely not travel on the Lord's day, bating necessity, and the tavern at Pittsburg is no place for Christian people on the Sabbath, for there will be brawling and fighting and mayhap bloodshed between the flat-boat men."

"Take the beasts by the bridles, Donald," said his wife, "while I put on the kettle. What ails ye that ye dinna do it? We hae room eneuch for ten people, let alone twa, and what's mair a hearty welcome."

THE SCOTCH SETTLERS' WELCOME. Page 284.

James could not have arranged matters so well for himself. Inwardly rejoicing, he assisted Miss Conly to alight, and they were ushered into the best room of the hospitable abode. While the travellers washed and rested a little from the fatigue of a long ride, Mrs. Cameron had prepared a backwoods supper.

"We have had worship," said Mr. Cameron, "before ye came, but an ye are not too weary I wad like to sing a psalm or two; it's seldom we hae any one wi' us can sing."

After spending an hour so pleasantly as to make James and Emily forget the fatigue of their journey, they retired for the night.

The evening had thus been fully occupied, and James, his courage screwed by despair to the sticking point, had as yet found no opportunity for a private interview.

When Sunday morning came, Emily told Mrs. Cameron if she would like to attend meeting with her husband, she would take care of the children and get the meals, to which the former replied that she would gladly go, as she seldom could leave the children, and Mr. Cameron's brother was to have a child christened that Sabbath.

Thus were they left alone, with the exception of the children, who were most of the time out of doors or in the barn. It seemed indeed a most auspicious moment; but, although ever approximating like a moth flying around a candle, James could not summon courage to declare himself in broad daylight. Mr. Cameron and his wife most likely would be inclined to sing till bedtime, and thus the opportunity that seemed at the outset so favorable, would in all probability have resulted in disappointment had not a fortunate circumstance prevented so untoward an occurrence.

Mr. Cameron was to deliver a load of wheat at Pittsburg by sunrise Monday morning, and intended to rise at twelve o'clock in order to eat, load his grain and reach the landing in season, as it was going into a flat-boat.

Her husband, unsuspecting soul, thought it was the most natural thing in life that Mrs. Whitman's sister should come to visit her, and come with this young man who was going right there; and was anxious even at the expense of his rest to indulge in a psalm or two. But his shrewder helpmeet divined that there was a feeling stronger than that of friendship between her guests, and when supper and worship were finished, ushered them into the best room, and begging them to excuse herself and husband, as he was to start at one of the clock or soon after, and she must rise at twelve to get his breakfast, left them together.

James found that, like many other things in life, the anticipation was worse than the reality, and though he could not the next morning have told the words he had uttered in that little parlor, he was very sure that Emily Conly had promised to be his wife, provided her parents were willing, and that he was the happiest fellow that night that the stars looked down upon.

They took no note of time till they heard Mrs. Cameron up stairs getting up, and had barely opportunity to scud to their beds before she came down stairs.

Mr. Cameron had seen William Whitman Sunday at meeting, and notified him of their being at his house, and when they arrived at Pittsburg they found William, his wife, with the baby, and Jane Montgomery. It was a joyful meeting, for the two sisters were tenderly attached to each other.

"James," said William Whitman, "we'll put everything into the birch and get in ourselves and go home in fine style. Jane Montgomery will take both the horses along."

When they had proceeded about seven miles and become a little satiated with conversation, William struck up a tune in which they all joined, for it was one which William and the sisters with the rest of the family were accustomed to sing sitting on the door-step at home. Before going into the woods James wrote to Mr. Conly and obtained the consent of the parents on condition that he should not carry her over the Alleghenies to live, for they could not bear to have the mountains between them and the remaining daughter.

They began trapping earlier this year; and abandoning the eastern branch of the stream that had been trapped out, took the western branch and went farther up, which necessitated the building of some new camps, but they found more beaver, and being so much earlier upon the ground, before the bears went into winter quarters, were enabled to kill several; likewise found more otters, and James, having had the advantage of a winter's practice, was more successful, and in the spring they divided six hundred and fifty dollars between them.

During the journey that James made on his way back the year before to the Susquehannah, he had been very much pleased with the beauty and fertility of the limestone soil in the valley of that stream. Settlements had been made there as early as 1778, but latterly a new county had been formed, a town had been laid out just above the mouth of Lycoming Creek that emptied into the west branch of the Susquehannah River, and a road had been laid out to a painted post, where it struck the road to New York.

The Susquehannah was navigable, spring and fall, down to the Swatara, the home of the Conlys and Whitmans, and with a birch at any time of year. This was quite different from a market at New Orleans by water two thousand miles away, with hostile Indians on the banks of the stream, or by wagon road to Baltimore, and across the mountains to Philadelphia, four horses being required to haul twenty hundred weight, and occupying six weeks' time. He now proposed to Emily that they should return that way and view together that country. They found that the lands in the valley bordering directly on the river were held very high, much above James' means, but that a short distance up the creek that was navigable for small craft, land equally good could be bought for two dollars an acre, and could be paid for in gales, as it was termed, that is, by instalments extending to three years or even five.

"I do not incline, Emily," said James, "to put myself in such a position that I must wait till I am past labor and enjoyment both, before I can obtain sufficient to be comfortable. I think it is better to pay more for land that is improved and nearer a market, even if you have to wait longer in the first place, for after you once purchase you must remain or sell at a loss."

The landlord of the public-house told James of two places in the vicinity that had been improved and could be bought; one of which, he said, was owned by proprietors, had a log house and hovel on it with twenty acres cleared, and which they held at ten dollars an acre, one hundred and sixty acres.

"That," said James, "is the asking price."

"They are rich and will not take less; they know land will never be worth less on this creek."

The other place, he said, was a great deal better place, better land and better location, because it was on the stream, while the other was a back lot. It had been bought and paid for by a Mr. Chadwick, but it took all he had to pay for the land, and having not a cent to help himself with, and having to work part of the time for others, he could not make much improvement, and became broken down with hard work and discouragement, and died in the struggle the winter before; that his widow and two little children were at her brother-in-law's at the mouth of the creek, and she was anxious to sell, but would only sell for cash; that it would have been bought long before but the majority of settlers could not pay down; he never had been on it, but believed the buildings were not much and the lot was a hundred acres.

"If the place is as good as you represent, and joins the land of the proprietors, and will be sold cheap for cash, why don't they buy it?"

"They mean to buy it, but are holding off to get it at their own price because she is poor, and they know she will be obliged to sell, and I wish that somebody would come along who has the money and take it from between their teeth."

"You don't know what she asks?"

"She did ask nine dollars; don't know what she asks now."

Obtaining directions from the landlord, they set out to see the places. After about four miles' travel over a good road they then struck into the woods over a road of very different character, but nevertheless a very good one for the backwoods. The stumps were cut low to permit the passage of wheels, many of them taken out, the large rocks removed and the brooks and gullies bridged in some places with hewn timber, in others with round logs or flat stones. They passed through clearings on which were log and timber houses, some of them underpinned with stones and pointed with lime mortar, and most of the houses built, of round logs, were chinked with stone pointed with lime mortar, the chimneys were all built of stone laid in lime mortar, and on most of the farms were peach orchards. This road had been made by proprietors to increase the value of their lands, and in dry weather was a very tolerable road for teams; they also passed a limestone quarry, near which was a rude kiln.

They now reached the proprietor's lot; a clearing of twenty acres had been made, ten of which were in grass, the rest pasture. A timber house of two stories, hovel built of logs, and hogsty and corncrib; the house had three rooms on the lower floor, stone fireplace, chimney and oven laid in lime mortar, two glazed windows in each room and in front; between the house and the road was a peach orchard in bearing, and a hop vine was clinging to the corner of the house. A spring in the head of a ravine ten rods from the dwelling afforded water.

James judged that the land was of fair quality, but broken and heavily timbered. After examining all that portion of the lot under culture, and the buildings, they rode on six miles farther, when they came to a very large pine-tree, hollow, blazed, and that bore the marks of fire. This tree had been given to James as a mark, and stood at the head of a bridle path which they followed, and soon came in sight of the creek, and rode through a beautiful stretch of level land, alluvial soil, and extending along the stream. In the centre of this clearing stood a great sugar maple, and beneath its lofty branches was nestled a diminutive camp, built of small logs, rather poles, stuffed with moss and clay. It was evident that stones were either not to be found upon this place or else the occupant had not cattle to haul them, as the fireplace was made of logs with a lining of clay, and small stones evidently water-worn and procured from the brook.

A large branch had been torn from the tree by the wind, and falling on the roof and chimney that was made of sticks coated with clay, had crushed in both roof and chimney. Within ten feet of the door a beautiful spring was bubbling out from beneath the spur roots of the maple. The hovel was much larger and higher than the dwelling, which would not have admitted a horse, being too low, and boasted a good bark roof; it was of sufficient size to contain six head of cattle and considerable hay.

It was already far past noon and they sat down by the spring to quench their thirst, bait their horses and partake of a luncheon.

"It is," said James, "idle for us to think any more of the other place at present, as it is beyond my means, and I will not run in debt, my only object in looking at it was to compare prices. It is possible this place may not do, but there is not time to examine as thoroughly as I should like, we will go back and come again to-morrow."

They returned again next morning in such season as to have the greater part of the day before them, and after a thorough examination, James said,—

"This place is worth two of the other for any poor man to get his living on, and I know if it will come within my means it is the place for me. What do you think of it. Do you feel as though you could ever make it feel like home?"

"My home will be where my husband finds it for his interest to be, and there shall I be content and happy, provided I can have sheep and cows, and flax, and spinning and weaving enough to do, that I may carry my part of the load in the way mother brought me up from childhood. But, to tell the truth, I should not have to try very hard to like this place, for it is the sweetest spot I ever saw."

"I like the place, but must be governed entirely by the possibility of being able to pay for it and to get my living from it afterwards."

"I can't help feeling a little sad as I sit by this spring of which they drank, look upon that roof that once sheltered them, now all fallen in, and recollect that they came here no doubt building castles in the air as you and I do, and full of hope as we are, thinking what they would do; and then the husband was taken sick and, as the landlord expressed it, died in the struggle for a homestead."

"The man died," said James, who had not one bit of sentiment about him, "of a broken heart, and the reason that his heart broke was because he paid his last cent for land, and looked no farther, a thing no man should ever do."

"Perhaps he liked the place, and his wife liked it, and wanted to live here and nowhere else."

"I like the place, but I shall not buy it and go on it without a cent."

James ascertained that the stream in its windings had formed a tongue of alluvial soil equal in extent to all the cleared land on the place, and which was concealed from his view the day before by the forest. It was overflowed and dressed by the spring and fall freshets and bore an abundance of grass, and by cutting a few bushes and removing the rafts of driftwood could be enlarged. This added vastly to the value of the land, particularly to an emigrant, as a stock of cattle could be kept at once, the openings in the woods affording with the browse sufficient pasturage in summer. He also found that the next lot of a hundred and sixty acres was government land, could be bought for two dollars an acre, or one dollar and sixty cents cash, and that on this lot was a mill-site.

"Now, Emily, we have seen all there is to be seen, and talked the matter over, I want to know if you like this place well enough for a home, because when I go to see this woman to know if she will take what I can give, I shall close the bargain. My own mind is made up that for me this is home."

"My mind is made up; this is my home."

The next morning, James went to find Mrs. Chadwick. She held the place at nine dollars an acre; said she had held it at ten; that everybody who was a judge of land said that it was worth more than the Ainsworth place, that the proprietors held at ten dollars, and that she must have cash.

James replied that the place had no buildings but a brush camp, only six acres cleared; that he expected to pay cash, but not so much as that.

Mrs. Chadwick said in reply, as James very well knew, that though there were but six acres cleared, yet by reason of the natural grass that grew on the intervale, it cut as much hay as the other place, that had twenty acres cleared by fire and axe.

After talking a while she fell to eight and a half. James replied that he compassionated her misfortunes, and wished she might get ten dollars, and even more, per acre, but that he was a young man just starting in life, had but seven hundred and sixty dollars in the world, but could get enough more to make up to eight hundred, and would give that, she replied,—

"Can I have any time to think of it? I would like to consult my brother-in-law."

"I am going through here to-morrow on my way home. I will call then and get your mind."

When upon his return, he told what he had said to Mrs. Chadwick, Emily replied,—

"I do not see how you could offer eight hundred for the land, when you have got but seven hundred and sixty, and you have always said that you never would spend all you had, to get a piece of land, and then be obliged to go on it without a cent to help yourself with."

"Nor do I intend to do it either. Arthur Nevins has been coaxing me for several months to sell the colt to him. He's an extra colt, and I don't know but he'll make as good a horse as old Frank. He has offered me a hundred and ten dollars for him. I am going to ask him a hundred and twenty. I know he'll give it; if not, there's another who will, and I shall have eighty dollars left."

"Is that enough to begin with?"

"Many have begun with less, but that is not my method of looking at things. I shall work for Mr. Whitman this summer, trap with William next winter, and if Mrs. Chadwick takes me up, go on to the place in the spring or early in the fall. If she won't sell, I shall by that time have sufficient, by the blessing of God,—as grandfather, if he was living, would say,—to buy a place in this region equally good. There are always people enough who are unfortunate or fickle-minded, who want to sell."

James slept but very little that night, for his heart was set upon getting that land, and more especially since he saw that his companion was equally desirous of making it her home.

Miss Conly had told the landlord's wife that James could run land, and by the time they were up in the morning, the landlord told James that there was a gentleman in the bar-room inquiring for a surveyor, for the only person in that place who surveyed land was sick with a rheumatic fever, and asked him if he could go, to which James replied that he had no instruments with him, but the landlord urged him to go and see the man, for doubtless they could obtain the sick man's chain and compass. James told the man if it was merely measuring land to ascertain the number of rods, feet or acres, he would go after he had met his engagement with Mrs. Chadwick, but if it was a matter of contested lines, he must get some person of more experience. The man replied there was no other person to be obtained without going a great distance, that there was no dispute about titles, but his work would be merely to divide a large body of land into lots, and lay out roads through it.

James lost no time in going to see the lady, who by the advice of her relatives, had concluded to accept his offer, and he paid her fifty dollars to hold the bargain till he could obtain the money at home. The next day he went on the survey, and was occupied five days, at two dollars and seventy-five cents a day, and paid but a trifle for the use of the instruments.

"Grandfather was right," said James, as they rode away from the inn, "when he urged me to study surveying, and would make me, when Saturday afternoons came and I wanted to work in the shop, go with Walter Conly and measure and plot land, and learn the use of instruments. He said it would put many a dollar in my pocket, and it has already put in almost fourteen."

CHAPTER XXI.
THE BRUSH CAMP.

Great was the uproar when Bertie and Peter found that James was going to sell the colt.

"Husband," said Mrs. Whitman, "I do hope you are not going to let James part with that colt he has brought up, and thinks so much of. Give him the money to pay for his land,—he only lacks forty dollars,—and let him keep his colt."

But Mr. Whitman was firm. "James," he said, "was getting along well, let him struggle, it was better for him, too much help was worse than none; when he is sick or unfortunate 'twill be time enough to give him. I had rather give him a chance to help himself," and with that view he gave him twenty-seven dollars a month for the summer, and also half an acre to plant or sow, and Bertie and Peter the same.

James sent on his money and received a deed of the land, and through Mr. Creech, the landlord with whom he had put up, made arrangements with Prescott, his nearest neighbor, to fell the trees on an acre of land.

When the time drew near for James to start for the Monongahela, Bertie said to him,—

"What will you do for a horse now you have sold the colt? I mean to ask father to let you have Frank."

"I don't want him, Bertie, as I shall go right to my place from trapping, and you will want Frank early in the spring. I have nothing to carry but a rifle; my traps are all there. I shall go afoot or in one of the wagons that haul goods over the mountains, and in the spring I can buy a horse there or a mule for ten dollars, and sell him this side of the mountains for seventy-five, perhaps a hundred."

The night before he started, Miss Conly said to him,—

"You will be at work on the place before we meet again, I want you to promise me one thing, and that is that you will not tear down the camp, for I intend to live in it."

"That is the very first thing I intended to do."

"I thought as much; well, don't you do it, I don't want you should."

"But you wouldn't think of moving into such a place as that, and I could not consent that you should."

"Why not? Did not Mrs. Chadwick live there four years with a sick husband and two little children? I hope I can do what any other woman has done."

"I don't doubt that, but there is no necessity. I intend in the spring to get Mr. Prescott's oxen and haul some of the trees he will cut this fall to the spot, hew them, and put up a comfortable timber house."

"You will have work enough to do without that. It is a great expense to *begin*; we must lessen it all we can. It will be but little work to repair that camp, and when we are on the spot and you have cattle of your own, and your tools are all there, you can do it in the intervals of other work, and can do it much more to your mind."

"That is all true, Emily, but——"

"But what?"

"Do you think I want to take you into the woods to suffer?"

"I have not the least idea of suffering unless I am called to. Then, I trust, I shall be supported. Tell me honestly, cannot such a camp be made comfortable? You know well enough what I mean by that?"

Thus appealed to, James hesitated, looked every way but at her, and finally said,—

"It is true that the camp can be made a shelter from rain and snow, and can be kept warm."

"Warm enough?"

"Yes, hot as an oven, for it is not much larger," said James, with a groan; "but what a hole to take you from a good home and put you into."

"I was born in a log house and passed my childhood in it, and one not much better than that camp, nor much larger, and there were seven of us. Sister and William tell of what they have been through. Father and mother and our boys are always telling the neighbors of how much William and Mary have been through and how resolute they are and faculized. I mean to have something to tell of and be praised for. Come, promise, you may put down a floor in the camp and make it three poles higher, that I may have room for my loom and

166

spinning wheel, and that the wheels and loom may stand firm on the floor. I don't care whether there's any chimney or not. We didn't have any in our log house for years, and the hole in the roof was about as good, for the clay was all the time falling off the cob-work and dropping into mother's pots and frying-pan."

"You won't want to stay there long, I hope?"

"Only till we can see our way clear to build a log house."

James reluctantly promised, and they parted. He set forth, mounted on Frank. Bertie took Dick and accompanied him to the foot of the North Mountain. He then took his pack and rifle, and proceeded on foot, while Bertie went back with the horses.

Starting much earlier in the season than before, they abandoned the Big Beaver and went on the Little Beaver, and far up that stream. They met with fewer beavers, but more otters, and took in log traps and in one large steel trap which they possessed, and by killing with the rifle, more bears than ever before, so that although they went farther and came out of the woods much earlier (as James wanted to go on his land), they obtained furs to the amount of five hundred and twenty-five dollars. When they were at the mouth of the Little Beaver, on their return, they met some Delaware Indians on their way to Pittsburg, encamped on the bank of the main river, their canoes turned up on the grass.

"I want a birch as I am going to live on a stream. I wonder if I can buy one, of these Indians?" said James.

"You can buy anything of an Indian, but his rifle or tomahawk, but if you buy one take that dark-colored one, even if they ask more for it, because the bark of which it is made was peeled in the winter and it is worth, double."

"I thought bark wouldn't run in the winter?"

"It will if you pour hot water on it or hold a torch to the tree."

James, after considerable talk with the Indians, who wanted him to take another one, bought the dark-colored birch. It was twenty-eight feet in length, twenty inches deep, and four feet six inches wide. It required a person possessed of the strength of James to carry it, as it was a load for two Indians, but James, much to the astonishment of the savages, turned the birch over his head and took it to the water. He now took all his traps and some tools that he had carried to make dead-falls, and parted with William and Mary, much to their regret, as they had cherished the hope that he would settle near *them*.

Jonathan Whitman had told him before he left home if he could find a good young horse that would weigh twelve hundred, and was used to team work, to buy him, for Frank was failing somewhat, and he wanted to favor his faithful servant and should not work him much more. He hired a wagoner to haul the traps and canoe and other articles to the Susquehannah at Harristown, bought a horse, pack-saddle, and some tools; an axe, auger, trowel, chain, and handsaw, irons made at a blacksmith's to peel bark, irons for a whiffletree. He also bought some white paper and oiled it, and a window sash with six squares of glass in it, put his traps and other matters into the birch, and managed at a small expense to send his horse to Mr. Creech his former landlord. He then got into the birch and, having a fair wind to start with, made a sail of his blanket, and by alternate sailing and paddling landed at length in the early twilight before his own camp. At the gray dawn and while it was still dark in the forest, he took his way to the brook with his rifle on his arm, and returned with two wood-ducks, one of which together with the provisions in his pack, furnished him with a substantial breakfast.

His nearest neighbor, Prescott, had been ten years on his clearing and kept a large stock of cattle. His family consisted of three strong, active boys, Dan, the eldest, being nineteen, which enabled him to work for others when disposed. James had engaged with Prescott the previous spring to cut all the grass to be found in the field pasture and openings in the woods, and to fell in the course of the summer an acre of trees; upon looking around he found the work all done, and the felled trees in just the right state to burn.

James now sat down under the shadow of the great maple to reflect, and lay his plans for a summer's work, and to make the most of his means. He had left in Bertie's care at Swatara, when he went into the woods, two hundred and fifteen dollars, after paying for his land. This money was the result of the sale of the colt, his summer's work with Mr. Whitman, the proceeds of his potato crop, and the money he had earned on his way home by surveying. He could not expect however to obtain two dollars and three quarters a day in future for surveying, two dollars was the customary price, but in the former case he was delayed on his journey, and kept on expense, and his employer had not the time to go for another surveyor at a great distance.

When James left Mr. Whitman's he took but five dollars with him. He obtained his birch of the Indians by barter, letting them have some of his traps in exchange. They had sold their furs at Pittsburg; but the buying of the horse, tools, and other expenses, and the money due Mr. Prescott for labor, brought it down to about one hundred and eighty-six dollars, and there was much still to be bought. The money for the horse, however, would be repaid by Mr. Whitman, who would take the beast off his hands, and in the meantime James would have the use of him. He had carpenter's tools enough for ordinary purposes, but not a single farming implement, not even a narrow axe, only a broad axe, and no seed to sow or plant, and all the harness he had in which to work his horse was a pack-saddle, an open bridle, and no description of cart or sled.

Having matured his plans, he cooked the remaining duck for his dinner, put in his purse the money he intended to use, hid the rest under a heap of stones, and swinging his pack started for Prescott's.

When settling with him he found that there was a great difference in wages between the place he was now in and Swatara. He could hire Prescott for fifty cents a day, his oxen at the same price, and Dan for two shillings.

Arriving at Creech's, he was received with great cordiality, and found there his horse and pack-saddle. He inquired in regard to the surveyor, and was informed that the rheumatic fever had left him a cripple on crutches.

"The best thing you can do, Mr. Renfew," said Creech, "if you mean to settle here, is to buy his instruments." James bought them for fifteen dollars, and told Creech if he heard of any one that wanted land run, to send them to him.

He bought a narrow axe, and what farming tools he needed for the present, and some rope and nails, and returned; put the fire into his trees, and got a good burn. With the rope and cedar-bark for a breastplate he contrived, by chopping the logs into short lengths, to twitch and roll them together sufficiently for a second burn, and planted his corn. He was dropping the last kernels of his corn when a man, sent by the proprietors, came to ask if he would go twenty miles into the woods to lay out a road, and measure some lots; that they would send three men to his place, one to carry the chain, and two to clear the way, if he concluded to go. They thought it would take about ten days.

James replied that he must have the next day to make his preparations, and would then be ready to go.

He hired Prescott to plough and sow to wheat two acres of ground; plant half an acre with potatoes, except a few rods reserved for beans.

When James returned, his first care was to peel hemlock bark, and put the bark under pressure to flatten the sheets to cover the roof, and to cut the timber for the roof, and logs to raise the walls, and haul them to the camp.

There was a mill at the mouth of the creek, and from thence he brought, in his birch, boards to lay a floor, make an outside door and a large chest, with a cover and partings, for cornmeal and flour.

James rather exceeded the instructions of Emily, and raised the wall high enough to make a good chamber above; laid the floor with boards, and made a ladder to reach it.

He went seven miles to a limekiln and brought lime in the pockets of the pack-saddle, that would contain half a bushel each, and built a fireplace and chimney of stones, with the chimney at the end of the camp and outside, thus affording more room.

The camp was twenty feet long by twelve wide; he put a bark partition across at thirteen feet, leaving a room of seven feet by twelve. This room he divided by a bark partition into a bedroom and a storeroom; the doors were a bear's skin and a blanket hung up. His single glazed window and two windows filled with oiled paper were put in the kitchen, as there all the spinning, weaving and sewing was to be done, and the most light would be needed. In the intervals of hoeing he cleared a road to the highway, and made it passable with wheels by great labor and two days' help from Prescott and his boys.

Haying and wheat harvest were now at hand. There was not a pair of wheels in the whole section of country in which James lived; the settlers hauled their hay and grain on sleds, or carried it on poles and hand-barrows. James contrived a singular vehicle for the present necessity. He hewed out two pieces of tough ash eighteen feet in length, fashioned one end of each into the form of cart-arms, and by pouring on hot water bent the other ends to a half circle; he then spread them the width of a sled, put cross-bar and whiffletree on, and two stakes behind the cross-bar and some light slats across. The trouble now was in respect to a harness; the rope traces did as well as leather, but the breastplate of cedar-bark needed constant renewal, and he had neither saddle or lugs to support the arms. He put a torch on the stem of the birch, paddled about five miles up the creek in the night, and shot a deer that attracted by the light came to the water's edge. With this rough hide he went to Prescott, who had shoemaker's tools, and by doubling the hide made a breastplate that would bear all the horse could pull; he also made lugs to support the arms and put them over the pack-saddle, and on this he hauled hay and grain, and even stones; it went much easier than a sled would have done, because there was less surface to drag on the ground, and a good portion of the weight was on the horse's back. As he had neither barn nor threshing-floor, when his grain was ripe he threshed it on a platform of timber placed on the ground, and the hovel being filled with hay, stored it in the kitchen as a makeshift, and went to ask advice of Prescott, who he knew began very poor and had passed through many similar exigencies.

"You may put it in my barn, Mr. Renfew, but there is a better method than that. There are a great many emigrants passing along the valley of the Susquehannah going west, and a good many settling round the mouth of the creek. They want supplies. Grain and pork have gone up, and the miller is buying all the old corn and grain he can get to grind, and all the new wheat, and storing it for a rise. I have no doubt you could sell it."

The next day James received a letter from Bertie, who informed him that during the winter his father and Peter had made him a wagon to move with, and his mother had woven the cloth to cover it, and as he was not much of a mechanic he was going to paint it as his share of the work.

James wrote Bertie to thank his father and mother and Peter, and to ask his father to put in a tongue suitable for cattle to work, as he should move with oxen.

He now went to the mill and sold his wheat for ninety cents, and carried it down in the birch; it measured sixty bushels. He brought back some flour, cornmeal, a grindstone, pork, and a keg of molasses.

"This is better than living on the Monongahela," said James to himself; "there wheat won't pay to carry over the mountains or down the Ohio, but it will pay to carry it yourself in a birch down a creek."

He now dug a potato hole in which to store his potatoes for the winter, and built over it a log house eight feet in width and fourteen in length, underpinned it, and pointed the underpinning with lime mortar, hewed the logs at top and bottom, put on a bark roof and laid a floor with flattened poles, and made a good door with wooden hinges and latch and two windows closed by shutters; here he put all his tools and traps, intending to make at some future time a workshop of it, and for the present it served as a convenient storehouse and protected his potatoes from freezing, otherwise he must have covered them with such a depth of earth that it would have been difficult to get at them during the winter.

He was now ready to set out for home; and mounting his horse rode to Prescott's, and exchanged his pack-saddle for a riding-saddle, and happened to mention to his neighbor that he had left a keg of molasses in the camp.

"You should not have done that, for if a bear happens to come along and smells it, he'll set his wits at work to get to it."

"Is that so?"

"Sartain; a bear is raving crazy after molasses or honey or sugar; he'll stave the door in or make the bark fly off that roof a good deal faster than you put it on."

"Then what will become of my corn while I am away?"

"There will be nothing to hinder all the wild animals from helping themselves."

"They'll destroy it all before I get back."

"Oh, no, they won't! They may hurt it a good deal, and they may not. There's one thing in your favor: it is a great year for acorns and beech-nuts, and hickory, and all kinds of nuts and cranberries,—the bogs are full of cranberries, and the bears and coons love them dearly, so they won't be so hard upon the corn as they would otherwise be. But I don't think there are many bears round this fall; the coons and the turkeys are the worst, because there are so many of them; but the coons are ten times as bad as the wild turkeys, because there are so many of them, and they come when you are asleep—the turkeys come in the daytime, and a shot or two at them scares them off for a week, and they are first-rate eating. If they take the bread out of your mouth, they put meat into it."

"I wouldn't object to the bears if I was to be here—a bear's skin is worth about thirty bushels of corn."

"Ay; but you might lose your corn and not get the bear."

"I wish I had sowed wheat on the burn, I could have taken care of that before I went; but I think I'll go back and get the molasses, and leave it here."

"I think I can help you, neighbor. Here's my Dan; he's the master critter for hunting and trapping you ever saw—plagues me to death with his nonsense. He'd sit up two nights to shoot one coon. We arn't much driven with work now, and shan't be till you get back, and if you'll let him use some of your traps, I know he'd be tickled to death to live in your camp and hunt and trap; and you may depend on it no wild critter will do any damage while he's around, for he'd take the dog with him, and nothing can stir in the night but the dog will let him know it."

"I should be very glad to have him, and will pay him."

"The traps will be pay enough and more too."

"I should like to have him pull my beans and thresh 'em out."

"Yes, he can do that, and dig the potatoes and put them in the pit; he can do it as well as not; he'll have a great deal of idle time, and I don't want him to get too lazy; and so you won't need to go back after your 'lasses."

"It must be a great change to Miss Conly to leave a pleasant home and kind neighbors and come here, and I had thought of getting some hens. It would make it seem a little more like home to her to hear the hens cackle and the rooster crow, and have eggs to get; and if Dan is going to be there to feed 'em, I can have 'em as well as not."

"We can find you in hens, and Dan can take 'em down with him."

"What are they worth apiece? I'll take half a dozen."

"Look here, neighbor, hens nor geese nor turkeys ain't worth anything here 'cept to eat; there's no market for such things here. I perceive you have carpenter's tools, and know how to use them, which none of us do. Take all the hens you want, for I believe we've got a hundred, and if you could make me a good ox-yoke I should be more than paid; and any little thing that you can't do alone just call on the boys, and they or I will help you, and we will change about in that way. I can make things, to be sure—have ter—but it takes me forever, and then I'm ashamed to have any body see 'em, only shoes. I can make a good shoe or boot, and I can tan a hide or skin as well as anybody."

"Can you curry?"

"No, but it isn't much to carry a hide to the village to get it curried."

"There's one thing, Mr. Renfew, that I want to tell you," said Mrs. Prescott, "that you wouldn't be likely to think of, and that is to get a pig and have it in the pen when you get there. When we came on to this place we were eleven miles from neighbors, and you don't know how much company and comfort it was to me when Mr. Prescott was away at his work and before we had so many children, to hear a pig squeal and to have him to feed; and so it is to have a cat or a dog. When we have no company of our own kind, we take to the dumb creatures."

"Have you any pigs to spare, Mr. Prescott?"

"We've got a whole litter of late pigs and a dozen shoats, and there's a black and white kitten you may have; and when you come with your woman we want you to come right here, because you'll both be fatigued, and the wife won't want to go right to cooking the first moment, and then you can take the kitten and the pigs along with you. I wish we had a puppy for you; a dog is valuable to a new settler as well as company."

"I've got a dog at home if he has not forgotten me. I do not feel that I ought to put myself upon you; perhaps I shall have four oxen and other cattle when I come."

"No matter if there's ten oxen. Thank God there's room enough in house and barn, and victuals enough, and nothing will suit the boys better than to wait on you. You must pass your word, and then we shall know, for the good Book says, 'Better is a neighbor that is near, than a brother afar off.'"

James promised.

James reached home safely.

CHAPTER XXII.
THE WILDERNESS HOME.

They were married, and instantly began to make their preparations for departure. Emily took none of her nicer articles of housekeeping, nothing in the shape of furniture but a small looking-glass, saying that there was no room or use for them in the camp; and as they were not going west of the mountains, and James had a birch, and could come down the river, they could get them when they had more room and it was needful; that what she wanted most of all were her tools and necessary things. And she carried not only the fixtures for a loom, but the loom itself, wool, flax, dye-stuffs, wheels to spin flax and wool, cards, warping-bars, a quill-wheel, reels, a flax-comb, a Dutch-oven, plenty of pots and kettles, but one large pewter platter, three pewter plates and two earthen mugs; three milkpans, and a churn and milk-pail and skimmer, and two good beds; not a chair, nor even a chest of drawers. But as the wagon was of great size, and the team strong, they were able to carry an abundance of the implements that would enable them, as they were possessed of both brains and hands, to manufacture these other conveniences and comforts, and be really independent. James did much after the same fashion, taking a good stock of carpenter's tools, some cooper's tools, a brick trowel, horse-nails, and a shoeing-hammer, harrow-teeth, the irons and mould-board of a plough, and the iron fixtures, and the tools pertaining to a lathe.

"Mother," said Bertie, "they are just alike; isn't it queer? They want to take the same things; it's all tools with 'em both. James hasn't taken hardly anything but tools, except books."

"That is because they are both gifted with common sense, and mean to be comfortable, and not to make a failure of it."

James bought four oxen that measured six feet nine inches in girth. Mr. Conly gave his daughter a cow, and Mrs. Whitman gave James another, and Maria gave him six sheep. James had the cows and oxen shod, put the cows in a yoke, and fastened them behind the wagon.

When Mr. Whitman asked James why he preferred to move with oxen, when he was so fond of horses and was accustomed to handling them, he replied:

"On the score of economy;" that he had bought a pair of oxen for what the harnesses of two horses would have cost him, and the four for what two good horses would have cost, and then had more strength; that there was not much difference in the rate of travel, on a long road, between oxen and horses when they were both heavily loaded; and as he should not at first have a great deal of hay and grain, oxen could be kept on browse much better than horses; that he could make yoke and bows and all the gear for oxen himself, and if he wished could, at any time, sell the oxen for beef and buy horses when better able to keep the latter; and, finally, if like to starve, could eat them, and thus had one winter's provision in possession.

Bertie insisted upon going with them, and driving the team as far as Shamokin, while James rode on old Frank with his wife behind him on a pillion.

When they parted, Bertie said,—

"You needn't be surprised to see me up there on a piece of land. I don't mean to stay at home; and if you'll let me stay with you, I may buy a piece of land, and come up there and work on it."

"Then you had better keep right on with us," said Emily, "for I have no doubt you have some one in view for a future housekeeper."

"No, truly, the fact is, I like all the girls so well that I can't like any one to pick her out. I romp with 'em, quarrel with 'em, and then make up, and they are all just like sisters. Expect I must go among strangers to get one; but if I thought I'd got to go through such a tribulation, and suffer so much as James did in getting you, I never would undertake it."

"It will pay if you do, Bertie," said James.

The emigrants slept in the wagon, built a fire at night and morning, and cooked beside the roads; stormy days, put up, milked the cows, and exchanged the milk that they did not need themselves at the farm-houses for other articles of food; and the latter part of their journey, as they came into the unsettled portion of the country, James killed game. They reached Prescott's upon a Thursday at noon, and stopped till the next morning.

Mr. Prescott, without their knowledge, sent Clarence, the second boy, to inform Dan of their coming, with the pig and the kitten; and his wife sent butter, bread, and a boiled ham.

When the married pair reached the camp, they found the provisions on the table, a good fire, a camp-kettle full of hot water, a birch-bark dish full of eggs, the kitten in Dan's lap and the pig was squealing lustily in the hovel; while the rooster, jealous of the intruder, was flapping his wings on the roof of the camp, and crowing in defiance. The walls of the hovel were hung with the skins of coons, foxes, and two otters stretched on hoops; the beans were threshed, and the potatoes in the pit. The boys were invited to dinner as the first visitors, and as they had but three plates and two mugs, James and his wife ate and drank out of the same plate and mug, and gave the other vessels to the boys, who, after the meal, helped to unload the cart, set up the loom, and make other necessary arrangements, and took leave after an early supper.

They now retired to rest, not without first returning thanks for their safe arrival to the Being whose hand, unseen, had brought them safely hitherto, and given to the pauper boy a homestead and a helpmeet.

It was quite an important matter for James to prepare his workshop, as he had brought only the iron portion of his farming tools; and they had not a bowl, nor barrel, nor even a wash-tub. So, after they had arranged matters, and he had built a pigpen and dug out a trough, he went to the mill in the birch, and brought home plank for a work-bench, and hardwood stuff for the framework of his lathe, and to make a wheel and footboard; and pine-boards for shelves and racks to put his tools in, and to make drawers; and before the ground froze, he had, mostly on stormy days, made bowls and plates and trays of wood, two wash-tubs and a trough to salt pork in, and the wood-work both of a plough and harrow, and had cut down the great wagon to proper dimensions for farm labor.

When James went to mill after his lumber, he felt quite uneasy lest Emily, left thus alone in the woods, should feel unhappy and homesick; but, upon his return, he heard, as he came up the bank, the whir of the shuttle, and found her singing at the loom, with the kitten on the bench beside her.

"You seem in excellent spirits," said James, delighted to find her in this happy mood.

"Why should I not be? Plenty to eat, plenty to do, and a nice young man to take care of me."

James bought three shoats, and let them run in the woods, and every night and morning they came up to the hovel, and he fed them with milk and a little corn, and then they were off to the woods nutting and hunting for rattlesnakes.

James ground his axe, to cut logs and hew them, on the two sides, for the walls of a house; but Emily persuaded him to cut and hew timber for a frame barn, telling him the camp was good enough; that she did not want a house to take care of; she wanted to spin and weave, and get something to keep house with; that she was just as happy as she could be in the camp; and that he needed a barn to hold the hay he was now obliged to stack out; he also needed a barnfloor to thresh his grain and to store it afterwards.

Thus exhorted and encouraged, James, convinced that his wife was really well content to live in the camp, cut and hewed his barn frame in the winter, and also cut logs sufficient to make boards to cover it, and hauled them to the bank of the creek, sawed up bolts for shingles, and in the evening split out the shingles, and shaved them before the fire in the camp, enough for the barn and house both; had also cut logs enough to furnish boards for the roof of the house and for doors, window-frames and sashes, for he had tools to make sashes. When the spring freshet came, he rolled his logs into the stream, and hired two men, who were river-drivers, to drive them to the mill, and the first of April raised his barn, and had it fit to put hay in by the time it was needed, though the doors were not made till after wheat harvest.

A Mr. Litchfield, an emigrant, had bought the farm that James first looked at; it had taken all his means, and he was obliged to work out part of the time to get a little money and provisions. While at work on his barn, James hired Litchfield to clear three acres of land, and paid him in pork, wheat to sow, wheat flour to eat, and by letting him have his cattle to plough. That autumn James dug a cellar and stoned it, and in the winter hauled the logs to build the walls, and hewed them on two sides; hauled bricks from the mouth of the creek to build a chimney and put them in the hovel, which now made an excellent storehouse for the materials to build the house. Indeed, everything was done that could be done till the walls were raised; but Emily manifested no more desire for a house than at first, and still clung to the camp; and James sold pork and corn and flour to emigrants, who began to multiply, going west, and had caught coons and foxes and otters enough, in the previous fall and winter, to pay all the expense incurred in building his barn, and after all his expense in outfits and labor, was a hundred dollars better off in money than at the time he left the Monongahela.

Just after wheat harvest, James received a letter from Bertie, saying that if he would come to Swatara in his birch, himself and Ned Conly would return with him, and bring his sheep.

"I know what they want," said James; "they want to come in the birch, and see the rough side of life, and that's the reason they want to come now, while we are in the camp; but I wish we had a good house for them."

"I don't. They wouldn't have half so good a time; they want to see just what beginning in the woods is, and what they must come to if they take it up, and perhaps it will sicken them."

"It won't sicken Bertie. But where shall we put them? In the loft they will stifle this hot weather. If we give them our bedroom, and put our bed in the kitchen, there won't be room to eat, for the loom and the spinning-wheels take up the greater part of it."

"Put 'em in the barn."

"Indeed I won't put Bertie and your brother in the barn. I shouldn't sleep a wink myself."

"Take the cloth that was on the wagon and make a tent. You make the poles, and I'll cut and make the rest; put a good bed in it, and they can build a fire before it, and make believe they are Indians, if they want to. I know that'll suit Ned; he is running over with that sort of thing."

"You don't want any bed, Emily, Bert won't want that, I know. I'll make a bed of cedar brush, and spread a bearskin over it; do you make a good bolster and stuff it with straw, and I'll spread a wolfskin over that. I have a lot of skins that I didn't sell, thinking we might need them for bedding. Give them a blanket, a birch bark dish to drink out of, and hang up some otter and coon skins, round the tent; pitch it near the spring, and they'll be in kingdom come."

"I believe you are going to turn boy yourself. I didn't think you had any such notions about you."

"True, I never had any boyhood like other children; but I know the feelings of Bert and Ned, for all that, and I think it is as much my duty to make Bert happy, as it is to pray to God."

James arrived safely at Mr. Whitman's. The return voyage was not difficult, as there were three to paddle, and carry the canoe when needful, Ned and Bertie bringing their packs, as they intended to go back on foot, and by their actions, seemed to be going into training for the backwoods.

It was now two days over the time James had fixed as the probable date of his return. The sun was setting, and Emily was looking forward to another lonely night, when the report of two rifles in quick succession, told her they were at hand. Before she could reach the spot, James was climbing the bank, and she almost fell into her husband's arms.

"I am going to have part of that, Em," cried Ned, clasping her round the waist.

"And I too," said Bertie, coming up on the other side, while the overjoyed wife and sister fairly cried with excess of happiness.

"What is that?" said Bertie, catching a glimpse of the white covering of the tent in the gathering twilight.

"That's where we are going to put you," said James.

Bertie turned aside the cloth and peered in.

"Come here, Ned Conly; this is worth coming all the way here for."

"How glad I am, Bert, that we didn't wait till they had got a good house; then we should have had to sleep in the best room, with a linen spread, all wove in patterns, on the bed, and curtains."

"Yes, and had to wipe our feet every time we came into the house; but now" (and he turned a somersault on the bearskin) "we can get into bed with our boots on."

After a most bountiful supper, for Dan had killed a wild turkey, they retired pretty thoroughly fatigued to their tent. In the morning Bert said,—

"Now, James, we want to go all over your place to-day, and see all you've got and all you've done, and talk and loll and fool round, and the next day we want to go over the next two places, above and below, and then we are going to work."

"You are not going to do a stroke of work. I didn't bring you up here for that; I suppose you could have done that just as well at home."

"We are going to help thresh your grain," said Ned.

"My neighbors have threshed it since I went away. You are going thirty miles up the creek with me in the birch to catch trout in a brook, and to hunt deer and perhaps a bear."

"I go in for that," said Bert; "but after that you need not think you are going to keep us from doing something; you are putting on too many airs, prosperity is injuring you. Remember, young man, you have been to school to both of us."

They went on the hunt, and took Dan Prescott with them, had a glorious time, and Ned and Bert brought home a bearskin each; it is presumed they killed the bears.

The first night after they arrived home, Bertie said,—

"Now prick up your ears and hear the news. Ned, you tell."

"No, you tell; you can do it best."

"James, can these two places above and below be bought, and for how much?"

"For two dollars an acre. I have got the preemption" (right to purchase before another) "of the one above."

"Then you must buy 'em,—the upper one for me, and the lower for Ned Conly."

Emily, during this conversation, sat with clasped hands; and then running to Bert, taking him by both shoulders, said,—

"Bertie Whitman, are you telling the truth, or are you fooling?"

"The truth and nothing but the truth, my dear girl. Walter has concluded not to go to college. Your father has given the farm to him to take care of the old folks; my father is going to do the same by Peter. Ned and I have got to shirk for ourselves, and are going to shirk up to Lycoming; that is, by and by, but we want to make sure of the land before we go back."

Ned Conly was an adept at handling tools, and as James had the materials for the house all on the spot, the cellar prepared, and the logs hewn, they put up the house, moved into it, and harvested the potatoes and corn before the boys went back. Ned Conly was engaged to Jane Gifford. He married her, and came on to his place the next year. Bert came the next year after Ned, built a log house on his place, and a saw-mill, as his father supplied him with abundant means, and boarded with James three years, when he married the daughter of Henry Hawkes, a neighbor of James; and in the course of five years more Arthur Nevins and John Edibean settled six miles above them on the creek.

They built a schoolhouse, and had meetings in it on the Sabbath, and got Stillman Russell up there to keep school in the winter for three winters in succession, and Mr. Whitman contributed to his support for the first winter.

Thus did the Hand Unseen, through the benevolent action of one man, and amid obstacles apparently insurmountable, lay the foundations of a Christian community.